Praise for *Up to No Gouda*

"Masterful misdirection coupled with a pace that can't be beat, Linda Reilly has grilled up a winner for sure!"

—J. C. Eaton, author of the Sophie Kimball Mysteries, the Wine Trail Mysteries, and the Marcie Rayner Mysteries

"A well-crafted and fun start to a new series! Carly and her crew serve mouthwatering grilled cheese sandwiches while solving crime in a quaint Vermont town. Plenty of twists and turns to keep you turning the pages and guessing the killer to the very end."

—Tina Kashian, author of the Kebab Kitchen Mysteries

"A delightful and determined heroine, idyllic small town, and buffet of worthy suspects make this hearty whodunit an enticing start to a decidedly delectable new series! This sandwich-centric cozy will leave readers drooling for more!"

—Bree Baker, author of the Seaside Café Mysteries

Also in the Grilled Cheese Mystery Series

Up to No Gouda
No Parm No Foul

CHEDDAR LATE THAN DEAD

A Grilled Cheese Mystery

LINDA REILLY

Published by Poisoned Pen Press, an imprint of Sourcebooks
P.O. Box 4410, Naperville, Illinois 60567-4410
(630) 961-3900
sourcebooks.com

Printed and bound in the United States of America.
KP 10 9 8 7 6 5 4 3 2 1

This book is for my aunt Deanna,
for always being there.
Love you, Auntie!

CHAPTER ONE

The door to Carly's Grilled Cheese Eatery opened on a *whoosh* of frigid air. Two women entered, and after shoving the door closed against the January cold, they stomped their boots on the mat. "Oh gosh, it's adorable in here!" the shorter woman chirped, sweeping her gaze over the exposed brick walls and the cozy booths upholstered in aquamarine vinyl. Wearing fuzzy white earmuffs that matched her ski jacket, she turned to her companion with a pout. "Dawn," she said in a girlish whine, "why didn't we come in here sooner?"

Dawn, who topped her friend's height by at least half a foot, shoved back the hood of her puffy purple coat. "Because you've been on a diet for almost a year, remember?" she said, a touch of tartness in her tone. "You told me not to let you near this place until *after* your wedding. I was only following orders."

Carly Hale, owner of the eatery, flipped over the Sweddar Weather she was preparing and peeked over the grill at the pair. The women, both around her own age, looked familiar. Had they graduated from high school with her? She thought they had, but after sixteen years, their names were eluding her.

Dawn. Yes! Now Carly remembered them—Dawn Chapin and Klarissa Taddeo. In high school they'd been an inseparable pair. Klarissa, the bubbly one with sparkling blue eyes and loose, titian-colored curls. Dawn, the quieter and more serious of the two, with hazel eyes and sculpted cheekbones, her straight brunette hair barely brushing the tops of her thin shoulders.

Carly handed over her spatula to her new assistant manager, Valerie Wells. "I want to say hello to these gals. Take over for me?"

Valerie smiled. "You betcha!"

Carly had barely made it around to the other side of the counter when Klarissa let out a squeal. "Carly Hale, is that you?" She rushed forward and threw her arms around her, mindless of the remnants of snow she was pressing into Carly's green knit sweater.

Carly hugged her in return. "Klarissa, you look great. I haven't seen you in so long!"

"I know. It's been like, *forever,* hasn't it?"

"Hey, Carly." Dawn leaned in for a brief hug, then brushed wet flakes from her coat sleeves. "Sorry about the snow."

"Oh heck, this is Vermont," Carly said with a smile. "We expect snow to sneak in with our guests.

Can I seat you in the booth at the back? It's close to the heat register so it's nice and cozy."

"We'll take it!" Klarissa pulled off her earmuffs and slid into the booth. Her curls spilled around her face and onto her shoulder.

Dawn settled in opposite her friend, then shrugged off her coat and set her gloves down on the bench seat. Carly gave them menus. After taking their orders and delivering their hot chocolates, she went back behind the grill.

"Old friends of yours?" Valerie asked. Her brunette topknot bounced slightly when she worked, which always seemed to be at warp speed. She slid a grilled cheese onto a plate next to a cup of tomato soup and a pickle.

Carly tucked her friends' orders on the strip above the grill. "Yup. I went to high school with them, although I haven't laid eyes on them since graduation." Carly delivered the sandwich plate to the elderly man seated at the counter.

"Thank you kindly," he said.

Carly had lucked out the day she interviewed Valerie for the assistant manager position. She'd been looking for a responsible helper, someone who could take over the reins for her when she was out of the restaurant and also feel comfortable in the role. In less than five weeks on the job, the forty-something Valerie had already proven herself. It was obvious to Carly that a gem had landed in her lap.

Suzanne Rivers, Carly's part-time server, came through the swinging door from the kitchen. The mom of a boy in grade school, Suzanne had been with Carly from opening day, nearly a year ago. Another lucky find.

"More tuna," Suzanne announced, a covered stainless-steel bowl in her hands. She shoved it into the mini fridge under the counter. "Seems like everyone's on a protein kick today."

"Must be the cold," Carly said, laughing. Her Farmhouse Cheddar Sleeps with the Fishes, the eatery's version of a tuna melt, had gained a sudden popularity.

When Klarissa's and Dawn's lunches were ready, Carly delivered them to their table. Klarissa had removed her gloves, displaying a colossal marquis diamond glittering on her left ring finger. Her gold-toned cell phone sat in front of her.

Carly set down their plates—a Vermont Classic for Dawn and a Smoky Steals the Bacon for Klarissa. "Beautiful ring," she commented to Klarissa. "Did I hear someone say you have a wedding in your future?"

Klarissa sat up straighter and wiggled her hand under the lights. A girlish flush colored her porcelain cheeks. "I do, in five weeks. I'm a very lucky woman, Carly."

"Congratulations," Carly said. "I wish you all the best."

Klarissa's glossy pink lips curved into a frown. "My shower is supposed to be a week from Saturday, if that idiot at the Balsam Dell Inn ever confirms it. You can't imagine the problems we've had with that place, Carly." She picked up a sandwich half and shoved a corner into her mouth. Her blue eyes lit up like tree bulbs. "This is what I've been missing," she said after she'd barely swallowed. "I can't wait till I'm officially Mrs. Tony Manous so I can start eating normal food again!"

Dawn glanced over at her friend but said nothing. She took a dainty bite of her sandwich.

"I'll let you gals enjoy your lunches," Carly said, mulling over the name. Tony Manous. She'd heard it before, but where?

Carly went through the swinging door into the kitchen. The familiar aroma of tomatoes and basil and—something else?—swirled around her. Grant Robinson, her other grill cook and a budding chef, was preparing another batch of his hearty tomato soup.

He grinned at her, his dark brown eyes twinkling. He'd been growing out his short dreads, and, in Carly's opinion, was getting handsomer every day. "You detected a new herb, didn't you? I can see it on your face." He gently stirred the large pot that was simmering on the stove.

Carly closed her eyes and inhaled. "It's…darn, I can't put my finger on it." She pinned him with a look. "Come on, don't keep me in suspense."

"It's thyme," he said. "Just enough to tantalize the senses but not overpower the soup."

"Mmm. I can't wait to taste it."

From the dining room, the musical ringtone from a cell phone filtered through the swinging door. It was the "Wedding March."

"Someone's getting married," Grant commented.

"Two old acquaintances of mine from high school came in for lunch," Carly explained. "One of them is engaged. You should see the rock she's wearing."

Grant shrugged. "Won't be long, you'll be wearing one of those." He gave the pot another stir.

Carly felt a flush creep up her neck. "It's way too soon for that," she said firmly, "Ari and I are taking our time, as every couple should." She wasn't sure she believed that, but it sounded good. It was her current mantra, anyway.

Truth be told, she'd been spending most of her free time lately with Ari Mitchell, the electrician who'd installed the pendant lighting in her eatery. Their relationship had blossomed over the summer and deepened during the holiday season. On New Year's Eve they'd celebrated as a committed couple, much to the delight of Carly's mom, Rhonda Hale Clark. Rhonda was currently on vacay in Florida with her hubby Gary, but she was itching for Carly to start sporting a diamond.

But that day, if it came, was in the distant future.

Retrieving a container of grated cheddar from the commercial fridge, she was picturing Ari Mitchell's adorable face when an angry voice erupted from the dining room. Carly set the container on the worktable and hurried out.

As she'd guessed, the commotion was coming from Klarissa's table. Klarissa's face had gone raspberry red, and she was shrieking into her cell. "Then you'd just better find a way to accommodate me," she threatened. "Otherwise, no one in the Taddeo family will ever patronize your moldy old inn again!"

Dawn reached over and touched her friend's arm in a calming motion. "Take it easy, and stop overreacting," she pleaded quietly. "Let me talk to her, okay?" She wiggled her fingers in a *give me the phone* motion.

Klarissa slammed her cell phone into Dawn's palm. "This is all your fault, so you'd better make it right," she ordered, and then took another massive bite of her sandwich.

Doing her best to appear like she wasn't eavesdropping, Carly busied herself clearing the table behind theirs. A few patrons sitting in the front booths had turned their heads to see what was happening. Rather than looking annoyed, they appeared to be enjoying the verbal tussle.

Carly listened as Dawn spoke calmly into the phone.

"I'm sorry, I know we didn't bring the check over on time," Dawn said patiently, "but your assistant led us to believe you would hold the date for us. And remember, it was she who did the booking." She listened for a moment, and then her eyes closed. "All right, thank you. I can see we're not getting anywhere." She disconnected the call and set the phone on the table. She shook her head. "They won't budge, Klar. I told you we needed to get that check over there by the first, didn't I?"

Klarissa's fist closed on the table. "How. Dare. You. Blaming me for *your* sloppiness. You're the wedding planner, and you're my maid of honor. This is all your fault."

Concerned over the mounting tension, Carly sidled over to their table. She spoke quietly. "Ladies, I couldn't help overhearing. Is there anything I can do to help?" She didn't seriously think there was, but she hoped her offer might calm Klarissa and get them to stop yelling in her eatery.

"I'm afraid not," Dawn said dismally, "unless you have connections at the Balsam Dell Inn. They double-booked the date of Klarissa's shower, and now we're fresh out of luck." She looked apologetically at her friend. "You're right, Klarissa," she said meekly. "This is my fault. But now we have less than two weeks, and I have no idea how to fix my mistake."

For several scary moments, Klarissa went silent. Then a sudden gleam shone in her blue eyes, and her lips curved into a smile. "I do. We'll have my shower at your mother's house. It'll be perfect!"

Dawn's mouth opened in surprise. "What? Klar, that's crazy. Thirty women will be attending the shower. Where will they all go?"

"In that vast drawing room, of course," Klarissa said airily. "Oh, Dawn, it'll be perfect. You'll have to arrange for table and chair rentals, of course, and someone will need to decorate."

"But...but we'd need a caterer," Dawn said, getting rattled now. "There's no way we can find one at this short notice. It's literally like, twelve days away."

Klarissa sat back against the booth, an impish smile on her lips. "Well, I can think of the perfect caterer. Carly, didn't you just offer to help?"

Carly nearly choked. She hadn't meant *that* kind of help.

"Klarissa, I'm...honored that you would consider me," Carly told her. "The thing is, I'm not a caterer. I run a small restaurant with a particular specialty. I wouldn't have a clue how to cater a shower."

Actually, that was a fib. She *did* have a clue, sort of.

Half a lifetime ago, or at least that's how it felt, Carly was working as restaurant manager at a historic inn in northern Vermont. One of her favorite employees had gotten engaged, and Carly had eagerly offered to host the bridal shower. From the sumptuous array of food to the decadent champagne cake, the shower had been a huge success—and a total blast.

Hard to believe that was only five years ago. Three years later, Carly would lose her husband, Daniel, to a tragic accident. It was months before she got her life back on track. She sold their small home and returned to southern Vermont, to her beloved hometown of Balsam Dell.

"You have an odd look on your face," Klarissa said, waving her beringed hand in front of Carly.

Carly shook off her memories. "Sorry, my brain went off on a tangent. Klarissa, I'd love to help, but like I said, I've never done any catering." That much, at least, was true.

Ignoring Carly's protests, Klarissa pointed a manicured finger at her maid of honor. "Donuts. Remember? They'd be perfect. I'll bet no one's ever served them at a wedding shower before!"

Dawn groaned and gave up a weak smile. "Grilled cheese donuts. Leave it to you to remember." She looked at Carly and explained. "We saw grilled cheese donuts at a diner in Maine last summer. Klar was already in high diet mode—determined to squeeze into a size eight wedding gown—so instead of trying one, she plunked them onto her bucket list. Her *postwedding* bucket list."

Grilled cheese donuts.

Carly had heard of them, but she'd never made one. She had to admit, the idea held a certain appeal. They weren't for everyone, but for sure they'd have some takers.

"It's an interesting idea," Carly said. "I hope you find someone who can cater for you, Klarissa. With my schedule, I can't possibly plan a menu for thirty plus people in such a short time."

As if Carly had turned suddenly invisible, Klarissa aimed a forefinger at Dawn. "It's your fault we lost the Inn, Dawn, so call your mom right now and firm it up with her. I came up with the solution. Now it's your job to make it work."

Dawn's expression hardened, and her slim nostrils flared. She dug out her cell phone from the pocket of her puffy coat and began tapping away.

Klarissa swerved her legs around in the booth and jumped up to squeeze Carly in a hug. "I just knew you'd save the day, Carly. And think what a feather in your cap this is going to be!"

"Wait a minute," Carly pleaded. "I'm not a caterer. You need to find someone who—" She halted midsentence, stilled by the look of desperation on Dawn's thin face.

Over Klarissa's shoulder, Dawn held up her

hands in a praying motion. *Please,* she mouthed silently.

I guess I'll be catering a wedding shower, Carly thought wryly. *And with grilled cheese donuts, no less.*

CHAPTER TWO

Carly was surprised at how little she'd had to negotiate with Dawn on the pricing. In truth, she'd felt bad for her, but she still had to charge for her time, for the supplies, and for recruiting Grant to help with creating grilled cheese donut recipes. Even after adding a surcharge for the short notice, Dawn had readily agreed to her quote. As for the double-booking mess, Dawn had hinted to Carly that there was more to that story but hadn't explained any further.

One thing Carly had insisted on was a tour of the area where she'd be doing the food prep. Sissy's Bakery, a favorite of Carly's, had agreed to supply the donuts for the grilled cheese sandwiches. Since they'd also be preparing the massive cake—a delectable raspberry concoction that was Klarissa's favorite—everything would be delivered on the morning of the shower.

On Sundays Carly's restaurant was closed, leaving her one day a week for personal chores and relaxation, whatever that might entail. Today she'd be spending her Sunday afternoon visiting the Chapin home and consulting with Dawn on the shower details. Not exactly the relaxation she'd hoped for.

Her thoughts drifting, Carly wondered how her mom was faring back at her old stomping grounds, as Rhonda referred to her former Vero Beach neighborhood. Rhonda and Gary had moved to Florida shortly after they were married, but one too many stray alligators and a particularly bad bug season had sent Rhonda almost virtually screaming into the night. She told Gary they were moving back to southern Vermont and that was the end of their Florida experiment. A yearly visit to the friends they'd made there was enough for her.

Meanwhile, Carly had Klarissa's shower to plan for. Dawn had agreed to give her a tour of both the kitchen and the drawing room ahead of the event. She'd even emailed Carly a preliminary sketch of how the tables would be arranged and asked if she had any suggestions. Impressed with the precision and detail of the sketch, Carly had nothing to add.

After three days of on-and-off snowfall, the roads of Balsam Dell were finally plowed clean. Sunlight glittered off the piled-high snowbanks, making the town center resemble a winter wonderland.

The ride to the Chapin home was a short one. Perched on a gentle hill overlooking a vast, snow-coated field, the mansion was impressive even from a distance. The private road leading to the house had been meticulously plowed and sanded, allowing easy navigation by Carly's aging Corolla.

As Carly drew closer, her eyes widened. The house was stunning.

Surrounded by wraparound porches swept clean of snow, its five brick chimneys jutted out from the expansive roof, puffing out wisps of whitish smoke. The house itself was white, the shutters black. The mansion seemed to sprawl the length of a football field, but that might have been an illusion. At one end, an octagon-shaped porch rested beneath a second porch that extended out from one of the upper rooms. The master bedroom, Carly guessed.

She was maneuvering her car around the circular drive when Dawn emerged from the front door and onto the wide porch. Dawn motioned her to a cleared area off to the side where she could park.

"Hey," Carly said with a smile, treading carefully up the steps. "It's great to see you. I'm looking forward to my tour."

"I am too." Dawn's thin face looked drawn and pasty, her hazel eyes underscored with dark pouches. Carly could only imagine the kind of stress she was under.

Dawn led her through the front entrance and into the marbled foyer. On the left, at the back, was an elegant, half-turn staircase with an elaborately carved handrail. It reminded Carly of something out of a fairy tale.

"You can leave your boots right here," she said, waving an arm at the floor. "Astrid will take your outerwear."

As if by magic, a short, stocky woman with straw-like hair appeared, her smile wide and her arms outstretched. She wore a long-sleeved fleece shirt over navy slacks and a pair of flat, rubber-soled shoes. "I'll hang these in the coatroom," she said in a sweet voice. "They'll be nice and toasty when you leave."

"Thank you," Carly said, handing over her coat and gloves.

The woman nodded and shuttled off, disappearing through a doorway on the right side of the foyer.

Carly was glad she'd thought to bring along a pair of loafers. It wouldn't do to tromp around this gorgeous mansion in her clunky rubber boots.

After slipping on her shoes, she followed Dawn into a cheery dining room. Slanted rays of sunlight streamed through the tall windows, casting tiny parallelograms on one papered, cream-colored wall. An oak table surrounded by eight curved chairs sat beneath a chandelier crafted from blue and white porcelain. In the center of the table, a cut crystal vase boasted a cluster of pale-blue hydrangeas, artfully arranged with what looked to Carly like sprigs of baby's breath. A mild floral scent permeated the room, a blend of lilac and vanilla.

The décor was simple, yet elegant—not as fussy as Carly had expected.

"Your home is absolutely beautiful, Dawn," Carly said. "And that flower arrangement is gorgeous."

Dawn smiled. "Thanks, but it's my mother's home, not mine. As for the flowers, Klar's auntie Meggs takes care of all our floral displays. It's kind of a side gig of hers. She and my mother have been friends since they were kids."

"So, your family and Klar's go back a long way?"

"You could say that."

Carly noticed an open doorway leading to another room, adjacent to where she was standing. Too nosy to resist, she stepped toward the entryway and sneaked a peek.

Unlike the airy dining room, this room was defined by dark paneling, Persian carpets, and heavy leather chairs. Brocade curtains hung from the soaring windows, blocking out most of the natural light. Two tall vases, ornately painted, bracketed a massive stone fireplace. In the center of the mantel, a large crystal vase held a cluster of red roses. Framed photos of sleek aircraft covered nearly one entire wall.

"That vase on the mantel is gorgeous," Carly commented. "Even from here I can see that it's engraved, but I can't make out what the engravings are."

Dawn smiled. "That crystal vase is one of a kind.

It was commissioned by my granddad from a glassmaker in France who created utterly unique pieces. Those lovely engravings you noticed are swallows. For him, swallows represented the freedom he felt when he was flying his jet planes. And per his strict instructions, that vase never leaves this room." She turned to Carly, the adoration in her eyes almost palpable. "He had an exact duplicate made for my grandmother, only hers was a perfume bottle."

"That sounds beautiful. Was your dad a pilot too?"

"No, only my granddad was. But Dad loves that room. It's his haven when he's around, which is almost never," Dawn added tartly. "Technically my folks are divorced, but Dad has visiting rights. When he's here, he purposely smokes cigars in there to irritate my mother. We've taken to calling it the smoking room." Her lips twisted in a mild smirk. "Come on, I'll show you the kitchen."

Carly followed Dawn along another hallway. "Is your mom home?"

"She's around somewhere," Dawn said flatly. "She wasn't exactly thrilled about hosting the shower, but, as they say, duty calls."

Interesting comment, Carly thought. Did that mean Mrs. Chapin felt obligated in some way to Klarissa? Or did Dawn herself feel duty bound to fix the mess created when the Balsam Dell Inn date fell through? She was mulling the question when suddenly they were standing in the most fabulous kitchen Carly had ever seen.

Stainless-steel appliances dominated, from the gargantuan refrigerator to the eight-burner Wolf stove, complete with double ovens and a griddle. A sink occupied one end of the granite island, the lower half of which was stacked with oversized pots. The wall behind the stove was white brick, a display of vintage blue Delft plates resting on the soffit along the top. If Carly had a kitchen like this, she'd want to live in it forever.

"My gosh, this kitchen is like something out of a dream. Is this where I'll be working?"

For the first time since Carly had arrived, Dawn actually looked pleased. Her smile was genuine, and her eyes bright. "It is. I had a feeling you'd approve." She aimed a hand at the stove. "The griddle is large enough to grill at least ten sandwiches at a time. We have two massive warming trays, which we'll set up in the drawing room, where the guests will be eating. Astrid will help you with anything you need, plus she'll do all the cleanup afterward."

"That's very nice of her, but I don't mind cleaning up after myself." She laughed. "I'm used to it."

Dawn waved a dismissive hand. "That's okay. She's looking forward to it. Will any of your helpers be with you?"

Carly shook her head. "No, I can't spare anyone, especially on a Saturday. Luckily, I have a terrific assistant manager. She'll handle everything at the eatery in my absence."

"Okay, then. Why don't you have a look around the kitchen, be sure it has everything you need?"

Carly did so, and after a few minutes was completely satisfied. "I can't think of anything I'll need to bring, except any food that's not being delivered."

"Excellent," Dawn said. "Would you like to see the drawing room now?"

Once again, Carly trailed in Dawn's wake. They passed through a small room that appeared to be a breakfast nook. A microwave, a toaster, and a set of flowered canisters rested on a counter opposite the table. Even without a window to the world, it was cozy and inviting. Beyond that was a pantry, where painted white shelves were jam-packed with foodstuffs and enough bottled water to last till the next millennium.

They made their way along a series of short hallways. If Carly lived here, it would probably take her a month to learn the layout. When they finally reached the drawing room, she had to stifle a gasp.

The walls were painted a dark teal, the wood trim a rich gold. A brick fireplace dominated one wall, its mantel adorned with two large porcelain vases, one at each end. Between the vases was an ornate, gold leaf mirror.

"These chairs and side tables are being removed temporarily," Dawn explained, indicating the gorgeously upholstered wingback chairs and cherrywood end tables. "Our RSVPs are all in, and the final head count is twenty-eight." She explained the seating and where the food and beverages would be set up.

"I'm...in awe," Carly said, gazing around with a grin. "No wonder Klarissa wanted her shower here."

They left the room through a different doorway. Carly realized they'd made a circle that had landed them back in the foyer.

Dawn's lips pursed, and she moved closer to Carly. "Carly, can I ask you something? In confidence?"

"Sure you can."

"You remember what Klar was like in high school, right? She was outgoing and fun, but always kind to everyone."

"She was," Carly agreed, sensing a "but" coming. "We were never close, but I always liked her."

Dawn crossed her arms over her chest. "Ever since she met Tony Manous, she's become a different person. And not in a good way, either."

"What do you mean?" Carly asked.

"She's gotten snappy, impatient. Like she's better than everyone else, you know? You heard the way she sniped at me in your restaurant. Like I was her...*servant*. I was mortified."

Carly had been too, but she'd chalked it up as a temporary aberration.

"Maybe it's just bridezilla syndrome," Carly

suggested. "I've heard it happens to the most mild-mannered of brides-to-be."

"I only wish that was the case." Dawn sniffled and her eyes misted. "Don't mind me. I'm a mess these days."

"Oh Dawn, I'm so sorry," Carly said gently. "I didn't realize any of this was happening. Tony's name sounds familiar. Is he a local guy?"

"A local *jerk*," Dawn said. "He's head of the town's Grounds and Recreation Department. Loves to show off his muscular bod in his official green polo shirt and tight khaki pants." She rolled her eyes in disgust.

Carly remembered, now, where she'd seen his name—in the town's most recent annual report.

"Have you shared your feelings with Klarissa?" Carly asked her. "Not about Tony, but about the way she treats you?"

"I tried to, once, but she laughed it off. She said that one day, when I'm in love with a wonderful man like Tony, I'll understand how she feels." Dawn swallowed, a deep sadness filling her eyes. "It doesn't matter anymore. After she and Tony move to North Carolina, I'll probably never see her again. At one time the thought crushed me, but now... I'm actually glad she'll be out of my life."

"They're moving?" Carly was surprised.

"Tony landed a job as head greenskeeper at one of the big country clubs down there. *Very* prestigious, according to him. I guess a big salary goes with it. The club where he'll be working is on the PGA tour, so a lot of the pros play there. If there's anything Tony loves, it's rubbing elbows with the stars," she said scornfully. "He and Klarissa already rented a condo near the golf club."

"But what about Klarissa's job?" Carly said, then realized she had no idea where Klarissa worked.

"She's an aesthetician at the spa that opened in Bennington a few years ago," Dawn explained. "According to her, getting another job in that field will be a breeze."

"Wow. That's a lot of change in a short time. How do Klarissa's folks feel about her moving?"

Dawn blotted her eyes with her fingertips. "Her dad's remarried and lives in Toronto, so he rarely sees her anyway. Her mom's disappointed, but it's her aunt Meg who's really bummed. Klarissa and Auntie Meggs are like this." She held up two fingers and crossed them.

Carly squeezed Dawn's arm. "I'm so sorry you have to go through all this. I can see you're struggling."

"Don't be sorry." Dawn gave her a tepid smile. "You're the one who saved my bacon, so to speak. I'll never forget what you did to rescue this shower for me."

"I'm glad I could help," Carly said, although she was beginning to wonder what she'd gotten herself into.

"If Klar had let me book the date at the Inn weeks ago like I told her," Dawn said through clenched teeth, "we wouldn't be here right now. I'm a wedding planner, for glory's sake! I know how these things work. But *nooo*. She loves to wait until the last minute, then expects everyone to do her bidding. It's like a control thing, you know? Only this time she got fooled, and I took the heat for it."

Carly nodded. She knew the type. Except that she'd have never guessed Klarissa Taddeo was one of them.

"To be totally honest, I *am* going to miss her," Dawn admitted. "We've been BFFs since we were kids. I guess now we'll have to drop the *forever* part, won't we?" With that, she burst into tears.

Feeling helpless and more than a little awkward, Carly hugged her and patted her back. "You'll feel different after the wedding," she soothed. "Once they settle into their new digs, I bet you'll be flying down to visit her."

Dawn pulled away. "No, I won't," she said bitterly, her face streaked with tears. "I won't even be invited." She lifted her gaze to meet Carly's, her eyes filled with pain. "I want my old friend back, Carly. And that's never going to happen as long as Tony Manous is in the picture."

CHAPTER THREE

On the day of the shower, Carly arrived at the Chapin mansion at 10:00, her cooler of cheeses in hand. The shower wouldn't start until 1:00, which gave her more than enough time to set up her supplies.

Dawn, clad in sweatpants and a gray fleece top, greeted her briskly and then escorted her into the kitchen. Her face was pale, devoid of makeup. After muttering her excuses, she disappeared in the direction of the drawing room.

A far friendlier face greeted Carly in the kitchen.

"Miss Carly, I'm so happy to be working with you," Astrid enthused.

Carly set down her cooler. "And I'm happy to be here." She glanced at the pink bakery boxes stacked neatly along one counter. "Are those the donuts?"

"They are, but first," Astrid said, "we will have our breakfast." She winked at Carly. "We need to keep up our energy if we're going to cook food to please all the visiting ladies!"

On the granite island, Astrid had set out a pot of

fragrant orange-flavored tea, along with a plate of warm raisin scones. Carly slathered her scone with clotted cream, relishing the rare treat. When they were ready to start the prep work, Carly gave Astrid a brief demonstration of how she would set up the sandwiches to prepare them for grilling.

For the sake of simplicity—serving thirty or so women would require speed and accuracy—Carly had opted to make only three versions of the glazed donut grilled cheese. One plain, one with crisp bacon, and one with thin-sliced tomatoes. Each sandwich would be made with a heaping portion of shredded orange cheddar. For anyone who wanted a more traditional grilled cheese, a non-donut version, made with country white bread in the shape of a gigantic heart, would be offered.

The dipping sauces she and Grant had made were Carly's favorite part. There was a tangy tomato soup, a pink-tinted sweetened whipped cream, and a spicy mustard sauce.

"You've thought of everything," Astrid said, clasping her hands together. "You're a clever lady."

"Thanks," Carly said, "but I have an excellent assistant at the restaurant who helped design most of the recipes."

Astrid turned to her with a quizzical expression, her hands pressed together. "Carly, is it silly that I'm so excited about this shower?"

Carly grinned at her. "Not at all. I'm excited too."

She was surprised at how much she meant it. "Do you know Klarissa very well?"

"Oh yes." Her expression was guarded. "Miss Klarissa and Miss Dawn have been friends for as long as I've been here. And Mrs. Chapin is friends with Miss Klarissa's aunt, Meg Gilbert. Miss Meg was here early this morning to help set up and do the flowers."

Carly wanted to press her further, but she sensed it wasn't a good time. Working assembly line style, they put together about four dozen sandwiches. Astrid's hands were quick and nimble. By 12:30, everything was ready for grilling.

After a brief trip to the restroom adjacent to the kitchen, Carly returned to find Dawn skimming her sharp gaze over everything. She'd changed into a long black skirt with a dove-gray blouse, her hair pulled back into a loose French braid. A touch of lip gloss and a few sweeps of blush had given her a bit of color. She smiled when she saw Carly.

"Carly, I'm sorry I was so abrupt with you earlier. It's just...the stress from this gig is getting to me."

"Don't give it a thought," Carly said. "I know you have a lot on your mind."

Dawn brightened. "I see you and Astrid have everything under control," she said, her tone laced with admiration. "Want a quick peek at the drawing room?"

"I'd love it."

Dawn turned to Carly's helper. "Astrid? The guests will be arriving soon."

Astrid nodded, as if she'd understood some secret code. She removed her apron, then darted through the doorway that led to the cozy breakfast nook Carly had seen on her first tour of the mansion.

The drawing room had undergone an amazing transformation. Low flames crackled in the fireplace. The dining room table was gone, replaced by six rectangular tables covered with white linen tablecloths. In the center of each table, an arrangement of red and white roses sat in a crystal swan. On each of the six tables, two fancy bowls of cut-up fruit had been placed—one on either side of the swan.

In a far corner, a round table covered with a dark red tablecloth had been designated for gifts. One sole present, meticulously wrapped in gold foil, sat in the center. Carly had brought a small gift for Klarissa—a set of elegant note cards engraved in gold with an "M" for Manous. She'd bought them at What a Card, the specialty card store owned by her bestie, Gina Tomasso. When she had a chance, she'd slip it onto the table with the other gifts.

Along the wall opposite the fireplace, a carved sideboard held a silver coffee urn and several wine carafes nestled in tubs of ice. Two silver-plated warming trays rested beside the wine.

"Dawn, this looks fantastic," Carly said. "Did you do all this?"

She shrugged, and then smiled. "I'm a wedding planner, remember? By now this is second nature." Her smiled faded, and her tone soured. "Being a wedding planner wasn't my first choice, but Mother thought I should have a career appropriate for a woman."

Carly was shocked. Any job a man could do, a woman could do. Her own mom had drilled that into her from birth. She couldn't resist asking, "What was your first choice?"

"I wanted to be an architect. I love to design things." Dawn's voice cracked. "Water over the dam, as they say, right?"

From the general direction of the kitchen, someone called out Dawn's name in a harsh, demanding tone.

Dawn froze, and her jaw went taut. She touched Carly's arm. "Excuse me, Carly. My jailer, aka Mother, beckons." Without another word, she hurried out of the drawing room.

Carly didn't have time to mull the interruption, because Klarissa chose that moment to sashay into the drawing room. Her cheeks pink from the cold, she looked radiant in a slinky, green knit dress with a tulip hem. A corsage of petite red roses was attached at her shoulder. Her diamond flashed under the glow of the overhead chandelier as she waved her hand toward the sideboard. "Oh, Auntie, look at this. Isn't it fabulous?"

A woman came in behind the bride-to-be, smiling from ear to ear. Carly pegged her at somewhere in her late forties, but her blue eyes were youthful and vibrant. Her auburn hair, cut in a stylish bob, was a few shades lighter than Klarissa's. Her wide-eyed gaze roamed the drawing room. "Oh, sweetie, you're right. This is absolutely perfect." She slipped her arm through Klarissa's.

Klarissa squeezed the woman's hand, then sidled over to Carly and encased her in a hug. "Thank you, Carly," she said in a soft voice. "You really did save the day. I don't know what we'd have done without you."

Carly smiled. "I'm glad I could help."

"Carly, this is my aunt, Megan Gilbert. Auntie Meggs, this is the superhero who saved my shower—Carly Hale."

The woman took Carly's hands in both of her own and gave them a squeeze. "It's a pleasure. And please, call me Meg. Or better yet, call me Auntie Meggs." She turned and cast a loving glance at her niece.

Astrid returned wearing a crisp black uniform with a white apron, a wool coat draped over one arm. She'd apparently been charged with taking everyone's coats as they arrived.

"I'd better scoot back in the kitchen," Carly said, excusing herself. "It was nice to meet you, Meg."

Klarissa blew her an air kiss, then turned to her aunt. "Now where the heck is Ron? If that idiot shows up late, I'll kill him."

Carly retraced her steps and retreated. When she got as far as the breakfast nook, she heard snappish voices coming from the kitchen. She halted in her tracks.

"You want your man back, don't you?" a woman hissed in a low voice. "Then do as I tell you, although I still can't fathom what you see in that moron. But if you're determined to have him, you need to act like Klarissa. She goes after what she wants, and she gets it."

"And just how do you suggest I do that, Mother?" Dawn's retort was sharp.

"You use your womanly wiles, my dear."

"I don't have *wiles,* Mother. I have a heart and a brain."

"Then put them to good use. You're smarter and prettier than Klarissa, so start using your head—*and* your natural assets. *If you get my drift.*"

Yikes. Carly needed to get back into the kitchen, but she was trapped.

Still, she had a job to do. She waited for a lull, then pasted on an innocent look and trotted into the kitchen. "Oh, hello there."

Dawn looked flustered. "Oh, um, Carly, this is my mother, Julie Chapin. Mother, this is Carly. I told you all about her."

Mrs. Chapin, who bore little resemblance to Dawn, held out a slender, manicured hand. Both her smile and her face were stretched tight. Her short black hair was expertly styled, with wispy bangs brushing her well-defined eyebrows. She was quite a beautiful woman.

"I'm so pleased to meet you," she cooed with a practiced smile. "I understand you're the heroine who rescued my daughter's reputation as a wedding planner."

Carly blinked, unsure how to respond to such a demeaning comment. She forced a cool smile and said, "Only the shower, and I had a lot of help with that."

She was saved from further awkwardness by loud chatter beginning to drift from the drawing room.

"The guests are starting to arrive," Julie Chapin said crisply. With a snap of her fingers, she steered her daughter out of the kitchen without so much as a backward wave.

To Carly's relief, Astrid returned a few minutes later.

"Everyone's here," Astrid said, looking a bit anxious. "Miss Klarissa insists that they all eat first and watch her open presents later. She says she is... *literally starving,* so we should start making the food now."

Carly nodded, then began preparing the sandwiches, the aroma of melted cheese and cooked bacon filling the kitchen. While she worked the griddle, Astrid shuttled trays of sandwiches to the drawing room. Carly was dying to sneak a peek at the guests as they ate, but she'd been hired to grill, not to gawk.

Slightly breathless, Astrid returned with an empty tray. "Can we make more bacon ones? The girls, they plowed through them already!" She set the tray next to the stove.

"You got it." Carly slid more donut sandwiches onto the grill, then grabbed her tote bag. She pulled out her wrapped gift. "Can you slip this onto the gift table for me?" she asked Astrid. "I should have done it earlier."

Astrid winked at her. "You got it."

By the time Astrid returned, Carly had another batch of sandwiches ready for her. She placed them on the tray.

"I'm going to cut the cake soon," Astrid said. "They want to eat it while Miss Klarissa unwraps her gifts."

Without warning, a man carrying a video camera shot into the kitchen. Carly jumped in surprise. "Oh my gosh!"

"Sorry," he muttered over a crooked grin. "Didn't mean to startle you guys."

His eyes were watery, but his face was rather handsome, with a neatly trimmed beard and long-lashed, expressive eyes. "Smile for the camera, ladies!" He held up his video cam and aimed it at Carly.

Astrid stepped directly in front of Carly and waved him away. "This is a kitchen. You go back to the party," she told him.

He shrugged. "Sorry. No can do. Klar told me to come in here and get a video of the chef making the donut grilled cheeses. Which, by the way, were *awesome.*"

"Thank you, but it's a little late for that," Carly bluntly informed him. "We're about through here."

"I know, but I got here kinda late and Klar is like, seriously ticked at me. By the way, I'm Ron Benoit, Klar's cousin. I don't suppose you could pretend to cook up one of those grilled cheeses so I can get a short clip? I'm only trying to prevent my cousin from serving my head on a platter." He made a sad, puppy-dog face.

Relenting, Carly went through the motions of putting together a donut grilled cheese. After barely a minute of filming, he said, "That was perfect. Thanks! Hey, can I have one of those?" He gawked at the fresh tray of sandwiches.

"Go ahead—" Carly started to say, when Dawn strode into the kitchen.

Dawn's cheeks pinked, and her lips curved into a slow, suggestive smile. She moved closer to him. "Ron," she said sweetly, "aren't you supposed to be at the shower?"

Averting his eyes he said, "Um, I'm going back now. Just had to get a clip of the kitchen help. Boss's orders, remember?" He grabbed a sandwich and dashed out of the kitchen.

Dawn watched him leave, her lips turning down into a disheartened frown. "I'm sorry about that, Carly. Would you mind coming with me to the drawing room? All the guests would like to meet you. They can't stop praising your wonderful food."

The idea didn't thrill Carly, but she didn't want to seem ungrateful. Especially since she'd charged plenty for her services.

"Sure. I'll be glad to meet them."

In the drawing room, she was greeted with a round of applause.

"Hail to the grilled cheese queen!" someone yelled. "Are there any more of those bacon ones?"

Astrid, who'd trailed in behind Carly and Dawn, nodded and placed the new batch of sandwiches into one of the warming trays. Three guests made a mad dash for them.

Before Dawn had a chance to properly introduce Carly, Klarissa strutted over and took Carly by the hand. She pulled her over in front of the sideboard. "Everyone," she began in a raised voice, "after those horrid people at the Balsam Dell Inn reneged on their promise, this beautiful and talented lady, Carly Hale, saved my shower."

More cheers went up. "Yay, Carly!" one of the women shouted.

"So, the next time you're downtown," Klarissa went on, "be sure to visit Carly's adorable restaurant." She beamed at Carly through watery eyes, then her voice hardened. "And please, for my sake, don't *ever* patronize the Balsam Dell Inn again. They screwed me over, and I'm not going to forget it. None of you should, either."

Inwardly, Carly cringed. Had Klarissa just used her as a sneaky way to bash the Inn?

Klarissa bounced her gaze around the drawing room. "Where's Auntie Meggs? She wanted to thank you too."

"Bathroom," someone called out.

"Hey, what about Tony?" someone called out. "When's he showing up?"

"Never," Klarissa said with a loopy giggle. "I told you before, remember? No men allowed!"

With that, Carly nodded and thanked everyone. She tried to excuse herself to return to the kitchen, but a slender blond woman wearing a leopard print designer dress stopped her midstride.

"I'm Ursula Taddeo, Klarissa's mom," the woman said, her breathy voice slightly slurred. Aside from her blond hair and overly made-up eyes, her features almost mirrored those of Auntie Meggs. "Thank you for everything, dear. The Taddeo family will not forget what you've done." She gave her a dramatic hug.

Carly started to respond when Julie Chapin pushed her way between the two. With a bright smile at the guests, she leaned her head close to Ursula's ear. "You have a nerve even setting foot in my home, Ursula dear. As I recall, you once called me the scum of the earth."

The words came out with such vitriol that Ursula stumbled backward.

I've got to get out of this room. I feel like a character in a cheesy soap opera.

To Carly's relief, Astrid had begun cutting the cake. Carly gave a final wave to the guests and backed away, wanting nothing more than to escape.

A thirtysomething blond wearing a beige pantsuit and a jeweled, cat-shaped brooch stood off to one side, her hands clasped in front of her. She gave Carly a sympathetic smile, as if to say, *I feel your pain*. Something about her was familiar, but Carly couldn't quite recall where she'd seen her. After acknowledging the woman with a grateful nod, Carly dashed off toward the kitchen.

She got as far as the breakfast nook when she saw a diminutive, dark-haired woman seated at the small table, sobbing. A tray of cream-filled pastries, artfully arranged on a fancy platter, rested on the table in front of her, next to a silver cell phone.

"Oh my gosh, are you okay?" Carly asked her.

"No," the woman said in a shaky voice. "I'm not okay. That girl is going to be my daughter-in-law, and she treats me like dirt!" She blotted her puffy eyes with a tissue.

Carly brought her a glass of water and sat down with her. "Is Tony Manous your son?"

"My stepson," the woman sniffled. "I knew when he brought that girl home, she was no good for him. But boys, they don't listen." She grabbed Carly's hand with her crooked fingers. "I'm sorry, I should introduce myself. I'm Rose Manous. I work at the Balsam Dell Inn, making pastries and cookies. Klarissa's been telling everyone what terrible people they are, all because *she* didn't turn in her deposit on time. How...how could she do that? She knows how much I love my job there."

Carly ached for the woman. "Sometimes people say things out of anger that they don't really mean," she offered gently. "I bet once she thinks it over, she'll apologize." She wasn't sure of that at all, but the woman was so upset she didn't how else to comfort her. As for Klarissa, her insensitivity shocked Carly. Why would she say such spiteful things about the Inn with her future mother-in-law right there in the room?

"I thought she'd appreciate my homemade pastries," Rose went on, "but then I found out Klarissa won't let me serve them, that she wants her fancy bakery cake to be the center of attention. I spent all day yesterday baking!"

"I'm so sorry," Carly soothed, her opinion of Klarissa heading further into a nosedive.

"And then she serves those silly...*donut* things with cheese to her guests! But my beautiful work isn't good enough for her," she said with disgust. "Oh dear, I'm so sorry. You're the girl who made the sandwiches, aren't you? I didn't mean any offense. Honestly I didn't."

"It's perfectly okay. No offense taken."

Rose abruptly got off her chair and pocketed her cell phone. "I need to go. I shouldn't have made that call."

"What call?" Carly asked, feeling completely at a loss.

"Can you get my coat, please? I have to leave right away!"

"Rose, maybe you should speak to Klarissa first—"

Rose shook her head firmly. "It does no good. I need to go. Now."

On Carly's first visit, the day Dawn gave her a tour of the mansion, Astrid had disappeared with Carly's outerwear through a doorway off the foyer. She'd start there.

Asking Rose to follow her, Carly wound her way through the kitchen and back to the foyer. The door in question was closed, but when Carly turned the knob, it opened.

"Oh my," she said, stepping into a vast coatroom.

The room was warm, scented with cedar. Racks of coats lined two walls. Boots and other winter wear rested on long rubber mats beneath the coats.

"There. That's mine." Rose pointed to a navy wool coat with a high button collar. She slipped it on, claimed her boots, and shoved her flat shoes into the deep pockets of her coat, digging out a pair of knitted gloves as she did so. After that she scurried out of the coatroom and made a beeline for the front door, Carly following close behind her.

"Rose, are you going to be all right?" Carly asked her when they reached the doorway.

"Yes, yes. I just need to go." She pulled on her gloves.

"Take care, then." Carly opened the door, and before she could ask Rose if she needed a ride, the woman was gone.

Shaking her head, Carly headed back toward the kitchen. She felt as if she'd stumbled onto the stage of a strange play, where every character she encountered nursed a grudge against another. She needed to exit stage left—or was it stage right?—clean up the kitchen, and get the heck out of there.

She'd gotten as far as the entrance to the airy dining room when a girlish giggle reached her ears. Something about the woman's tone made Carly halt on the spot. She pressed herself into the corner of the walls in the foyer, praying no one would notice her.

"You're a naughty boy, you know that? Sneaking in here half-snookered." Dawn's voice, lilting and slightly off-color.

Her mouth forming an O, Carly squashed herself close to the wall.

"I didn't *sneak* in here." A man's voice, his words thick. "I'm only sampling your granddad's aged whiskey, which wasn't even my idea." The sound of ice cubes clinking in a glass reached Carly's ears. "I came here because I have a bone to pick with my beautiful bride." His tone had an edge.

Dawn laughed—a fake, fluttery sound. "Don't you mean your beautiful *future* bride, Tony?"

Tony!

Carly clamped her hand over her mouth.

A loud gasp suddenly burst from Dawn. "Ron, what are you doing? You're supposed to be at the shower."

Ron—Klarissa's videographer cousin. He must have entered from the other doorway.

Ignoring Dawn's question, Ron said, "Tony, my man, what are you doing here? I waited for you at the pub, but you never showed up. I ended up being late for this chick fest. Klarissa was royally PO'd at me."

"I already told you, *man*," Tony retorted. "I'm not interested in what you're peddling. Sinking money into anything you do would be like pouring it down the hopper. I didn't even want you for our wedding videographer, but it turns out blood is thicker than water."

"Fine, but it's your loss," Ron snapped. "And Dawn, don't waste your time trying to make me jealous. It only makes you look more pathetic than you already are."

Dawn sucked in a whimper and a scary silence fell over the trio. At that moment, if Carly could have melded with the wallpaper, she'd have done so in a heartbeat. She held her breath.

Finally, she heard the click of Dawn's high heels rushing from the dining room. Dawn left through the opposite doorway, toward the kitchen—a stroke of luck for which Carly was immensely grateful. One of the men—Ron?—lingered for at least half a minute, but then finally followed in the direction Dawn had gone. To Carly's dismay, the other man was heading into the foyer.

Please don't see me, please don't see me.

The man, who had to be Tony, came through the doorway. Without a glance in her direction, he strode toward the elegant staircase, his steps unsure, his drink still clutched in his hand. His wavy hair was coal black, and he wore a gold knit sweater over faded jeans.

Carly knew she had only seconds before he'd turn around and see her. She fled into the dining room—thank heaven for rubber-soled shoes—her heart flogging her ribs so hard she had to catch her breath. After several more seconds, she quick-stepped on tiptoe back into the kitchen. Dirty plates were stacked next to the sink. Flatware soaked in a plastic tub.

"Miss Carly, I wondered where you were!" Astrid's face looked strained.

"I know, and I'm sorry if I worried you. I had to find a coat for one of the guests who wanted to leave. You were cutting the cake, so I didn't want to bother you."

Astrid ran steaming water into the stainless-steel sink. "It was for poor Mrs. Manous, wasn't it?"

Carly sighed. "It was. She was very upset."

Astrid tapped her fist to her heart. "Makes me hurt, the way Miss Klarissa talks about her." Her face flushed. "Please don't tell anyone I said that."

"No, I won't. Astrid, did Dawn just come through the kitchen?"

"She did," Astrid confirmed. "After her, that Ron fellow came in too. He tramped right through my kitchen like it was a…an outdoor market. Not even a 'hello' or an 'excuse me'!"

"I'm so sorry," Carly said. "I'll help you get these dishes cleaned up."

Astrid fluttered her hands. "No, I'll do that. It's my job. You take your things and go, Miss Carly."

Carly smiled at her. "But it'll be faster if we both pitch in, right?"

Within fifteen minutes, the kitchen was spotless.

Carly packed her few leftovers in her cooler and snapped it shut. Then she sent off a text to Dawn, telling her she was leaving and that they'd settle the bill on Monday. Given what Carly had overheard in the dining room, she had no desire to seek out Dawn and communicate that to her in person.

Astrid offered to fetch Carly's coat, but Carly refused, giving the woman a grateful hug. "You've done enough, and I know exactly where my coat is. Relax and have a cup of tea."

The dull cacophony of voices coming from the drawing room suddenly rose in pitch. Someone—Klarissa?—was weeping loudly, her voice a grating blend of a screech and a wail.

Carly hurried from the kitchen. Once in the foyer, she'd almost reached the door to the coatroom when she spotted something at the corner of her vision. A figure lay huddled at the foot of the exquisitely carved staircase.

A sense of dread filled her—a growing feeling of déjà vu that chilled her to the bone.

She moved closer to the figure, her heart smacking her ribs with every step. A man was lying face down, a broken cocktail glass splattered on the floor beside him. Next to the glass, an amber liquid puddled on the marble floor, a sole ice cube melting in the center. Even without seeing his face, Carly recognized him from his gold sweater and jeans.

Tony Manous.

He fell, Carly told herself. *Too much to drink had sent him tumbling down the stairs. But why had he gone upstairs in the first place? Hadn't he said he had a bone to pick with Klarissa?*

Carly dropped her cooler and her tote and went over to him. "Mr. Manous?" she managed to squeak out. "Tony?" She reached down and jiggled his shoulder, but he didn't move.

Her vision swam, and her throat closed. *Do something,* she told herself.

She retrieved her tote from where she'd tucked it in the coatroom and rummaged through it for her cell. Her fingers fumbled to punch in 911. She'd barely tapped the last "one" when Klarissa stormed into the foyer from a rear doorway, a posse of guests at her heels. Klarissa got one look at her fiancé's crumpled form before she threw herself over him. A high-pitched whine issued from her lips, and she cried out his name repeatedly.

The operator came on. Carly gave a rapid-fire explanation of the emergency, along with the address. She was instantly pelted with questions, but over the growing clamor she could barely hear.

She stepped backward, away from the gathering crowd, her gaze drifting up to the staircase. Descending the marble stairs was Dawn Chapin, her expression a mixture of disbelief and horror.

In the next instant, Dawn collapsed onto the stairs in a dead faint.

CHAPTER FOUR

CARLY POCKETED HER CELL AND STUMBLED UP the stairs toward Dawn. Dawn's face was a ghostly white, her eyelids closed, her head hanging over one stair. With everyone's attention on Tony, no one had even noticed that she'd passed out. One of her five-inch heels had tumbled to the bottom stair.

"Please, someone, I need help here," Carly announced to the growing throng. She wrapped one arm around Dawn and carefully lifted her head with the other. Cradling her as best she could, she massaged her forehead and cheeks. "Dawn? Can you hear me?"

Someone finally saw Carly struggling and rushed up to help her. It was Klarissa's Auntie Meggs, her kind face creased with concern. "Oh my gosh, what happened?"

"She passed out, I think," Carly said, swallowing back a lump.

"Dawn? Sweetie? It's Auntie Meggs, honey. Wake up." She pulled Dawn away from Carly, wrapping her gently in her own arms and rocking her as if she were a child.

In the distance, a siren blared. Only seconds

later, it seemed to Carly, the front door banged open and responders rushed inside.

To Carly's relief, an EMT immediately took over Dawn's care. He snapped open a vial and waved it under her nose. Dawn's eyelids fluttered, and she began to cough. Auntie Meggs reached for Carly's hand and squeezed it. "Thank you."

The EMT checked out Dawn thoroughly before moving her to a comfortable position. He probed her scalp lightly, then pushed her hair back from her face. "Hey, there. How are you feeling?"

"I'm…I'm okay," Dawn said in a choked voice. "What happened?"

"You fainted," the EMT said. "We're taking you to the hospital to be sure you don't have a concussion. I didn't feel any lumps, but we want to be sure." He smiled, but Dawn only scowled.

"I don't need to go to the hospital. What happened to Tony?" she asked urgently. "Is he okay?"

By that time more police were streaming into the foyer. Faces grim, they disbanded the growing horde of onlookers and escorted guests from the area. A tall man with a full head of gray hair and wearing a gold badge that said CHIEF broke from the others and came over to Carly.

"Say it isn't so," the chief said tightly, shoving his hands onto his hips.

"Hi, Chief," Carly greeted him. "Can you tell me what's happening?"

He graced her with a full-on glare. "Excuse me," he said to the others. "I need to talk to Carly privately."

Fred Holloway was a longtime family friend, but he'd warned her twice before about getting involved with criminals. He'd halfheartedly threatened her with jail time if it happened again.

He led her to a corner at the entrance to the dining room. The same corner where, only a short time ago, Carly had unwittingly eavesdropped on Tony, Dawn, and Ron. "What in tarnation are you doing here?" the chief demanded.

Carly was not happy with his tone. "I was asked to cater a wedding shower," she bristled. "That's what I *was* doing. I was just leaving when I saw a man lying on the floor near the staircase. I couldn't rouse him, so I called 911. After that all...you-know-what broke loose. Are they taking Tony to the hospital?"

The chief ignored her question. "You just referred to him as a man. Now he's Tony?"

Carly had to resist an eyeroll. "You're splitting hairs, Chief. I'd seen Tony earlier, and I knew he was wearing a gold sweater. Except for the videographer, he was the only man here."

"So you'd met him then?"

"No, not exactly," Carly admitted. "But I saw him talking to Klarissa's cousin earlier, and someone called him Tony. That gold sweater was sort of a giveaway."

The chief rubbed his hand over his forehead. "I suspect there's more to this story, but right now I have more immediate issues." He lifted his chin toward the dining room. "I want you to sit down in there and wait for an officer to interview you. Don't talk to anyone who isn't official police, and that's an order. I'll get back to you as soon as I can."

Slightly incensed at his commanding tone, Carly craned her head toward the area where Tony lay on the floor. A man and a woman Carly suspected were detectives crouched beside him, blocking her view. "Chief, is Tony going to be all right?"

The chief looked away, then shook his head. "No, Carly, he's not going to be all right. I'm sorry, but Tony Manous is dead."

~

Dead.

The word reverberated in her head.

She lowered herself onto an upholstered chair. She'd dropped her tote and her cooler in the foyer, and now she had nothing except her cell phone. Thank heaven she'd stuck it in her coat pocket.

The chief had ordered her to talk to no one, but surely he'd been referring only to the people in the mansion? Either way, she needed to let Ari know what happened. They'd planned to meet at her apartment later for a pizza, but now she was delayed indefinitely. She couldn't just let him wait and worry. She punched in his number.

"Hey, what's happening?" His deep voice gave her chills—the good kind, the kind that sent a zing of electricity through her. "Are you home already?" The smile in his voice was obvious.

Carly kept her voice quiet. "Not yet. Um, there's been kind of a glitch, so I'm going to have to stay at the Chapin house for a while."

His voice morphed instantly into one of deep concern. "What kind of glitch? Should I come over there?"

"No, they probably wouldn't let you in anyway." She swallowed, then related what happened as succinctly as she could.

"Oh, honey, that's awful." Ari's voice softened. "I'm guessing right about now it's chaos over there."

"Controlled chaos is probably a better description. The chief told me to stay in the dining room and not to talk to anyone except official police."

"Are you okay?"

"I'm okay," she assured him, although that wasn't the entire truth. She agreed to call him the moment they released her, which she hoped would be sooner rather than later.

After they disconnected, Carly studied the beautiful room. The chief had closed both doors, so the clamor from the foyer was muted. On the oak dining room table, large clusters of hydrangeas—the same blue flowers she'd seen on her first tour of the mansion—nestled with sprigs of a lacy white flower in a crystal vase. Not baby's breath this time. More like Queen Anne's lace, Carly thought. A few drops of water had spilled onto the polished table. Her normal instinct would be to blot it with a tissue, but without her tote she had nothing.

"Carly?" Holloway had opened the door so silently behind her she hadn't heard a sound. She jumped in her seat and turned around. A short, plump man with a wide face and a sharp gaze stood beside the chief.

"Yes?"

"Lieutenant Granger from the state police has some questions for you." With that he ushered him into the room and closed the door, leaving Carly alone with the man.

"May I sit?" Granger said in a voice that was surprisingly soft.

"Of course," Carly said, adjusting her chair a bit.

Instead of taking a seat on the opposite side of the table, Granger pulled out the chair next to Carly's. Facing her at an angle, he removed a vinyl-covered notepad and a pen from the inside of his tweed jacket and set them down in front of him.

Granger's questions were brief and to the point, and he scribbled a few notes as she spoke. How she knew the Chapins, what her role had been in the wedding shower, if she'd met Mr. Manous before today. Carly answered as carefully as she could, but after twenty minutes or so her throat was growing dry. She began to cough.

"Do you need water?" Granger asked her when her cough was beginning to wane.

Carly shook her head. "I'm okay. Thanks."

After a few more questions, he closed his notebook and looked her straight in the eye. "You a football fan?"

Inwardly, Carly sighed with relief. Granger was wrapping things up. With any luck she'd be allowed to gather her things and leave. More than anything she wanted to be home, where sanity, not turmoil, reigned.

"You mean, pro football?"

Granger nodded.

"Um, kind of. My boyfriend is a bigger fan than I am, but we enjoy watching the games together. I know there's a big playoff game tomorrow, but I'm not even sure who's favored."

He nodded without comment. "Ms. Hale, how well do you know Dawn Chapin?"

The question threw her. Had he planned all along to catch her off guard? Was that the purpose of the random football question? "Well, I've known Dawn since high school, but we were never best buds, if that's what you mean." She gave him a brief recap of how she happened to be catering the shower at the Chapin home.

"I see. Do you have any reason to believe Ms. Chapin might've had a beef with Mr. Manous?"

And there it was. The real reason for all the probing questions.

Dawn's expression when she came down the stairs and saw Tony on the floor flashed in Carly's mind. It was a mixture of horror and fear, Carly thought. Had it been laced with a touch of guilt?

"I'm...not really sure how to answer that. I only reconnected with Dawn and Klarissa a few weeks ago, at my restaurant. Before that I hadn't seen either of them since high school. And I'd never even met Tony Manous."

But Dawn's words that day, when she gave Carly the tour of the mansion, rattled in her brain.

I want my old friend back, Carly. And that's never going to happen as long as Tony Manous is in the picture.

CHAPTER FIVE

Carly's tote had been returned to her, but her cooler was being retained by the police. She didn't know what they hoped to find, but at least she didn't need it for the restaurant. Granger had dismissed her with instructions to stop by the police station the following day to give an official statement.

A state trooper had been stationed at the door, no doubt to screen anyone who was either coming in or leaving. Since Granger had escorted Carly to the door, she'd been allowed to leave without explanation.

Just as she was leaving, a man was attempting to enter. Blond and handsome, he looked nervous, his face flushed and his eyes darting all around. "I'm Adam Bushey, the best man." He showed the trooper his ID. "Will you let me inside?"

"Sorry, sir." Granger came up alongside him. "Only official personnel are allowed in."

The man started to argue, but Carly didn't stick around to listen. She hurried out to her car and flipped the heat on high, then immediately called Ari. They agreed to meet at her apartment in thirty minutes. She weaved her car out of the parking area, now crammed with official vehicles. Her insides turned over when she saw a large van nearly blocking her exit. Unfortunately, she'd seen that same vehicle before. It belonged to the state's crime scene investigation unit, which suggested only one thing.

Tony Manous's death had not been accidental.

Carly was making her way down the driveway when another vehicle caught her attention. An olive-green car—a hybrid of some sort—was parked off to one side on the road leading to the house. A large sign on the passenger's side door read: Bushey's Pet Grooming, along with a local phone number. Below that was an image of a dog and a cat, each with big fluffy tails. Carly tried to get a better look at the sign, but she was too far away.

Adam Bushey, the best man. That had to be his vehicle.

It didn't matter. All she wanted was to go home to her cozy apartment and her sweet dog, Havarti. She'd adopted the little Morkie about six months earlier, and he'd proven to be a wonderful companion. Ari would be arriving soon too, a thought that would normally give her a warm, tingly feeling. But after the bizarre events of the day—*a day that ended in death,* she thought soberly—romance was the furthest thing from her mind.

Carly had no sooner shut off her engine when her cell pinged with a text. Ignoring it, she headed upstairs to her second-story apartment, swept Havarti into her arms, and laughed as he licked her face. "You're happy to see me, aren't you? I'm happy to see you too."

After setting him down, she freshened his water bowl and fed him a few treats. Her neighbor, Becca, had been taking care of his bathroom breaks, so she didn't worry about rushing him outside.

Minutes later, Ari arrived. The moment he stepped into her apartment, he wrapped her in his arms and pulled her close. For a few luxurious seconds she melted into him, feeling the tension slip out of her limbs.

"I need coffee," Carly said, and Ari laughed.

"Of course you do. Relax while I put the pot on. I don't like seeing you so stressed."

While he prepared the coffee, Carly flopped onto the sofa. Her head was beginning to pound. Closing her eyes, she rested her head back. Her lips formed an automatic smile when she felt a furry form crawl into her lap.

In her mind, she pictured Tony, Dawn, and Ron in the dining room, sniping at each other while she hid from their line of vision. *There was no love lost in that trio*, she reflected grimly.

Ari came in with two coffee mugs.

"Thank you," Carly said. "I need this for my headache."

After a few sips, she told him everything, from working with Astrid right down to finding Tony's prone form in the foyer.

"You've sure had a day," he said, touching her cheek. "Lots of drama, a million unanswered questions." He drained his coffee mug and his brow furrowed thoughtfully. "I actually worked with Tony Manous on a project for the town last year."

Carly sat up straight. "You knew him? What did you think of him?"

"He was okay," Ari said. "A little brash for my taste, but he was fair and not bad to work with. The lighting in Ledyard Park was being upgraded, and the town had accepted my bid. Even so, Tony and the town manager bickered about everything before the contract was finalized. It's a miracle the lighting ever got installed."

"What did they argue about?" Carly asked him.

"You name it. The timing, the suppliers, the subs. Then one day, the town manager suddenly agreed to Tony's demands, and the project moved forward immediately."

"Strange," Carly said, mulling that. "Small town politics, right?"

"Pretty much," Ari agreed, "but it was definitely odd."

"By the way, I should know this, but who's the town manager?"

"Her name's Gretel Engstrom. She's a pleasant

woman, and a very competent one. In the four years she's been town manager, she's done a lot for Balsam Dell. Tony seemed to be the only one who had a problem with her."

Carly made a mental note of that.

Ari frowned. "Carly, if this turns out to be murder—" He broke off and shook his head.

"I know what you're thinking, honey, but please don't worry. Believe me, the state police are all over this. By the time I left, the Chapin mansion looked like a cop convention."

He gave her a weak smile. "I can only imagine. What's that place like, anyway?"

"Gorgeous. Every room that I saw had décor to die for." She smacked her fingers to her lips. "Sorry, I said that without thinking."

"It's just an expression. Did you tell the police about that argument you overheard in the dining room?"

She groaned. "No, not yet. I'm not sure what to do. I mean, people argue all the time, right? It doesn't mean they have violent tendencies." Carly paused. "What would you do?"

"That's a tough call, but I think I'd mention it to the police. I'm sure they're questioning Dawn and Ron anyway, but what you overheard might give them something to work with."

"What I'm afraid of," she said darkly, "is if I do that, I'll be throwing innocent people under the bus, so to speak."

"The truth will always shine through, eventually," Ari said. "Even if it has to sneak around a few dark corners to get there."

She knew he was referring to a few short months ago, when he himself had been suspected of murder. He'd been cleared once the killer was caught, but for a while, things had been dicey.

"I haven't even checked on my restaurant today," Carly said. This was the first day since she'd opened that she hadn't made an appearance at her eatery.

"I was there earlier," Ari told her, "and everything was running smoothly. Gotta say, your new assistant manager is a whirlwind. She never seems to get tired, and Grant and Suzanne like her a lot. Customers do too."

In a prior life, Valerie Wells had been half owner of a country store in the Rutland area, where a bustling lunch counter had been the main attraction. Her partner had been a man named Luke, but that's all Carly knew about him. For reasons Carly had never been clear on, the store closed abruptly, leaving Valerie jobless. She was currently living with an elderly aunt on the outskirts of Balsam Dell.

Carly smiled. "That's good to hear about Valerie. I'll shoot her a text later and check in." She felt her smile collapse. "I dread telling them all about what happened today."

"Honey, none of it had anything to do with

you," Ari soothed. "You were an unlucky bystander, period."

Unlucky for sure, Carly thought. She'd overheard so many prickly conversations that her ears were still ringing.

Ari went to the kitchen for the coffee pot and refilled their mugs. "Still feel like a pizza?" he asked her.

Carly wrinkled her nose. "I'm hungry, but I'm also a bit queasy. If you order it half-plain, I'll eat a slice."

"Is it okay if I order a meatball for Havarti?"

She smiled. Ari was more indulgent with "people food" than she was, but they both loved to spoil Havarti. "That's fine, as long as we give him half tonight and save the other half for tomorrow."

With that decided, Ari called for delivery of the pizza from Louie's, their favorite pie joint. While he set the table, Carly fetched her phone from her tote. Three voicemails had come in, but it was the text message she wanted to read first.

It was from Dawn.

Carly tapped open the message, her mouth going dry as she read: Carly, U have to help me. The police think I killed Tony!

Carly stared at the message. Was Dawn serious, or was she exaggerating? Had the police already determined Tony was murdered?

"Carly, you're so pale," Ari said, returning to sit beside her. "What's wrong?"

She showed him the text.

His expression tightened. "I can guess why she wants you to help her," he said quietly.

She nodded. Twice before, Carly had gone against her better judgment and delved into murders. Neither experience had been pleasant.

On the plus side, two murderers had been caught. She had to keep reminding herself of that.

"I'll tell her she needs an attorney," Carly said firmly. "I have a restaurant to run, and I am not an investigator."

Ari gave her a half chuckle. "When I look into your eyes, I can already see the wheels turning," he said. "You were there when it happened. You probably know more than you realize."

"I'm supposed to give my official statement tomorrow," she said. "I'm going to tell the police what I overheard, but I'm also going to tell them something else."

"What's that?"

Dawn's face flashed in Carly's mind—her genuine smile that first day when she showed Carly around the mansion's magnificent kitchen. Despite her feelings about Tony, Dawn had gone to great lengths to put together a beautiful shower for Klarissa. That the day ended in death had been a tragedy, but it had nothing to do with Dawn. Deep in her bones, Carly felt sure of that.

She looked at Ari. "I don't believe for a minute that Dawn Chapin murdered Tony Manous."

CHAPTER SIX

On Sunday morning, Carly steeled herself for the dreaded appointment at the police station. Ari had offered to accompany her, but she declined. He had projects to work on, and she didn't need a babysitter. She'd gotten through similar interviews before, and she'd get through this one.

At the Balsam Dell Police station, the state police had set up two interview rooms. Carly was graced, once again, with having Lieutenant Granger as her interviewer. Wearing a long-sleeved knit shirt over neatly pressed corduroys, he escorted her into a windowless room with a table, three chairs, and a mirrored wall. A microphone rested in the center of the table.

"Coffee?" he offered.

"No, thanks." Glancing up at the camera perched in one corner of the ceiling, she loosened her scarf and shrugged out of her coat. The room was stifling. She wondered if they used it as a trick to get prisoners to spill their stories more quickly.

"Ms. Hale, I'll get right to the point. With so

many people at the Chapin home yesterday, these interviews are taking a long time. I don't see any need to waste mine or yours with pleasantries, so let's get started."

She nodded agreeably at his curt statement.

"It came to my attention yesterday that you talked to several guests at the shower. Guests you might not have encountered if you hadn't veered from your assigned job of making grilled cheese sandwiches."

Carly felt her hackles rise. "I didn't intentionally *veer*, as you put it. At one point I was asked by the hostess to accompany her into the drawing room so the guests could thank me for the sandwiches. Everyone enjoyed them quite a bit, I guess. After I did that, I left as quickly as I could."

"In the drawing room, do you remember who you came in direct contact with?"

Carly mulled his question, then named everyone she could recall speaking to. There was at least one guest whose name she didn't know—the woman in the beige pantsuit.

Granger scribbled something on his notepad. From Carly's angle, it looked like he was making a grocery list, but she couldn't be totally sure.

"And after that?"

"After that I went back to the kitchen. The house is a bit of a maze, but I knew the shortcut through the breakfast nook."

He nodded slowly, then rubbed his jaw with his hand. "Did you encounter anyone on the way?"

Carly's heart suddenly clutched. *Rose Manous.* Until now, she'd forgotten about her. The poor woman must be devastated over her stepson's untimely death.

"Yes," she said. "Mrs. Manous, Tony's stepmom. She was sitting alone at the table in the breakfast nook. She was upset because she hadn't been allowed to serve her homemade pastries to the guests."

"Did she seem angry?"

Carly shrugged, but the question irked her. "It's hard for me to judge, since I'd never met the woman before. She'd been crying, so I'd say she was more sad than angry."

"Do you know what she did with those homemade pastries?"

"Sorry, I'm not sure where they ended up. She wanted to leave right away and asked if I'd get her coat."

He looked surprised, but Carly suspected he was acting. "Didn't that seem odd to you? I mean, you were there to grill sandwiches, not to host, isn't that correct?"

"I didn't really think about it, Lieutenant," she said, trying to keep her tone even. "The housekeeper, Astrid, was busy serving cake to the guests. Rose seemed so anxious to go I agreed to help look for her coat."

She recounted her path through the dining room and into the foyer to the coatroom.

Granger flipped to a new page in his notebook. "So, Mrs. Manous left without incident?"

"Yes, she did," Carly confirmed.

"After that, did you return to the kitchen?" He pierced her with a look that made her want to squirm.

Forcing her limbs to relax, she said, "Yes, but as I reached the entrance to the dining room, I overheard two people talking. It seemed rather personal, so I...sort of squeezed into the corner so they wouldn't see me. I wasn't trying to eavesdrop, but I didn't want to embarrass them by scooting past them, either."

She related what she'd overheard, including the part about Ron, the videographer, joining the conversation. From there, she retraced her actions until she found Tony on the floor and called 911.

"I find it curious," Granger said, "that you didn't think to disclose all this yesterday during our interview. Is there a reason you omitted it?"

"You said I'd have to come in to give an official statement today," Carly responded coolly. "That's what I'm doing." She softened her voice. "Lieutenant, do they know how Tony died?"

"At the moment, no. It appears to be from something he consumed, but tests are still being performed. We probably won't know for another day or two at the earliest."

"I see." Carly thought back to the spilled drink on the floor where Tony had lain. "Was it something he drank?"

"I'm not at liberty to say. Ms. Hale, I have one more question, and then you can go. But please be prepared to come in again if we need more information."

"I always cooperate fully with the police," she said, then wished she could take her words back. It made her sound like a habitual offender.

He quirked a smile. "Yes, word has it around the station that you've had more…experience with murder than the average citizen."

Carly felt a flush creep up her neck. "Only because I happened to be at the wrong place, at the wrong time," she defended. "What was your question?"

For one long moment, Granger stared at her. "When Dawn Chapin came down the stairs after you discovered Mr. Manous's body, what, exactly, did she say to you?"

Carly hesitated. What *had* Dawn said? She thought back.

After squeezing the memory back into her brain, she told Granger the truth. "She didn't say a word, Lieutenant. She just dropped to the stairs like a rock and passed out."

~

Though she was sorely tempted to fly out of the interview room, Carly forced herself to maintain her composure. She made her way calmly along the tiled corridor, keeping an even but unhurried pace. She didn't want Granger to think she'd gotten rattled by his questions and that she was anxious to bolt.

It was only after they'd concluded the interview that she realized she hadn't given Granger her opinion—that she was sure Dawn wasn't a killer. Not that he would have put any faith in it, but she wanted to make it known.

Carly was buttoning her coat, heading toward the exit when she spotted the woman in question. Clad in her puffy purple coat, her complexion close to gray, Dawn was walking beside a tall, silver-haired man wearing a heavy overcoat. In one hand he carried a briefcase. With his other hand, he clung to Dawn's elbow as he steered her toward the lobby.

When she saw Carly, Dawn's face crumpled. She tore her elbow from her companion's grasp and threw her arms around her. "I knew you'd help me," she whispered.

Carly hugged her. She didn't have a clue how to respond. The man beside Dawn was staring hard at Carly, as if trying to place her. "Brett Farnham," he said. He removed his hand from Dawn's elbow and held it out. "Ms. Chapin's attorney."

Thank heaven. She has an attorney.

Carly introduced herself and accepted his handshake. His grip was firm and dry, his blue eyes intense.

"Dawn told me about you," he said glibly. "You've been a good friend. We very much appreciate that."

We?

"Carly, did the police ask you about me?" Dawn said urgently.

Carly hesitated. "They asked me about a lot of people, Dawn. The guy threw so many names at me, my head was spinning like a top." At Dawn's bereft expression, she softened her voice. "Yes, he mentioned you. Along with at least a dozen guests."

Dawn swallowed, then grabbed Carly's arm. "Listen to me, Carly. I didn't do anything. I didn't poison Tony!"

Poison. Is that what Granger meant when he mentioned something Tony had consumed?

"Is that what they said?" Carly asked her. "That Tony was poisoned?"

Farnham gripped his client's elbow again, so tightly that Dawn winced. "Ms. Hale, it was a pleasure meeting you. Dawn and I are heading to my office now. Have a good day."

Before Dawn could utter the word "goodbye," Farnham whisked her through the lobby and out the main entrance.

Carly watched them leave. Dawn's head was down, and Farnham was rushing her toward the parking lot as if a snaggled-toothed gremlin was nibbling at their heels.

Grateful to be done with her interview, Carly hurried toward her car. The parking spaces along the street had all been taken, and she'd been forced to park almost a block away. A TV cable van was double-parked along the side street next to the police station.

"Hey! Carly!" The voice came from behind her.

She turned and saw Don Frasco jogging toward her. The sole owner and editor of the town's free weekly paper, Don was always on the lookout for a breaking story—one that would put him on the national news map. Mostly what he published were ads from area merchants, along with the usual stories covering local events.

"Hey," he repeated, coming up alongside her. "Did you hear about Tony Manous? It's all over the news. I'm bummed I didn't get the scoop. The cops won't tell me a thing. They're being extra tight-lipped on this one."

"I'm sure everyone in town's heard about it by now," Carly said carefully. "Was it on TV last night? I didn't watch the news."

He ran a gloved hand through his dark auburn hair, which was nearly the same color as his eyes. "Yeah, it was on TV, and stop walking so fast, will ya?"

"I have to walk fast. I'm freezing."

As if a light suddenly snapped on in his head, he said, "Hey, were you at the police station just now?"

Carly suppressed a groan. If Don found out she'd been at the Chapin home when Tony Manous passed, he'd badger her for details until chickens gave milk. "I'm not really supposed to talk about it," she said evasively. "You know how the police work. Mum's the word, and all that."

"*Oh. My. Gosh.* You weren't just at the police station. I bet you were at the Chapin house yesterday, weren't you?"

Carly knew her telltale flush gave her away, but she kept her lips closed.

Don turned and began trotting backward in front of her, his freckled face morphing into a grin. "Don't deny it. I can tell just by that look on your face I'm right."

"Don, stop walking backward. You're going to trip."

"I will if you'll grab a coffee with me. You can tell me all about it. Besides, I might know some things you don't."

Carly stopped walking. She wasn't going to be drawn into figuring out who killed Tony. For all she knew, the poisoning—if that's what it was—had been accidental. Whatever the case, it was in the hands of the police. It wasn't her job to intervene.

"I'm sorry, but Ari and I are spending the

afternoon with my sister and her friend. I'm in charge of appetizers, so I need to get home and make something."

His eyes glittered. "Is her *friend* that famous opera singer?"

Carly wasn't sure how famous Nate Carpenter was, but he was a fantastic performer and a kind man. More important, he adored her sister, Norah, and made her happy.

"He's the guy," she said brightly.

"Thought so. Anyway, about Tony Manous. What if I know of someone at the town hall who *really* didn't like him?"

Carly halted. "You're trying to trick me into talking to you, but it won't work. Have a nice day, Don. Stop by the restaurant tomorrow and I'll give you a root beer." She moved to go around him.

"It's a woman," he said in a teasing tone.

Do not get involved. Do not get involved.

She sighed and lifted her chin. "I'll give you five minutes. My car is right up there."

~

Carly started the engine of her aging Corolla. "Should be warm in a minute," she told him. *Or three.*

Don had plunked himself onto the front seat and was frowning at the windshield. "For criminy's sake, Carly, there's a coffee shop right up the street. Aren't you afraid we'll die of carbon monoxide poisoning this way?"

She rolled down her window a crack. "We're out in the open, Don, not in a garage. So, tell me who *really* didn't like Tony Manous."

"What'll you tell me in return? Come on, Carly. I need something."

Carly thought back to the events of the day before. She gave him a brief overview of how she'd ended up catering the shower.

"So, that's why you were there," he said slowly. "You were hired to be the cook. What was that place like, anyway?"

"Gorgeous," she said, her mind's eye skipping through the stunningly appointed rooms. "Simply...beautiful."

Except for the body of Tony Manous lying in the foyer.

"While you were there," Don pressed her, "did you notice anything unusual? Anyone skulking around? Anyone who looked out of place, like they didn't belong there? Come on, Carly. I need something I can sink my investigative teeth into."

She had to admire his determination. If nothing else, he was relentless.

Carly had been about thirteen the day Don's mom called and asked her to babysit him for an afternoon. She hadn't been there ten minutes when it became obvious why his mom had trouble keeping sitters. Don was the most boisterous, overactive, vocal kid she'd ever met. When she began making him a grilled cheese for lunch, he'd issued a shriek so deafening Carly feared for Mrs. Frasco's crystal. He'd finally settled for a PB&J, and Carly was grateful she'd never been asked to sit for him again.

"Don, even if there was something I could tell you, you can't just go around questioning people based on stuff I might have overheard. I'm sure the state police will be having a press conference later today or early tomorrow. You can ask your questions then."

He looked deflated. "But don't you get it, Carly? You were right there, in the belly of the beast. In a way, you had a ringside seat."

A ringside seat to murder. Every restaurateur's dream.

When she didn't respond, Don bit down on one chapped lip and shook his head. "Okay, let me ask you this. While you were there, did you happen to meet a woman named Gretel?"

"Not that I recall," Carly said truthfully. "I wasn't hired to mingle, only to grill sandwiches. At one point, Klarissa Taddeo introduced me to the guests, but I can't say many of the faces looked familiar."

Don dug his cell out of his jacket pocket, pulled off a glove, and tapped at the keys. He held it out to her. "Was this lady one of them?"

Carly stared at the photo of the attractive, thirty-something woman. High forehead, streaked blond hair, plump lips. The memory came to her—she was the woman in the beige pantsuit.

"I *did* see her there. Did you say her name's Gretel?"

"Gretel Engstrom. Shame on you, Carly. I'm surprised you don't recognize our very own town manager."

Of course! The town manager. The woman Ari had told her about.

"I should have remembered that. Ari mentioned her to me yesterday. I won't reveal the details, but he said Gretel Engstrom and Tony clashed over a town contract."

"Clashed is a polite word, and I already know the details. Gretel Engstrom is a 'by the book' type, and Tony is…well, *was* more of a 'work around the rules' sort. He came up with all kinds of demands, some of which were reasonable, others, not so much. When Ms. Engstrom suddenly caved, the Select Board members were shocked. No one really knows what happened, but Ledyard Park got its beautiful lighting, along with a landscape upgrade and a few other things Ms. Engstrom hadn't been thrilled over. She thought the town had wasted too much money on frivolous things, like crawly tubes for kids, complete with skylights."

Carly shrugged. "They sound nice. So you never

found out what happened to make her change her mind?"

"No. Which is exactly why I did some online digging on Ms. Engstrom."

Now Carly's interest was piqued. "What did you find out?"

"Not as much as I'd hoped," he said, looking troubled. "Ms. Engstrom has a stellar reputation. She's saved money for the town. She pushed for the construction of the new senior center at least a year earlier than the scheduled groundbreaking. The entire project came in at below cost, which made her a hero with our budget-conscious locals. Everything about her seems competent and genuine."

"Then I don't get it. What's the problem?"

"The problem is that her history is a mystery. I can't seem to figure out where she came from. It's like, she materialized in Vermont one day, presented her credentials to the Board, and was appointed town manager."

Carly swallowed. She'd known someone like that in the past. Someone's whose history turned out to be not very savory.

But this was different.

"A lot of people keep their private lives private. I'm sure the Select Board checked her out thoroughly. Does she have a Facebook or Instagram page?"

"Not that I could find." He chewed on his poor lip again like Havarti with a meatball.

"Something doesn't make sense," Carly mused aloud. "If she and Tony didn't like each other, why was she invited to Klarissa's shower?"

Don pointed a finger at her and smiled. "That, Ms. Carly Hale, is an excellent question. Maybe you should pop into her office tomorrow and chat her up. As a local businessperson, you should be able to dream up some bogus reason."

She shot him a look. "Thanks for the vote of confidence. But I'm curious about something. How did you know Ms. Engstrom was at the shower yesterday?"

His eyes gleamed. "I didn't. I knew about Manous's death, obviously, and where it took place. That much was splashed all over TV. I figured if I was going to get any of the deets, I'd have to start at the police station. I strolled in casually, sat on a bench, and opened my newspaper like I was waiting for someone. No one even questioned what I was doing there."

"Very clever," she said wryly.

"Wasn't it?" he said, without a hint of irony. "I tried signaling to a few of the cops that I wanted a statement, but they walked past me like I was invisible."

"Once more, how did you find out about Ms. Engstrom attending the shower?"

"I made an educated guess when I saw her coming out of the restroom at the station. She looked like the devil, her face all pale and pinched. But I still didn't know for sure"—he grinned—"until you just confirmed it for me."

Carly groaned and shook her head. She had to admit, he'd gotten her. "You're a trickster."

"I'm a reporter," he corrected. "Come on, Carly. I've been sitting here almost five minutes, possibly breathing in dangerous exhaust, and you haven't given me one helpful tidbit of intel. What really happened at that gig yesterday?"

How much should she tell him? So many guests had attended that fateful shower. Half the town was probably already gossiping about it. At this stage, was anything she witnessed unknown to the police?

Yes. I was the only one who overheard the argument among Tony, Dawn, and Ron.

"I'll tell you one thing," Carly said. "There was a videographer at the shower. It struck me as odd, until I learned he was Klarissa's cousin. I'm guessing by now the police have asked him to turn over his video cam, or at least see his films or whatever they call it."

That got Don's attention. "Was it a video cam or a camcorder?"

Carly shrugged. "I don't know. Is there a difference?"

"A camcorder is better, depending on the model. The newer ones can convert the optical signal to an electronic one *and* store it, as well."

"I can't help you there, Don. I wouldn't know one from the other." *I wouldn't even know one from a toaster oven.*

A slow smile spread across his face. "Hey, by any chance, was the videographer a local guy? Like maybe, Ron Benoit?"

"Ah, so you've heard of him. But since you already guessed who it was, you can't say I spilled the beans."

Don's expression bordered on gleeful. "I actually know Ron Benoit. A few years ago, when I was honing my photography skills, I took an adult education class from him at the high school."

"Was he good?"

"He was okay. Maybe a little full of himself. Rude to some of the students he didn't like. I'll say this about him, though—he won't be working in Hollywood any time soon."

"Was that one of his goals?"

"I had the sense it was on his bucket list, but it could've been just talk. He's a bit of a blowhard." Don's face turned suddenly pensive. "Something just struck me. With all the money the Chapins have, I'm surprised there weren't any hidden cameras in the house." He turned sharply toward Carly. "Or were there?"

Stumped, Carly looked at him. "I didn't even think of that, but I never saw any. If there were cameras anywhere, they were well disguised." She blew out a sigh. "Listen, Don. I know you're doing your job, and I get that you have to dig for information. But a lot of people were at that shower yesterday. Most, if not all of them, are innocent of any wrong-doing. Reputations can be easily damaged by careless gossip."

He narrowed his gaze. "But if Manous was poisoned—which is the current rumor—it's possible, actually likely, one of them is guilty. I think I'll stop by Benoit's studio tomorrow. Remind him I took a class from him. Maybe I can squeeze something juicy out of him for this week's issue." He looked hopefully at Carly. "Want to go with me?"

"No, I do not," Carly said firmly, but a part of her was itching to hear what Benoit had to say. "Asking questions is the job of the police. I'm sure they'll do it efficiently and professionally. Without any help from me."

At least I can tell myself that.

"Suit yourself," Don said ominously. "But keep one thing in mind. If you hadn't gotten involved in the last local murder, Ari Mitchell might be wearing prison orange. For a *long, long* time."

Carly looked at Don, and her heart sank. He wasn't totally right. The police would've nailed the real killer eventually. But Carly's interference had sped up the process, and the killer was now awaiting trial.

"You know, Don, for what it's worth, you've

acquired some pretty decent investigative chops since last year's nightmare. I mean, considering what you have to work with in a small town like this one."

His jaw hanging open, he gawked at her. "I… geez, thanks, Carly. So maybe I'm not just that dopey little kid who hates cheese anymore?"

"Oh, you're still that," she said, deadpan. "But you're a reporter too. Now get out of my car before I rev up the engine and ramp up the fumes."

With a chuckle, he opened his door. "No problem. I wanna get to the deli before it closes, anyway. I've got a bone to pick with the clerk. Yesterday, I asked for a half pound of sliced ham. When I got home, I had bologna."

She grabbed his jacket sleeve. "What did you say?"

He gave her an odd look. "I said I got bologna instead of—"

"Before that."

"I had a bone to pick with the clerk?"

I came here because I have a bone to pick with my beautiful bride.

It was the phrase Tony had used when he was talking to Dawn in the dining room.

"Thanks, Don, for jogging my memory. Now go get yourself some ham."

CHAPTER SEVEN

SUNDAY'S VISIT WITH NORAH AND NATE HAD been the perfect distraction from talk of poison and murder. Carly had prepared some cheesy hors d'oeuvres, and Norah had supplied the wine, although the men opted for beer. They'd all enjoyed watching the NFL playoff game, in spite of Norah's disdain for the sport. In fact, Carly had never seen her sister look happier.

Even so, Carly had trouble pushing dark thoughts out of her mind. Why had Tony shown up at the shower? What was the bone he had to pick with Klarissa?

The thought had nagged her all night. She'd awakened Monday morning with jumbled images floating through her brain.

Her spirits lifted instantly when she strode through the back door of her eatery. Valerie and Grant had both come in early. They greeted her with hugs, and Valerie patted her back soothingly.

"Before you even ask, I'm fine," Carly said. She peeled off her coat, scarf, and gloves and draped them over a bench seat in one of the booths. "So, how did Saturday go?"

Grant poured her a cup of coffee. "It went fine. Super busy, but that's how we like it. How about a breakfast biscuit?"

Cheesy bacon breakfast biscuits had become a morning staple for the trio, although Valerie only indulged about twice a week.

"Thanks, but I'll pass on the biscuit today," Carly said. "I stuffed myself silly on snacks at Norah's yesterday."

Valerie sat on one of the stools at the counter and patted the one beside her. Her topknot was fuller than usual, and her cheeks had the tiniest hint of blush. "Come on. Sit here," she told Carly. "You sure you're okay?"

"Totally." Carly slid onto the stool beside her. "It feels good to be back to work."

Suzanne arrived a few minutes before 11:00, and the day turned into one of the busiest Mondays ever. Carly couldn't help wondering if word had leaked out about her presence at the shower on Saturday.

Grant was quieter than usual. Carly knew something was up. She approached him in the kitchen when they had a lull in customers. "Come on, spill it," she said, trying to sound casual. "What's wrong?"

"Nothing's wrong. I'm worried about you." He

removed a container of washed field greens from the commercial fridge. "Word around town is that Tony Manous died of poisoning, not from natural causes."

"So far, that's the theory," Carly said, "but I don't think there's been anything official. Grant, I know what you're thinking before you even say it. You're worried that I'll get involved in another murder."

Avoiding her gaze, he pulled the lid off the greens. "If someone poisoned him during the shower, then the killer was there, Carly. Right there while you were making sandwiches!" His voice rose. He tossed handfuls of dried cranberries into the greens.

"You need to stop worrying," she said. "Nothing's going to happen to me."

She wanted to ease his mind, to assure him that she wouldn't get involved. But deep down she knew it was a promise she wouldn't be able to keep.

Suzanne came in through the swinging door with a tray of dirty dishes. She set them on the counter next to the dishwasher. "Carly, Dawn Chapin is out there. She wants to speak to you."

"Thanks. I'll be right out."

Dawn was standing near the front door, huddled in her puffy purple coat. Her face was wan, her expression bleak.

"Hey, there." Carly gave her a brief hug.

Dawn handed her an envelope. "This is for

Saturday," she said. "The rest of what we owe you. The guests were all thrilled with the food. It was probably the only thing that went right."

"I don't want to accept this, Dawn. Not after what happened."

"I want you to have it," she insisted. "Plus, well...I have a favor to ask. I have an appointment tomorrow morning with the accounts manager at the country club. You know, where the wedding was supposed to be?"

With so much emphasis on the botched shower arrangements at the Balsam Dell Inn, Carly had nearly forgotten about the wedding. They'd booked it at the country club because they needed more room than the Inn could offer. "What's the favor?"

Dawn pulled in a slow breath. "It's going to be a battle trying to get the deposit back this close to the wedding date. It's not like there's time to book another wedding." She gave Carly a pleading look. "Would you go with me, Carly? Maybe with two of us there, she'll feel bad enough about Tony to give us a refund. The Taddeos are starting to pressure me. It's probably my last chance to save my friendship with Klarissa," she added in a strangled voice.

Carly's heart broke for her. It must have taken every ounce of her pride to ask for help. Now that Tony was out of the picture, getting that deposit back might be Dawn's only shot at keeping her friendship with Klarissa intact.

"I guess I can go with you, Dawn, but I'm not sure my presence will add anything."

Dawn pressed a finger to one eye. "Please, Carly? I honestly don't have the strength to do it alone. Mrs. Taddeo told me, in no uncertain terms, it was my job to get that money back. Besides, they're all grieving for Tony. They're in no position to talk to anyone."

How could Carly refuse? Besides, she had to admit that a tiny part of her welcomed the chance to get some answers from Dawn. "Sure. What time shall I meet you there?"

Dawn looked so relieved Carly wanted to weep for her. "Nine-thirty? I'll wait for you in the lobby, near the coffee bar."

"I'll be there. In the meantime, try not to worry about it, okay?" In a lower voice Carly said, "Have you heard any more from the police?"

Dawn swallowed. "Only that they're still trying to identify the...substance that killed Tony. They think it was in his drink."

That was bad. It meant the substance, whatever it was, most likely came from the house.

"But you have an attorney now, right? That must be a relief."

"Not really. He's pushy, arrogant, and a know-it-all. I don't trust him one bit. I told Mother I want a different lawyer, but she insists he's the best."

Carly didn't understand why Dawn allowed her

mother to intimidate her. She was around Carly's age, so thirty-two more or less. Why hadn't she moved out of the house by now and gone out on her own?

Fortunately, Dawn hadn't said anything more about being considered a suspect. Maybe the police had other fish on the line and were checking into alibis.

"See you tomorrow, then," Carly said, watching Dawn leave.

Grant had returned to the dining room. Carly felt his gaze on her. She summoned Valerie and Suzanne and told all of them her plan for the following morning. She also asked them to keep it to themselves, for the sake of the Taddeo family's privacy.

"My lips are sealed, but good luck," Suzanne said, sounding doubtful. "I heard the accounts manager at the country club is a piranha."

"Gee, that's comforting," Carly said with a mild chuckle. "At least I know what I'm in for."

Valerie sighed. "I hope someday I'll know the locals as well as all of you do. I love living here, and Aunt Flo is thrilled to have me as a roomie. But I still feel like an outsider."

"Don't worry. Before long, you'll be a regular Balsam Deller," Grant joked.

Valerie's eyes clouded. "I hope so. I truly hope so."

CHAPTER EIGHT

By Tuesday morning, a warming trend had crept into southern Vermont. Temps in the forties, along with blindingly bright sunshine, heralded a pleasant winter day.

Instead of heading to the eatery, Carly worked at home for an hour. Gina had given her some ideas for menu designs, so she toyed with those on her laptop. And since the two hadn't seen each other since before the shower, Carly had invited her friend to stop by that evening. Gina was bringing tacos from their favorite Mexican restaurant, and Carly offered to make a salad.

After taking Havarti outside for one last visit to the backyard, she kissed him on the snout and left. The drive to the country club took only about ten minutes. The walkways had been shoveled and sanded, snow melting along the edges.

The moment she stepped inside the lobby, the scent of apples and cinnamon wafted over her in a veil of olfactory nirvana. The club was known for its apple-stuffed breakfast popovers, but she'd never been lucky enough to sample one. No doubt the aroma was drifting from the dining room, which was the large, sun-filled room straight ahead.

Off to the right was the coffee bar, which was pretty much self-serve. Dawn was seated in a chair next to the bar, her fingers twisted in the handle of her purse. When she spotted Carly, she nearly leaped off her seat. "I'm so relieved that you're here! My nerves are already jumping."

"You'll do fine," Carly assured her, hoping she was right.

"Do you want a coffee first?" Dawn offered.

"No, I've already had two cups, but you go ahead." Carly removed her coat and draped it over her arm.

"Are you kidding?" Dawn shuddered. "Coffee would do a number on my already ragged nerves. I'll text Tabitha to let her know we're here."

A few minutes later, the accounts manager strode into the lobby. Barely five feet tall, she had a cluster of dark curls that framed a tiny, elfin face. She stuck out one beringed hand. "Dawn, always a pleasure," she said. Before Dawn could introduce Carly, Tabitha's piercing green eyes swiveled sideways, and her jaw lowered. "Carly? Carly Hale?"

Carly gawked at the woman. "Oh...my gosh. Tabitha? The dragon lady of Balsam Dell High?"

"In the flesh!" She grabbed Carly in a bone-crushing hug. "So, how's my favorite frog champion?

I heard all about your restaurant. Keep meaning to pop in, but this place keeps me chained to the desk."

Dawn stared at them both. "You know each other?"

Tabitha slid her arm through Carly's and grinned. "Don't be fooled by Carly's mild-mannered demeanor. Back in the day, she and Gina Tomasso sneaked five fat frogs out of the science department and returned them to their natural habitat. It was the talk of the school for weeks."

Carly laughed. "Yeah, but we got detention for it too. And what about you, pulling a bully off a kid half his size?" She turned to Dawn. "We were all dressed for a Halloween fundraiser we'd set up near the bleachers. Tabitha had on this adorable dragon costume she'd made herself. Anyway, some kids were hanging around behind the bleachers, and we noticed this one boy, a senior, taunting a skinny freshman. Tabitha marched over there with steam coming out of her ears, grabbed him by the back of his shirt collar, and pulled him right to the ground. When all his buddies started cheering, the bully brushed off his pants, turned on his sneakered heel, and bolted."

"Hence the dragon lady moniker," Tabitha explained. "Come on, gals, grab your coats and we'll go down to my office."

They followed Tabitha along a carpeted hallway.

Her office was a square, tidy room with file cabinets lining one entire wall.

Tabitha took a seat behind her desk. "Have a seat." She softened her voice to a reverent tone. "First of all, I want to extend my sympathies to Klarissa and to the Taddeo and Manous families. Tony's death must have been a terrible shock. I am truly sorry for their loss."

Dawn cleared her throat nervously. "Thank you. I know they'll appreciate that. Given the tragic circumstances, the Taddeos are hopeful that the club will return their deposit, which, as you know, is substantial."

Stone-faced, Tabitha opened the folder resting in the center of her desk. "You've worked with us before, Dawn. You know the contract calls for surrender of the deposit if cancellation is less than three months from the event." She shot Carly an odd look that was impossible to interpret.

Dawn nodded. "I do. But on the family's behalf, I'm asking if that can be waived so they won't be forced to suffer a financial hardship. You can probably imagine what they're going through right now."

Well said, Carly thought.

Tabitha sat back in her chair and thought for a moment. "Tell you what I'm willing to do. If the Taddeos will agree to pay a small fee to cover my time"—she scribbled on a slip of paper and showed it to her—"I'll refund the remainder of the deposit."

Dawn looked at the paper, then sagged with relief. "Thank you, Tabitha. This is more than fair. On their behalf, I accept."

"Good. I'll prepare an amendment to the contract and email it to you later."

Dawn's face had brightened considerably. "Again, thank you. May I use the restroom before we leave?"

"Of course. Meet us in the lobby."

Dawn went off to the restroom. Tabitha walked Carly back to the lobby, a twinkle in her eye.

"You took a beating on that, didn't you?" Carly gave Tabitha a fist bump to the arm.

"Hey, listen, if it got around that we didn't refund the deposit for a deceased groom, our reputation would be toast." Tabitha grinned. "Besides, when I heard what happened Saturday, I found a gig to replace the wedding. A ski club was looking for a venue to host a jack and jill for two of their members who're getting hitched. It was kind of a last-minute deal, and they'd been going nuts trying to find a place that wasn't booked. I offered them the date, added a 'late booking' surcharge, and they happily took it."

Carly smiled. "Well, you did good. And don't pretend it was all for the good of the club."

Dawn returned to the lobby. After a round of hugs, she and Carly said their goodbyes.

"I can't thank you enough," Dawn said on their

way to their cars. "When Auntie Meggs hears this, she'll probably want to throw you a party."

"Dawn, I really didn't do anything."

"Your friendship and support helped me deal with it, though."

"Then I'm glad I could help. I'm surprised you didn't remember Tabitha from high school, though."

"I think Klar and I traveled in a different crowd," Dawn said by way of explanation, and then a flush crept up her neck. "Look, Carly, I have a confession. I remembered that you were friendly with Tabitha in high school. That's partly the reason I wanted you to come with me today. That story you told about her and the bully? I vaguely remembered that, but I didn't want to say anything. I-I'm sorry if I deceived you." She lowered her head. "It's just...I had a feeling you'd have more influence with her than I would."

A pinch of annoyance tightened Carly's gaze, but it softened at Dawn's penitent expression. "That's okay. Don't give it a thought. But now that you mentioned Klarissa, how is she doing? Out of everyone, she's probably the most devastated by all this. Well, her and Rose Manous," Carly added.

Dawn frowned and walked slowly toward Carly's vehicle with her. "Right now, Klar's a mess. I tried talking to her a few times, but her mom said she just stays in her room, crying. At the police interview on

Sunday she got nearly hysterical, according to her mom. They almost had to get a stretcher for her."

"I'm so sad for her," Carly said, noticing she didn't mention Tony's stepmom. "I lost my husband in an accident a few years ago, so I understand her pain."

"That's right. I remember reading about that. I'm…sorry for your loss, as well, Carly."

"Thank you. Do the police consider Klarissa a suspect?"

Dawn blinked and looked away. "No, but they probably would if they knew everything."

Carly's pulse jolted. "Everything?"

"There's so much you don't know, Carly. Tony and Klar fought all the time about his stepmom. At one point they almost broke up. But the police don't know all that, so I'm still the primary person of interest, only because I happened to be upstairs at the same time Tony was." Dawn's lip trembled.

"Klarissa disliked Mrs. Manous that much?" Carly asked.

"She did. Klar was convinced that Rose only married Tony's dad for his money."

Carly digested that for a moment, then said, "Dawn, why *were* you upstairs that day?"

"My feet were killing me, so I went up to my room to change my shoes. I heard someone in the bathroom. I knew it was Tony because I recognized his voice. He was coughing a lot, almost like he was gasping for breath, but I heard him yelling at Klarissa on his cell."

"You're sure about that?"

"Totally sure. He called her by name and screamed at her to stop lying. That's about all I heard before I ran into my room."

Something baffled Carly. "But why would he go upstairs to find a bathroom when there were bathrooms downstairs?"

"I don't know. I'm guessing he didn't want to be seen."

"Did he know the layout of the house?"

Dawn used her hand to shield her eyes from the sun, which was rising higher in the sky. "Not really, but obviously there'd be bathrooms upstairs. Why are you asking that?"

Conflicted, Carly mulled whether she should confess to Dawn that she'd overheard her squabble with Tony and Ron. If she did, she might get answers to some of her questions. Should she let Dawn know she'd been privy to the contentious argument?

"No particular reason," Carly said. "I'm just wondering, since Tony was right there in the house, why didn't he just confront Klarissa in person? It wouldn't have been hard to find her, even if he didn't know the layout of the rooms."

"I wondered that too," Dawn said. "I didn't even know why he came over. But I'm sure he knew Klar would throw a hissy if he embarrassed her in front of her guests, especially since he'd been drinking. He probably figured they'd hash out the rest of their argument later, after the shower was over."

"I guess that makes sense," Carly agreed. "Dawn, I really have to get to work, but I have one more question. Is there any word on what Tony...died from?"

"Not yet," Dawn said quietly.

"Did he have any allergies?"

"He did, but nothing that would have been fatal." Dawn gave her an impulsive hug. "Thanks again for coming with me today. Do you think we can get together again? Like maybe tonight after you get home?"

Tonight? Dawn really must be worried.

"Sorry, but I can't do it tonight, Dawn. My friend Gina's coming over to visit. Maybe tomorrow?"

Dawn's face drooped with disappointment. "I guess tomorrow will be okay. You're so lucky to have a friend like Gina Tomasso. I worked with her on a few of my clients' wedding invitations. She's a super lady, and so talented. I really admire her work."

Was Dawn hinting to be invited?

In truth, Gina would probably be delighted if Dawn joined them. Dishing about locals was one of her favorite pastimes, and when it came to grudges and animosities, she often had helpful insights.

“Let me see what I can arrange,” Carly offered. “Can I get back to you?”

“You sure can,” Dawn said with a hopeful smile. “I’d better go. Now that Klar’s wedding is off, I’ve got a long list of people I need to notify. Talk to you later?”

With a wave of her hand, Dawn crossed the lot toward her own car. Carly hopped into her Corolla and dug out her cell. Instead of texting, she called Gina.

“Hey, any chance we can add Dawn Chapin to tonight’s gab session?”

“Dawn?” Gina squawked. “You’re serious?”

“Totally.” Carly explained why she wanted to invite her.

“This will be *most* interesting,” Gina said eagerly. “I hope she likes tacos and refried beans.”

“Don’t worry. If she doesn’t, I’ll make her something else.”

That plan made, Carly headed to work. She’d call Dawn once she got there and ask if she’d like to join her and Gina. She was confident Dawn wouldn’t refuse.

In her mind, Carly was already composing a list of questions she wanted to pose to Dawn.

At the top of her list?

If Dawn had gone upstairs that day to change her shoes, why was she still wearing her high heels when she fainted on the stairs?

CHAPTER NINE

GRANT WAS STIRRING A POT OF TOMATO SOUP and Valerie was wiping down the tables in the dining room when Carly arrived at the eatery. Valerie followed her into the kitchen.

"How did it go?" Grant asked, wiping his hands on a towel.

Carly hung her coat in the closet. "Surprisingly well. The Taddeos are going to get most of their deposit back."

"As well they should," Valerie said a bit sharply. "Anyway, that's good news."

Carly smiled at her. "Did you do something different to your hair?"

Valerie fluffed her topknot with her fingers. "I added a few highlights. You know, just the stuff you use at home. Nothing special."

"Well, it's very attractive."

"Hey, Carly, Chief Holloway was looking for you this morning," Grant said. "He banged on the front door, and I let him in. He was surprised your car wasn't out back."

Due to limited space, the only cars that parked behind the historic building in downtown Balsam Dell were Carly's and Gina's. About three months earlier, to Carly's delight, Gina had moved into the apartment above the eatery. Even so, with their busy schedules they struggled to find enough time together to catch up on their lives.

"Why didn't the chief call me?" Carly said, puzzled. She pulled her cell from her tote and saw that she missed a text from him. She quickly punched in his number.

"Carly, thanks for getting back to me." The chief's voice sounded strained. "Can you come over to the station sometime today?" The note of urgency in his tone set her nerves on high alert.

"I can, but would you give me a clue why?"

"Not on the phone. By the way, I have your cooler here. The forensic team finished its examination."

Carly had almost forgotten about the cooler. In the scheme of things, it was last on her list of concerns. "Okay, how about if I leave here around two?" she suggested. "We're usually in a lull around then."

"You got it, Carly. See you then."

A thread of worry wove itself into Carly's psyche. Why had he sounded so secretive? Did he want to see her about Tony Manous, or something else?

"He wants to see me at the station this afternoon. Are you guys okay if I leave again?"

"Of course we are," Valerie said, "but are you okay? You look a bit shaky."

"I'm fine. It's just that he sounded so mysterious. I can't imagine what he wants that's so pressing."

"Well, you'll know soon enough." After a pause, Valerie brightened and said, "He's a nice man, isn't he?"

"Who? The chief?"

"Yes, the chief. That's who we were talking about, wasn't it?"

Carly smiled at Valerie's odd reply. "Well, you're right. Chief Holloway is a good man, and an excellent police chief. He's been a friend of my family for years. In fact, his daughter Anne is Havarti's vet."

Valerie's eyes took on a dreamy look. "I think it's wonderful how everyone is so friendly around here and how everybody knows each other. I'm loving this town more and more every day. Sometimes I...wish I'd been born here."

Carly didn't know what to make of that. "Where *were* you born, Val?"

Valerie's lips pursed. "Rutland."

Grant shot Carly a look as if to say, *What gives with Val?*

"From what I've observed, you've already made a ton of friends since you started working here."

Valerie shrugged. "I know. I just wish I knew them all better."

"It takes time to get to know people," Carly said

with an encouraging smile. "Trust me, after a little more time, you'll feel like you were born across the street."

Carly knew that didn't make an ounce of sense, but Valerie's relaxed smile in return made it worthwhile.

Valerie blinked. "You guys are the best, you know it?" She grabbed two aprons from the linen drawer and tossed one to Carly. "Come on, let's get cracking. Our customers will be flocking in any minute!"

~

Before she got started on her daily tasks, Carly texted Dawn and extended an invitation to join her and Gina. Dawn was more than happy to accept. She loved tacos and insisted on bringing dessert, plus she was looking forward to seeing Gina. She'd sounded so grateful that it tore at Carly's heart. Had Klarissa been Dawn's only friend? Did she have no one else she could turn to for comfort during rough patches?

Suzanne arrived at 10:58. Minutes later, the eatery bustled with activity.

Carly was setting a box of chips next to the grill when Suzanne came over and grabbed three sandwich platters from the end of the counter. "Hey, Carly, a man sitting in one of the back booths asked me if we're gonna start serving grilled cheeses on donuts. He said he heard about them from someone who knew someone who was at the Taddeo shower."

Oh, no. Had word already traveled through the gossip network about Carly's role in the shower?

"What did you tell him?"

"I gave him my finest 'Dora the dunce' look and said I never heard a thing about it."

"Good."

Suzanne raised her eyebrows. "Gotta tell you though, Carly, it might not be a bad idea."

"What? Telling people I was at the shower?"

"No." Suzanne lowered her voice. "I meant trying out donut grilled cheeses on customers. I read about them online. In some areas, they're pretty popular."

Carly blew out a breath. "Grant and I discussed it. I'm not sure—"

"Gotta go. But think about it, okay?" Suzanne zipped away to deliver the platters to a booth of three hungry telephone linemen.

By the time 2:00 rolled around, business had quieted. Carly removed her apron, donned her coat and gloves, and headed to the police station. When she saw Chief Holloway waiting for her in the lobby, her nerves almost shot into space.

"Hey," he said and ushered her down a corridor. "How're things going?"

"Not bad." She didn't say another word until they were inside his office with the door closed.

One corner of his desk was graced with pictures of his daughter Anne and her partner Erika, posing with various dogs and cats. The other corner was stacked with folders. A lovely photo of his wife, who'd passed years earlier, took up prime space behind his desk blotter.

"What's up, Chief?" Carly asked, dropping onto the chair opposite his desk. She noticed her cooler on the floor beside it.

"Can I take your coat?"

"Nah. I can leave it on the chair," she said, removing her arms from the sleeves.

His face tense, Holloway opened a drawer on the left side of his desk and pulled out a handful of photos. He drew his eyebrows together. "Carly, we have a situation that requires the utmost confidentiality. Before I reveal anything, you need to promise not to breathe a word, to anyone."

She swallowed. "Okay, I promise, but now I'm officially scared. Is it about...Saturday?"

"Yes, but it's not what you might think." He flipped one of the photos around and set it down in front of her. "Do you know who this woman is?"

Carly was staring at a headshot of Gretel Engstrom, the woman in the beige pantsuit at the shower. "I do, although I didn't until a few days ago. She's our town manager, right?"

"Correct, and she's been a fine one too. Exemplary, in my opinion."

"You said she's *been* a fine one. I'm almost afraid to ask, but why the past tense?"

"Because," he said, in a grim voice, "Gretel Engstrom is *un*officially missing."

Carly felt her insides cinch. "What do you mean, missing?"

"I mean she didn't show up at her office yesterday, and no one's been able to locate her. She hasn't been seen since she left the police station on Sunday."

"Maybe's she's sick?" Carly offered weakly. "I was once so sick with the flu I couldn't even dial the phone. She didn't text anyone?"

"That's the thing. Around 3:00 yesterday she texted her assistant, Penny Harper. Here's a screenshot of the text." He handed her another photo.

Carly read the text: Sorry to bale on everyone. Mom took a bad turn and I need to be with her. I am taking Uber to the airport & heading west. Will get in touch when I know more.

"Does anything strike you about it?" the chief asked.

Carly stared at it again. "Other than the wrong spelling of 'bail,' not really."

The chief folded his hands on his desk. "Penny Harper said there's no way Gretel would've made that error. Bad spelling was her top pet peeve."

"But sometimes the cell phone autocorrects and gets it wrong," she pointed out.

"True, but Ms. Harper said Gretel never even sent a text that she didn't proof to the nth degree."

"Does Gretel live alone?" Carly asked him.

"She does, in a pretty Cape Cod on Western Avenue. Early yesterday afternoon—this was before Penny got the text—the police quietly went to her house to do a wellness check. There was no sign of foul play, but her cat was locked in the master bedroom. The kitty had plenty of food and water, and a litter box, but all the curtains were tightly closed. They're the kind that block light, so no one could see in."

"In a way that's good, right? Maybe Gretel asked someone to look in on the cat while she's gone?"

"We checked around, and that doesn't seem to be the case. One of her close friends, Megan Gilbert, told us Gretel would've never left her cat that way if she was leaving town. She'd have boarded her or made other arrangements. Ms. Gilbert is pressuring us to ramp up our efforts to find her."

Megan Gilbert.

"That's Auntie Meggs!" Carly said, nearly leaping off her seat. "Megan Gilbert is Klarissa Taddeo's aunt."

"Exactly, and that's why I asked you here. Carly, you're one of the most observant people I know, not to mention the most curious, to put it mildly. At the shower on Saturday, I know you spent most of your time in the kitchen. But I understand you also went into the party room to greet the guests at one point."

"The drawing room," she clarified. "Klarissa wanted to introduce me to the guests, so Dawn brought me in there. Some of the women were a bit tipsy, which added to their jolly mood."

He smiled flatly. "I can imagine. Did you see Gretel Engstrom?"

"I did, but at the time I didn't know who she was. She was standing kind of apart from the others. She was wearing a plain beige pantsuit with a sparkly, cat-shaped brooch attached to the jacket. I had the sense she didn't feel totally comfortable there. Some of the guests were getting a bit raunchy, but I don't know if that was the reason. I was heading back to the kitchen when she smiled at me, but we never actually spoke."

The chief leaned back in his chair and gripped the armrests. "This is exactly why I wanted your input. Let's face it, who else could describe the outfit of a woman she'd only seen for a few seconds?"

"Most other women, I suspect," Carly said wryly.

"No, Carly. You notice way more than most people do. And, let's be honest, you're nosier than most people."

"Hey," she said with mock offense.

"Think back. You said she might have looked uncomfortable. Did she seem upset, or distracted? Did you notice anyone close by?"

Carly reeled her memory backward to Saturday afternoon. Most of it she wished she could erase, but there were a few high points—like working with Astrid in that glorious kitchen.

When Carly saw Gretel on Saturday, she'd been standing alone. A few women had drifted past her, wineglasses in their hands. If they knew who she was, they didn't acknowledge her. Then again, everyone had been at the shower for a while, so they might have been previously introduced.

She related all that to the chief. "I wish I could pinpoint something in particular that would help," Carly said, feeling frustrated. "I can't say she looked especially worried. More like a fish out of water."

He nodded absently and shuffled papers on his desk. "Carly, there's a reason I feel personally invested in this. Gretel Engstrom called me twice on Sunday. Once late that morning, once around midafternoon. Both calls went to my voicemail. With all the hoopla going on that day, I didn't get a chance to return her calls until Sunday evening."

"And by that time, you couldn't reach her," Carly finished for him.

"Exactly. Now I'm kicking myself for not seeing those messages sooner, but people had been calling and leaving messages for me all day. I barely had time to breathe, let alone screen messages and call people back."

"I'm sorry, Chief. I wish I had more to offer,"

Carly said. She saw how stressed he looked over Gretel.

"If this turns into a missing persons case," Holloway went on, "every observation will be important, even if it seems trivial. Keep that in mind, okay? In case you think of anything else?"

"I sure will. Chief, did Gretel drive herself home from the shower Saturday?"

"No, Megan Gilbert was her ride, so she drove her. With so many guests invited and so many cars, they'd decided to double up and go together. Everyone's departures were delayed, of course, because of Manous's untimely death. Ms. Gilbert told us that after she dropped off Gretel at her house, she watched her go inside, turn on her lights, and wave from the window. That's the last she saw of her. I'm curious why you ask that, though. We know Gretel didn't disappear that night. She gave a statement to the detectives the following morning."

"I know. I was just wondering who spoke to her last after that nightmare of a shower. Is Gretel's car missing too?"

"Nope. It's locked in her garage, but her keys are gone, as is her purse."

"Which would make sense if she left of her own accord and took an Uber," Carly told him, although a few things nagged at her. "Has anyone tried to reach her mom or her family? Was she seeing anyone?"

"Tried and, so far, failed. As close as Ms. Harper is to her boss, she had a devil of a time finding any contact info for Gretel's family. As for whether she was seeing anyone, we don't know that either."

"Have you checked with Uber?" Carly asked him.

"That's in process now, as is checking the airports. Most people think the police have instant access to information." He made a sweeping motion with his arm. "We wave a magic wand, and everything drops into our laps. The truth is—it takes time, legwork, and patience. Right about now I'd kiss the tile floor if Gretel walked in and asked us what all the commotion was about. Of course if that happened, I'd have so much egg on my face it would be dripping onto my shoes."

Carly smiled. "True, but that would still be the best outcome. Chief, you obviously know about the bad blood Gretel had with Tony Manous over a town contract."

He nodded. "We're looking into that angle, but I think it's a dead end. Manous might not have been Gretel's favorite person, but she attended the shower because of her friendship with Ms. Gilbert. Besides, from what I've heard, there were no hard feelings between Manous and Gretel. I don't think Ms. Gilbert and Gretel would've remained friends if Gretel was still nursing a grudge against him."

Carly wasn't sure she agreed with that, but she

kept the opinion to herself. "Chief, I'm almost afraid to mention this, but after I gave my statement to Lieutenant Granger on Sunday, Don Frasco caught up with me on the sidewalk."

"Oh boy."

"Turns out he'd been hanging around the police station that morning, hoping to get someone to talk to him. When he spotted Gretel coming out of the restroom, he connected the dots. He figured that for her to be there, she must've been at the shower. I had to give him credit for nailing it," she said with a touch of admiration. "He said Gretel looked awful, which I took to mean stressed. He gave me a few of the details about the contract battle."

"None of that is news, Carly."

"I know, but—" She hesitated, then revealed what Don told her about Gretel's history being a mystery.

"He investigated her background?" the chief sputtered. "Good grief."

"Only because Gretel caved so suddenly to Manous's demands. That does seem a little odd, doesn't it? And you have to remember, Don *is* a reporter."

Holloway splayed his fingers over his eyes. "Listen, I like Don, and I know he tries hard. But please don't talk to him about Gretel, or about Tony Manous. Something smells wrong about all of this, and I don't need to add him to my list of worries.

Remember what happened the last time he poked his nose where it didn't belong?"

"I do, indeed," she admitted, knowing he could say the same about her. "He put himself at grave risk." She didn't add that in doing so, Don had inadvertently helped the police solve crimes that had stymied them for months.

Carly jumped in her chair. "Chief, I just thought of something. What did you do about Gretel's kitty?"

"Not to worry." He put up both hands. "Turns out Anne is her vet, so one of the officers delivered Buttercup to her clinic. The cat is in good hands."

"Thank goodness. But what if Gretel comes home and finds her cat missing?"

"The police left a note explaining the cat's whereabouts. Carly, I hate to toss you out, especially since I invited you here, but I've got phone calls and texts up the you-know-what to return. And remember, this cannot be shared with anyone, although I'll make an exception for Ari. I trust him completely, and I know he won't breathe a word. If Gretel doesn't turn up soon, word's going to leak out. We need to keep it under wraps as long as we can."

"I totally understand, Chief. Just…please keep me updated, okay?"

"I will. You'll be one of the first people I call if we hear anything. Don't forget your cooler."

She shrugged on her coat and rose from her chair. "I give you my word that I will share it with Ari, but no one else."

"Good. One last thing," he added, his voice sharper now.

Here it comes.

"Do not even *think* of getting involved in investigating Tony Manous's death. If it turns out he was intentionally poisoned, it's almost certain the culprit was someone who attended that shower."

"I hear what you're saying," she said carefully. "You don't need to worry."

He narrowed his gaze at her, then cleared his throat. "By the way, how is your new assistant manager working out?"

The question surprised Carly. "Valerie? She's great. Everyone enjoys working with her, and she's terrific with customers."

He nodded. "That's good. Good to hear."

Before he could issue any further admonitions about Tony Manous, Carly picked up her cooler and bade him goodbye. On her way out of the station, the one question she'd refrained from asking rolled through her mind.

Had the police ever considered that Gretel left town because she poisoned Tony Manous?

CHAPTER TEN

It was Grant who'd come up with the idea of taking turns working shorter days. Having Valerie on board gave them the flexibility they didn't have before. So far, it was working perfectly.

Two days a week, Grant, Valerie, and Carly each worked from 8:00 to 4:00. Carly's days were Tuesday and Friday. Grant's were Monday and Saturday, and Valerie's were Wednesday and Thursday. It gave them all a chance to make evening plans or enjoy activities such as book club, bridge night, bowling, and the like. Suzanne was happy to be excluded because she worked only part time.

Luckily it was Tuesday—Carly's day to leave work at 4:00. That gave her plenty of time to prepare for her evening with Gina and Dawn.

Carly had told Dawn to come by around 6:00, but she'd asked Gina to come a bit earlier. She wanted to fill in Gina on what went down at the shower, and she wanted that conversation to be private.

"Hey, everyone, I'm heading out," she announced at 4:01. "Gina's bringing tacos for dinner."

"Sounds like fun," Valerie said, a bit wistfully. "Hope you guys have a good time."

"Thanks," Carly said. "After the past few days, it'll be a welcome break."

She didn't mention that Dawn Chapin would be joining them. It would only elicit questions she wasn't prepared to answer.

Once she was buckled in the front seat of her car, she checked for messages on her cell. She'd missed one from Don Frasco a few hours earlier. It was short and to the point: R Benoit wants your cell #. OK to give?

R. Benoit. Ron Benoit, the videographer?

While she waited for her engine to warm up, she tapped out Don's number. "Hey, what's the scoop? I'm guessing you talked to Ron?"

"I did, but I didn't learn much," Don groused. "He promised me a short interview, but only if I could get him your phone number."

"I appreciate your asking me first, Don. Go ahead and give it to him, if you don't mind."

"I don't mind, but let me know if he calls you, okay?"

"You got it."

Don hadn't mentioned Gretel, so word of her disappearance hadn't yet traveled that far. Carly disconnected and drove home, her thoughts whirling. Ron obviously remembered her from the shower. She'd made a donut grilled cheese while he videotaped it. So why did he want her number?

Whatever the reason, for Carly it was a stroke of luck. Ron had been on her radar of people she wanted to talk to. Even better if he sought her out so it wouldn't look as if she was prying.

The moment she unlocked her apartment door, Havarti greeted her as if she'd been absent for weeks. Carly fed him and took him outside for a short break. The balmy weather of earlier in the day had switched from near springtime temps back to a good ole Vermont freezing cold winter. The dog seemed happy to take care of business and trot right back inside.

That taken care of, Carly put together a green salad with the same ingredients they used in the eatery—field greens, dried cranberries, crumbled goat cheese, and sunflower seeds. Customers were loving the combo, especially when blended with Grant's featherlight salad dressing.

Gina arrived early, her round cheeks pink, her dark curls framing a beaming face. Lately Gina had been looking more radiant than usual. Carly suspected it had something to do with her significant other, Zach Bartlett, who she'd been seeing for several months.

Havarti launched himself at Gina's knees, begging to be picked up. Gina lifted him into her arms with a laugh and hugged him soundly. "Are you glad to see your auntie Gina?" She set him down and removed her outerwear, revealing the intricately woven gold chain Zach had given her for Christmas.

Carly poured them each a glass of white wine while Gina set the tacos in the oven to keep them warm. "That salad looks delish," she said peeking into the fridge. "I'll zap the refried beans right before we eat."

They relaxed in Carly's cozy living room, Carly on the sofa with Havarti and Gina in the rocking chair. Carly brought her friend up to speed on the events of Saturday, touching lightly on her and Dawn's meeting with Tabitha that morning. She kept her promise to the chief and didn't mention Gretel Engstrom being MIA.

Gina took a sip of her wine. "Good heavens, you've had quite the adventure. *Not,*" she added sarcastically.

"That day at the shower," Carly said, "it started to feel so surreal. Kind of like scenes from a play, only I wasn't sure what role I was supposed to have. So tell me, what do you know about the main players? Dawn's and Klarissa's moms, for starters."

Gina rocked back in her chair. "I'll start with Julie Chapin. From what I've heard, she keeps her personal life close to the vest. Alcoholism in her past, and maybe in her present. Husband, or rather former husband, Anthony Chapin, travels internationally for business, so he's almost never around. Julie's father was Wesley Walker Stone, a hotshot pilot during World War II. He and his wife had Julie late in the marriage, and they doted on her. Hence the reason she inherited that fabulous mansion."

Carly recalled the photos of aircraft that graced nearly an entire wall in the dark, paneled room adjacent to the dining room. It was the same room Tony Manous had emerged from moments before Dawn and Ron came into the dining room.

"One thing was painfully obvious," Carly said. "Julie Chapin and Ursula Taddeo have no love lost between them. I sensed that Dawn's mom wasn't thrilled about hosting the shower."

Gina nodded. "There were rumors a while back, and I mean *way* back, about Julie having a fling with Ursula's ex-husband—before the Taddeos were divorced, that is. I have no way to confirm it, but if it's true, Ursula was probably relishing the fact that her nemesis, or former nemesis, had been strong-armed into hosting a shower for her daughter in that fabulous mansion."

"That's an interesting take on it," Carly quipped. "It's weird, because their daughters are so close. If the fling rumors are true, I hope the girls never found out about it."

"Yeah, me too. As for Ursula," Gina continued, "I really don't know very much. She bought cards at my shop a few times. She seemed pleasant but aloof, not one to chatter." She shrugged.

"Auntie Meggs, on the other hand," Carly said, "seems like a total sweetheart. She clearly adores Klarissa."

Gina smiled. "Yeah, she's Ursula's sister. Super nice lady. Years ago she worked at Balsam Dell Floral, but I'm not sure where she works now."

"What do you know about Ron Benoit and Adam Bushey? Either of those names ring a bell?"

Gina twisted her lips. "I don't know anything about Adam Bushey, but I know a little about Benoit. He has a reputation for using people to get what he wants. You know who Sybil Cobbett is, right?"

"Sure. She's been starring in some of the mystery movies on TV."

"Exactly. Well—this was a while back—she and her entourage were in town filming some winter scenes for a holiday movie. Benoit managed to worm his way into her manager's trailer to give the guy a thumb drive with samples of his videography. Supposedly the manager thanked him, said he'd be in touch when the right movie came along. After that Ron bragged around town that he was a future videographer to the stars, like any day he'd be getting *the call* from Hollywood." Gina rolled her dark brown eyes. "Sorry for knocking the guy, but he really is an obnoxious dude. A gal pal of mine went out with him a few times. She said he talked nonstop about himself all evening but didn't show an ounce of interest in her. She dumped him before it went anywhere, if you get my drift."

"I do." Carly ran her fingers absently through Havarti's soft fur. "From what I saw, Dawn's really hung up on him. She must see *something* good in him, right?"

Gina shrugged. "I suppose if you're smitten, you can delude yourself into believing anything. I'm guessing since she's a wedding planner, he schmoozes her when the mood strikes him so he can get more gigs."

"Maybe, but he didn't act very friendly toward her. You know what else Dawn told me? Her mother pressured her into having a career appropriate for a woman—that's how she worded it. Dawn originally wanted to be an architect."

"Whoa. Poor Dawn! Sounds like mommy dearest hasn't stumbled into the twenty-first century yet. Why didn't Dawn just tell her to get stuffed and do her own thing?"

"Who knows?" Carly took a sip of her wine. "Family dynamics can be complicated."

Gina looked suddenly troubled. "Carly, before Dawn gets here, should I assume you're officially investigating what happened to Tony Manous?"

Carly frowned at the question. Had she been that obvious? "I'm only trying to help Dawn," she defended. "Okay, yeah, I guess I am trying to figure out who poisoned Tony. I told myself I wouldn't get involved—and the chief already warned me not to—but Dawn says the police are treating her like their prime suspect."

For a moment, Gina said nothing. "Did it occur to you there might be a reason for that?"

"Yeah, it did." Carly heaved a sigh.

Until now, she hadn't wanted to consider that Dawn might've done away with Tony. She couldn't picture Dawn poisoning anyone, but stranger things had happened.

Gina set down her empty wineglass. "Listen, I'm starting to feel weird about this. Maybe we should wait until Dawn gets here to talk about this stuff. I feel like I'm dissecting her life behind her back."

"You're right," Carly said. "She'll be here soon, so I'll set the table. Want another glass of wine?"

"No, I'll wait till— Hey, wasn't that a knock?"

"Yup." Carly opened her door to find Dawn standing there holding a pink bakery box. "Hi, I'm not too early, am I?"

"Not at all. Come on in. You know Gina."

She took Dawn's coat, along with the box. Gina rose and gave Dawn a warm hug. "It's great seeing you, Dawn."

"Thanks. You too. Oh! Who's this?" Dawn looked down at the small dog who was sniffing her leather boots with gusto.

“This is Havarti,” Carly introduced, pulling the dog gently away. “Are you okay with dogs?”

“Oh, sure. I like animals, even though Mother never lets any in the house.” She gazed around at the papered walls and the cozy décor. “What a nice apartment you have. By the way, I brought frosted cookie hearts from Sissy’s Bakery. I hope you both like them.”

Gina grinned and clutched her chest. “Be still my heart. Pun intended.”

“I had to go there today to cancel the wedding cake,” Dawn said sadly. “It was going to be so beautiful. Sissy was nice about it, though. She refunded the entire deposit.”

“She’s a good person,” Carly agreed. “Since the tacos are warm, shall we eat?”

They went into the kitchen. Carly set out plates, napkins, and flatware. Dawn seemed to enjoy everything, although she ate in small quantities. After they were finished, Carly shooed Gina and Dawn into the living room while she cleaned up the table. Everyone wanted coffee, so she brewed a pot.

A few minutes later, Carly handed out coffee mugs and set down a plate of cookies. Dawn had settled in the rocking chair, so Carly sat on the sofa next to Gina. Havarti snuggled between the two, his head on Gina’s thigh.

“Dawn, Carly and I were talking earlier,” Gina began. “She told me some of what happened at the shower on Saturday.”

Dawn nodded, her eyes dropping to her lap.

When she didn't respond, Carly said, "The thing is, we didn't want to discuss it further unless you were okay with it."

"No…I mean, yes, I'm totally okay with it." Dawn looked directly at Gina. "Carly probably told you the police think I'm a suspect. I want both of you to know that I did not poison Tony. Maybe I wasn't crazy about the guy, but I certainly wouldn't have done something so horrible." She swallowed hard and shook her head.

"Then let's talk about it," Carly said quietly. "Gina wasn't there on Saturday, but you and I had front row seats, so to speak."

Dawn gave a sarcastic chuckle. "Yeah, weren't we lucky?"

It was time, Carly decided, to let Dawn know about the argument she overheard.

She explained the whole mess, how she'd gotten trapped hiding in the corner in the foyer when Tony, Dawn, and Ron were having their contentious conversation.

Dawn covered her eyes with her fingers, and her cheeks flushed. "My mother advised me to use my womanly wiles to make Ron jealous and try to get him back. I can't believe I was dumb enough to actually listen to her. So much for motherly wisdom," she added sourly.

"Don't beat yourself up," Gina said. "Believe

me, I've done plenty of things for love that make me cringe now." She tickled Havarti's chin, and the little dog nuzzled her palm. "Dawn, do you love Ron?"

Dawn's expression was hollow. "At this point I'm not sure anymore. And Carly, I'm so mortified that you overheard us in the dining room that day. I can't even imagine what you were thinking, hearing me, you know, sort of flirt with Tony. I knew Ron was close by, and I was hoping he might overhear me."

"Don't give it another thought. I could tell you were faking it. What I'm more curious about is what Tony meant when he said he wasn't going to sink money in whatever Ron was peddling."

Dawn's eyes widened. "Oh, that. Ron wanted Tony to invest in his new startup venture—R.B. Videography Productions. Ron had visions of Hollywood that never panned out. But with investor funds, he thinks he can expand his business and attract commercial customers. Right now, he does mostly weddings. I'm sorry to say he's gotten some mediocre reviews. Anyway, Tony wanted no part of the deal. He didn't even like Ron. He only tolerated him for Klarissa's sake."

"Do you think Ron was angry about that?" Carly asked her. "About Tony not investing, I mean?"

"I'm sure he was disappointed, but he—Oh my gosh, you're not insinuating Ron could have poisoned him, are you?" She sounded horrified.

"No, I didn't mean it that way," Carly said quickly, but it had crossed her mind. "But Dawn, think about it. If someone did poison Tony, then that someone was either *really* mad at him, or had another motive."

"I…never even thought about a motive."

"It's one of the first things the police look for," Gina piped in. "Means, motive, opportunity. Right, Carly?"

"Um, right. Dawn, didn't you think it was odd that Tony showed up there at all?"

She shrugged. "I guess it was strange, but I never got a chance to ask him why he came over. He did say something about a bone to pick with his beautiful bride, but I didn't know what he meant. At that moment, I was more focused on Ron, I'm embarrassed to say." Her cheeks flushed pink.

"Okay, I'm asking you to think back now," Carly continued. "When you and I spoke earlier, you told me you'd gone upstairs to change your shoes, right? That's when you overheard Tony on his phone in the upstairs bathroom."

"Right," she said, nodding. "My heels were killing me, so I went up to switch into flats. I noticed the bathroom door was closed, and then I heard Tony's voice from behind the door. I was surprised because I didn't even know he'd gone upstairs."

"And you heard him say Klarissa's name and tell her to stop lying, right? Did he say anything else at all?"

Dawn looked away, thinking. "I thought he said something like 'I'm in trouble,' but it was garbled. I might've heard that wrong."

Interesting, Carly thought. Dawn hadn't mentioned that before.

"And after that?" Carly asked her.

"Like I told you before, I ran to my bedroom. I stayed there for a while, then figured I should go back to the shower before people wondered where I was."

Carly puffed out a breath. She still struggled to make sense of Tony going upstairs. "Dawn, this is a touchy question, but what did you think of Rose Manous?"

"Honestly?" Dawn said. "I never thought she married Tony's dad for money. I've seen Rose with Gordon. She loves him dearly."

"How did they meet?" Gina asked.

Dawn crossed one slender leg over the other. "When Gordon Manous was in rehab for his broken hip, Rose was working there as an aide." She smiled. "I guess the two of them sort of clicked. Rose was always sneaking him her buttery homemade pastries, a big no-no for a patient with a heart condition on top of a broken hip."

"I would guess so," Carly said.

Dawn's smile dimmed. "But then Rose pulled an even bigger no-no, or at least she was accused of it. Another aide claimed she saw Rose slip Gordon a pain pill that hadn't been prescribed for him."

Gina gave a low whistle. "That's a major no-no, if it's true."

"Exactly," Dawn said. "Gordon reluctantly agreed to a blood test, but the results were inconclusive. Rose vehemently denied any wrongdoing, but she was let go anyway. Without any real evidence, there wasn't much else they could do. It wasn't like there were cameras in every room spying on the patients."

Cameras!

"Dawn, when you said cameras just now, I thought of something. With all the beautiful things in your...mom's home, didn't she have a security system?"

"If you're thinking cameras, no. There are motion sensors covering all the main entry points, but there's nothing to spy inside the house. Not anymore, anyway." She picked a cookie crumb off her slacks.

"So, there used to be?" Gina prodded, wiping crumbs off her lips.

Dawn heaved a sigh that sounded infinitely sad. "Up until my parents got divorced, there were cameras in nearly every room. Discreet, very well-hidden cameras. You wouldn't know they were there unless...well, unless you knew. Dad had them secretly installed so he could spy on Mother."

Gina gasped, choking on her coffee. "Oh...my. Why would he do that?" She swiped a napkin over her mouth.

"To see if she was lying about her drinking," Dawn said tightly. "Unfortunately, he got more than he bargained for. Not only was she still drinking, but she was drinking with a gentleman friend. And that wasn't all they were doing." Her lips twisted.

Carly felt her face redden. "Dawn, I'm so sorry. That must have been devastating. For all of you." She refrained from asking if Dawn had known about the "friend."

"Dad, of course, was forced to confess about installing the hidden cameras. When he confronted Mother about her indiscretions, she flew into a rage. She had every single camera ripped out the next day."

"Is that when your parents got divorced?" Carly asked.

"Yes, but Dad still comes over and stays once in a while, when the mood suits him. He loves that house. He always has."

"Your mom lets him do that?" Carly was flabbergasted.

Dawn smirked. "She has no choice. Mother's lawyer was no match for the one Dad hired. The settlement Dad got from Mother would blow your mind, but more important is that Dad has a life estate in the house."

"And that means what?" Carly was intrigued now.

"It means that even though the title's in mom's

name alone, the house can never be sold or even mortgaged without Dad signing off."

Carly was stunned. Virtually tongue-tied. She had no idea how to respond.

Why did Dawn stay in that dysfunctional household? Sure, it was luxurious, and Astrid was a gem. But it was also an emotional minefield.

Gina spoke first. "Dawn, I'm sorry you had to go through all that. That's...really a shame."

Dawn flashed a fake smile. "Not to worry. I'm used to it. I have a beautiful room with its own private terrace and a view of half the estate. Whenever I need my own space, I lock myself in there and chill with my audiobooks. It's a great way to tune out the world. Anything else you want to know?"

Her question was so out of place that all three abruptly fell silent. Even Havarti sensed the tension. He buried his nose under Gina's arm and hid his eyes.

And then Dawn started to cry. Deep, bone-racking sobs that shook her entire frame. Carly went over and wrapped her arms around her, but Dawn continued to weep.

After a minute or so, Gina brought her a glass of water and a box of tissues. Dawn accepted the water and slugged back a few gulps. She snatched a handful of tissues from the box.

"I'm...I'm so, so sorry," Dawn stuttered out, blotting her face. "I haven't cried like that in ages.

It's just...with everything...I couldn't..." She sucked in a deep sniffle.

"It's okay, Dawn," Carly soothed. "We all need a good cry now and then." She smiled at her. "I know I do."

Gina nodded in agreement.

"You're both so kind, and you both really listen," Dawn said. "Klar has Auntie Meggs to confide in and care about her, but I haven't had anyone like that in a long time. Is it okay if I wash my face?"

Carly directed her to the bathroom, then she and Gina brought the empty coffee mugs and the one remaining cookie into the kitchen. Carly saw that her friend's eyes were damp.

"That was hard to hear," Gina murmured, then bit into the remaining cookie.

"I know," Carly whispered, "but I think she got some of the pent-up anxiety out of her system. In a way, it was probably cathartic."

When Dawn returned, her face was dry but deathly pale. The little bit of makeup she'd sported earlier was gone.

"I guess I better go," she said. "Carly, I think I know what you wanted to ask me before when we were talking about Tony in the bathroom. You wanted to know why I still had my heels on when I fainted on the stairs. Am I right?"

Carly winced at how easily Dawn had read her mind. "It wasn't that I doubted your story, only that

I want to be prepared in case the police ask me for another interview."

Dawn's face fell. "Do you think they'll do that?"

"I'm hoping not, but they warned it was a possibility. When the police questioned you, did you tell them why you'd gone upstairs?"

Dawn sighed. "I'm sure I did. I was trying to be honest and forthcoming about everything I remembered from that awful day. When I heard Tony talking in the bathroom, I flattened myself against the wall and listened. Like I said, I only caught a few tidbits before I escaped into my bedroom. I was so distracted I forgot all about the shoes. After that...well you know what happened."

"Thanks for clarifying that," Carly said. She gave Dawn her puffy coat.

"No, I should be thanking you, both of you," she said. "Gina, it was great to see you. Maybe we can all get together again soon?" The raw hope in her eyes was unmistakable.

"I'd like that." Gina hugged her and Carly walked Dawn to the door.

"Call me tomorrow, okay?" Carly grabbed her hand and gave it a quick squeeze. "I want to be sure you're okay."

Dawn smiled, her swollen eyes brightening a bit. "I will. I promise. Thank you both for dinner."

The moment the door closed, Carly sagged against it. She looked at Gina. "I feel so sad for her."

"I do too." Gina dropped onto the sofa again. "I'll tell you one thing. Dawn might be an emotional wreck right now, but there's no way she poisoned Tony Manous."

Carly lifted Havarti and sat beside Gina, the dog snugged in her lap. "I agree. I think she'd have confessed by now if she had." She puffed her cheeks and blew out a breath. "You know what would help?"

Gina looked at her. "What?"

"If we knew what Tony was poisoned with."

"Yeah," Gina said, "but even when the police figure that out, they might keep it under wraps."

"They might." Carly bit her lip and then sucked in a breath. "Gina, something else just hit me. When I was hiding in the foyer and heard Dawn talking to Tony, she was teasing him about sneaking in there half-snookered. Tony retorted that he was only sampling her grandfather's aged whiskey, and that it wasn't even his idea."

"Whoa." Gina's eyes widened. "If it wasn't his idea..."

"Then maybe it was the killer's idea," Carly slowly finished. "*If* the poison was in the drink, that is. As far as suspects, Dawn actually gave us something to work with. Right now, I can think of three people with a motive to want Tony out of the picture." She could actually think of four, but because she'd been sworn to secrecy about Gretel Engstrom's disappearance, she needed to keep that name to herself. For now.

"Three?" Gina sat up. She ticked them off on her fingers. "Ron Benoit, for one. Tony refused to invest in his company."

Carly nodded. "That's the first."

Gina ticked off another finger. "Rose Manous. I know she's his stepmom, but we can't rule her out if she had a financial motive. But if she poisoned Tony, she had to have done it earlier, before you escorted her to the door."

"Exactly. Not likely, but not impossible."

Gina looked at Carly. "So who's the third suspect?"

"The third is Klarissa herself," Carly said. "Maybe when they were arguing about Rose on the phone, Klarissa decided she'd had enough and decided to end it."

"A pretty extreme reaction," Gina said doubtfully. "But if that was the case, when would she have done it? Remember, we still don't know how Tony was poisoned."

"I know. She also had nothing to gain by losing Tony. It would have been a self-destructive act of pure rage. That's why she's not at the top of my list."

Gina smirked. "Your list?"

"Oh, let's face it, Gina. We both know I'm not going to rest until I figure out who killed Tony Manous."

CHAPTER ELEVEN

After Gina left, Carly called Ari. She filled him in on everything, beginning with her visit to the country club with Dawn, right down to her dinner with the ladies. And since the chief had given his blessing, she also gave him the details surrounding Gretel's disappearance.

"So, no one's seen or heard from Gretel Engstrom since Sunday?" Ari said, sounding concerned.

"That's right, unless the chief knows something he hasn't told me."

"Maybe she really did fly out to help her mom," Ari said. "If her mom's seriously ill or in the hospital, Gretel would certainly give that priority over making phone calls."

"I know, but I still think it's strange. I don't even know the woman and I'm worried about her." *In addition to wondering if she poisoned Tony.* "Do you know if she had a significant other?"

"Not a clue," he said, and then a smile widened his voice. "Listen, honey, I can hear how tired you are. Get a good night's rest, okay? By morning, the chief might have positive news about Gretel."

"Fingers crossed," Carly said. "Love you."

"Love you too."

The first thing Carly did on Wednesday morning, after walking and feeding Havarti, was text Chief Holloway: Any word on G?

His response was short and to the point: Negative.

Which meant Gretel Engstrom was still unaccounted for.

Had Tony known something about Gretel that she didn't want revealed? If so, did he threaten to use it against her unless his demands over the town contract were met? Had Gretel bided her time, waiting patiently until she saw her chance to get even with him?

Gretel's face flashed in Carly's mind. Was the mind of a killer hidden beneath those gentle features? She hated to think it might be true, but she knew from past experience that anything was possible.

Her history is a mystery.

Don Frasco's exact words.

Cereal bowl in front of her, Havarti nestled at her feet, Carly pulled over her laptop and fired it up. She entered Gretel's full name in the search bar. Several hits popped up. Most were unrelated—different Gretel Engstroms—but a few matched the woman in question.

The first was a short article, accompanied by a photo, announcing Gretel's appointment to the position of town manager. In the photo she's smiling, but in Carly's opinion, it looked like one of those forced smiles you flash when the photographer tells you to "say cheese" for the camera.

A few other articles popped up. All of them related to town matters—including the brouhaha over the improvements to Ledyard Park. Carly perused the articles briefly. The battle had ended abruptly after Gretel caved, and the park went on to have one of the most impressive—and most costly—playgrounds in the state. Beyond that, Carly found nothing relating to Gretel's background or education, or even her past employment.

Did she have a different name in the past? An ex-husband's, maybe?

Someone has to know something. Gretel didn't suddenly appear out of a cloud of smoke and get appointed as town manager.

But maybe there was someone who did know something. The chief mentioned Gretel's close assistant. Penny Harper, was it?

Carly checked the online directory for the town. Sure enough, Penny Harper was listed as "administrative assistant to the town manager." Her contact info, including email address, was also shown.

The problem was how to approach Penny. Carly

couldn't reveal that she knew Gretel was missing. She needed to come up with a ploy—something that wouldn't make it appear she was spying. She googled Penny Harper.

And hit the jackpot.

Carly scribbled it all down and shoved it into her tote, then cleaned up her few dishes and headed to the eatery.

Grant had arrived first. He stood behind the counter, putting together his usual cheesy bacon biscuit. Although Carly was accustomed to it by now, the combined aroma of coffee and bacon never failed to ignite her taste buds.

She sat on one of the stools near the grill while Grant poured her a coffee. "Biscuit today?" he asked her.

"You bet."

He smiled. "How was your evening with Gina?"

"Um, interesting. Dawn Chapin joined us." She took a long sip of her coffee.

Grant's smiled faded. "Are you serious?"

"Totally. Dawn knows Gina—we were all in school together. Gina was happy to have her there. She brought tacos for everyone, and Dawn brought cookies."

Grant layered shredded cheddar onto half of a biscuit. "So, what'd you all talk about?"

"We talked about what happened on Saturday. Dawn told us a lot about her mom, and Klarissa's mom, and—" Grant's anxious expression stopped her cold. "What's wrong?"

"What's wrong," he said, keeping his tone soft, "is that you're doing it again. You're trying to solve a murder."

"I...never said I was doing that." Carly stuck her mug under her lips too quickly, nearly burning her mouth.

"You didn't have to say it," he said, placing the stuffed biscuit onto the grill. "Come on, Carly, don't you think I know you by now?" He smiled, but the worry lines between his eyes deepened.

"Yeah, I know you do. But think about this. It was my grilled cheeses that were served at that shower. When word gets around, people might leap to conclusions and think the poison was connected to my food." It was a weak excuse, but it was all she could come up with.

As the biscuit sizzled on the grilled, Grant remained silent. When it was golden brown on both sides, he flipped it onto a plate and set it down in front of her.

"Listen," Grant said, "I can't tell you what to do, nor would I ever want to. I'm just begging you, please, to think about the consequences before you start asking questions. Whoever poisoned Tony Manous has a lot to lose if they're caught."

Carly knew he was recalling her past experiences with murderers and was worried about her safety.

"Grant, don't you think I know all that?" Carly

gave him an appreciative smile. "Let's talk about something else. Any plans for the next few days?"

His eyes popped wide, and his smile broadened. "Actually, I've been working on a project I'm kind of psyched about—getting kids to eat healthy, delicious lunches. Balsam Dell Elementary agreed to be my test site."

"Grant, that's fantastic!"

Munching on her biscuit, Carly listened in awe as he described the lunch packets he designed with sections for fruit, cheese, trail mix, and gluten-free cookies.

"I bought tiny cookie cutters to make shapes from the cheese and the fruits," Grant went on, his eyes beaming. He shrugged. "I know it's nothing revolutionary, but you'd be surprised at how many kids still eat junk for lunch."

"I'm so impressed, Grant," Carly said. "Let me know if I can contribute in any way, okay?"

He grinned. "You'll be the first one I ask."

Carly finished her biscuit and drained her mug. "I want to head over to the town hall this morning, if you and Val can spare me for a bit. There's a woman there who's putting together a fundraiser for shelter animals, and I want to see if I can help." She felt her cheeks flush slightly with the subterfuge, but the fact was—she really did want to help. She also wanted to poke into Gretel Engstrom's past, and Penny Harper was the perfect starting point.

"Sure, any time. Hey, here she is now." He smiled at Valerie, whose face was visible through the glass door.

Valerie came inside, wiping her boots on the bristled mat. "Morning guys," she said in a monotone.

"Hi, Val," Carly greeted her. "Everything okay?"

"Yes. Fine."

Valerie beelined for the kitchen. She returned wearing a crisp apron. Her topknot was slightly crooked, and her eyes bloodshot. "It's my day to do bathroom duty, so I'll get started."

"Wait, no coffee first?"

"I had some at my aunt's." Valerie started to fetch cleaning supplies when Carly pulled her aside.

"Val, I can see that something's wrong," she said quietly. "Want to talk about it?"

Valerie swallowed, and her eyes watered. "Not now, okay?"

Carly nodded and left her alone. She'd talk to Valerie later, when she was ready to share whatever was bothering her.

With her other mission in mind, Carly waited until 10:00 and then drove to her apartment. Havarti leaped off the sofa the moment she opened her door, and when she fetched his leash, he danced circles around her feet. "You're going to be my goodwill ambassador this morning," Carly explained to him with a grin. "Think you're up to the task?"

Havarti gave out a tiny yip, which she took as a *yes*. She kissed him on the nose and off they went.

The town hall building, which was next to the police station, was a decades-old, colonial-style home that had been remodeled and expanded to house the town offices. A directory in the lobby listed the various departments. The town manager was on the second floor.

Carly wasn't sure if dogs were allowed inside the building, so she lifted Havarti into her arms and smiled at everyone she passed. She made her way along the hallway to the elevator, and within moments found herself standing before Room 211. The door was closed. Letters painted on the frosted glass read: Gretel Engstrom, and below that: Town Manager.

Carly knocked on the wooden doorframe. After nearly a minute, a slightly plump woman with short black hair opened it. She looked surprised to see a visitor, but then her gaze melted at the sight of the little dog. "Hello? Can I help you with something?"

"I hope so." Carly smiled. "I'm looking for Penny Harper. Do I have the right office? The door says town manager, so I wasn't sure."

The woman's eye twitched, but she didn't smile. "I'm Penny Harper. What can I do for you?"

"Hi, Penny. It's nice to meet you. I'm Carly Hale, owner of the local grilled cheese eatery. And this is Havarti." She beamed at the dog in her arms.

At the sound of his name, Havarti licked Carly's cheek. Penny's face relaxed slightly, and she smiled at the dog. "I've eaten there. You make delicious sandwiches."

"Thanks, that's good to hear." When Penny made no move to invite her into the office, Carly said, "Anyway, I saw something online about you heading up a fundraiser for shelter animals?"

"That's correct, I am," Penny said, her tone a bit less tense now. "Are you looking to volunteer?"

"Um, yes, I am, in a way." Carly was winging it now.

Penny visibly relaxed. "Well, then, why don't you and Havarti come into my office and we can chat?"

She ushered them into a large office with pale green walls and fabric blinds. An antique oak desk facing the door dominated one corner. Save for a framed photo of a tuxedo cat with bright green eyes, only a blotter and a pencil holder graced the desk. A desktop computer rested on an adjacent table. On the wall behind the desk, a college diploma hung in a plain silver frame. From where Carly was standing, she couldn't quite make out the name of the university.

"My office is this way," Penny said.

She led Carly through an adjacent doorway into a smaller, plainer office. "If the arrangement looks odd, it's because decades ago, when the town offices were first laid out, they believed the secretary to the town manager should have to pass through the manager's office to reach her own. That way the secretary wouldn't be tempted to make unnecessary trips to the restroom or take too many breaks, et cetera."

"Sounds archaic," Carly said, trying to lighten the mood.

"Yes, apparently back then, people of my lowly ilk couldn't be trusted." She rolled her eyes with disdain, then nodded at the chair opposite her metal desk. "Have a seat."

Carly lowered herself onto the indicated chair. "If I hold onto Havarti's leash, is it okay if I set him down? He's very well behaved."

"Of course! Whatever is most comfy for him. He's really a darling."

"Thanks. Ms. Harper—"

"Please, it's Penny."

"Penny," Carly continued, "given my long hours at the restaurant, I'm not sure how much time I can devote to the fundraiser. But the online article mentioned a raffle you were having to benefit the shelter." She smiled down at Havarti. "In honor of my own rescue dog, I'd love to contribute a few gift certificates."

Penny clasped her hands together. "That would be fabulous. We're putting together three raffle baskets. Each will be stuffed with goodies from local businesses. Can you part with three? One for each basket?"

"I sure can. Consider it done." Carly quietly let the leash slide off her wrist. Havarti sniffed the carpet, then moseyed around the desk toward Penny's chair.

In the next instant, Penny jumped slightly, then she beamed down at Havarti. "Oh my, did you come to pay me a visit?" Havarti gave out a tiny bark, and to Carly's surprise Penny lifted him onto her lap.

"Sorry, the leash slipped out of my hand," Carly fibbed, "but he made you an instant friend, didn't he? I hope he's not coating you in dog hair, though."

"I don't mind dog hair," Penny scoffed, and then rubbed the dog's furry face. "I'm sure I'm already wearing cat hair."

While Penny's attention was focused on Havarti, Carly peeked sideways at two wooden frames propped on the desk. In the larger one, a happy young couple posed with two little boys. In the other, three black cats nestled together in a padded basket. She turned the smaller frame for a better look. "Aw, are these your cats?"

Penny's face softened. "Yes, those are my rescue babies. I adopted them from the same shelter I'm raising money for."

"They look so sweet." Carly shifted in her chair. "Speaking of cats, does the tuxedo cat in that other picture belong to Ms. Engstrom? I sneaked a peek at her desk when we were walking past it." She tried to look apologetic for being so nosy.

In the next instant, Penny's entire demeanor changed. She set Havarti gently on the floor, then tented her hands over her mouth and hitched in a ragged breath. "I'm…sorry, I'm having kind of a bad week. Do you have a business card you can leave?"

"Well, sure," Carly said, digging one out of her tote. She set it on the desk. "I'm sorry if my question upset you. Is there anything I can do to help?"

For a long moment Penny said nothing, as if debating how much to share. "It's just…I haven't heard from my boss all week, and I'm worried sick. I'm so afraid something's happened to her."

Carly set her tote on the floor. "Ms. Engstrom, you mean?"

Penny looked at Carly, her eyes full of pain. "Yes, she sent me a text Monday afternoon saying she was heading west to care for her sick mom. I've tried reaching her, but…nothing. She doesn't call. She doesn't text. I'm just so worried. It isn't like her to be…incommunicado."

Carly thought for a moment. More than anything, she wanted to search Gretel's desk, but she needed an excuse. "Have you tried calling her mom's home?"

Penny threw up her hands. "That's just it. I can't even find a contact number for her. Gretel never talked about her family, and I never wanted to ask. I'm at my wits' end."

"Have you searched her desk? Some people still keep contact names in an address book."

Penny's gaze narrowed, and then her face dropped. "The police asked me the same thing. Gretel didn't use an address book. She kept all her contacts in her desktop. Since I know her login, I went through it myself. I didn't find a single contact name from out of state. They were all Vermont numbers."

The mystery deepens.

"So the police know she's missing?" Carly said.

"They do. They're making quiet inquiries. They don't want a repeat of the Hollis Batchelder debacle. I assume you know that story."

"Actually, I don't." Carly explained that she'd only returned to Balsam Dell less than two years earlier.

"Well, this goes back a bit. Batchelder was a volunteer on the Zoning Board at the time. Likable guy, a bit full of himself. One night he didn't return home after a meeting, but his car was found parked on the side of a dirt road. His wife was frantic, positive he'd met with foul play. The police launched a massive search, practically called out the National Guard. They found him three days later, drunk in a motel room with a paid escort, as she called herself. Batchelder claimed he'd been drugged and robbed, but the facts didn't support that."

"Oh my! That's quite a story."

"It gets worse. After his wife kicked him out and he was fired from his bank job, he sued the town and the police department for creating the hubbub and sullying his reputation."

"But that's ridiculous!" Carly said.

"Thankfully the lawsuit went nowhere, but I think it's why the police are keeping Gretel's sudden disappearance tightly under wraps. They don't want to look like dolts if she suddenly turns up."

Carly blew out a sigh. "My gosh, I wish I could help in some way. I don't mean to pry, but was she seeing anyone?"

"Not that I know of," Penny replied. "She never traveled anywhere, not even on vacation. I thought it was odd, but she told me one day her work was her life. In a way it made me sad—I can't imagine my world without my son and his family. But to each her own, so more power to her, right?"

"Right." *Unless she's hiding something she can't afford to reveal.*

"She must have a close friend or two, doesn't she?" Carly suggested.

Penny nodded. "The police have already talked to them. No one has a clue. They're just as stymied as I am."

Carly folded her hands. "I can see why you're concerned. It sounds like disappearing this way is totally out of character for her. You said you *did* search her desk?"

Penny paused, as if formulating an answer. "I did. There was nothing that would help the police."

Something in her tone was off. *She's lying, but why?*

"Carly, I'm sure you have a busy schedule," Penny said, "but would you be willing to sell some raffle tickets too?" It was clear that Penny was done with the conversation and was hinting for Carly to leave.

"Absolutely," Carly told her. "I'm happy to help."

"Oh, good. The more we sell, the more money for the shelter." Penny tried to sound upbeat, but her tone was lifeless. She pulled open a lower drawer on the right side of her desk. Havarti, who hadn't left Penny's side since she'd set him down, trotted around the desk and poked his nose into the drawer.

"Havarti, remember your manners," Carly said lightly. She gathered her tote and rose from her chair, then picked up the leash and tugged Havarti gently away from the drawer.

"He probably smells my peanut butter crackers," Penny commented. Her voice rattled. She sounded anxious to find the tickets and send Carly on her way. When she finally pulled out a cardboard box, Carly stole a glance into the drawer. Tucked away at the back was a clear plastic bag with several envelopes sealed inside. Penny slammed the drawer shut.

"Here we go." Penny removed two packages of

tickets from the box and wrapped them in rubber bands. She handed them to Carly, then escorted her out of her office and into Gretel's.

Reluctant to leave, Carly thanked her. She hadn't really learned anything, but she couldn't think of a valid reason to stall any longer.

"Oh, where is my head today?" Penny scolded herself. "Let me get you an envelope for those." She turned and went back to her desk.

Carly quickly whipped out her cell and took a photo of Gretel's diploma. If nothing else, it was a starting point.

"Here you go." Penny gave her a manila envelope with a clasp, and Carly stuck the raffle tickets inside. "Thank you so much for wanting to help the shelter." She leaned over and gave Havarti one last tickle under the chin. "Most people have to get roped into volunteer work."

"I'm happy to do it," Carly said. "And, if I can help with the other matter, please let me know. Sometimes it helps to brainstorm with someone who's looking at it from a fresh perspective."

Carly thought Penny hesitated for a moment, but then she ushered her and Havarti out the way they came.

By the time Carly returned Havarti to the apartment, gave him a treat for his fine performance, and got back to the restaurant, it was nearly 11:00. Suzanne had arrived, and Grant was setting up the grill. Valerie was filling napkin holders and wiping down the tables. She'd straightened her topknot and swished on a touch of lip gloss, which Carly took as a sign that she was feeling better.

"You doing okay?" Carly said quietly to Valerie.

Valerie gave her a tepid smile. "Yes, better. Thank you."

The eatery got busy quickly. Shortly before noon, a man wearing a heavy blue jacket with a fleece collar came in. Carly knew him immediately—Ron Benoit.

He wiped his booted feet on the mat—at least he had manners—and looked around the dining room. Carly was removing plates from one of the booths when his long-lashed gaze landed on her. He sauntered toward her. "Hey, got a minute?" He flashed a smile totally lacking in warmth. In fact, it gave her a chill.

Carly straightened, clutching the tray of dishes. "Mr. Benoit. Lovely to see you again." Her tone held a touch of sarcasm, but he didn't seem to notice. Or maybe he didn't care.

"Yeah, and it's Ron, okay? I was going to call you, but I decided to do this in person. You and I need to talk."

"Well, that's getting straight to the point." Carly glanced around. "There's a free booth at the back. Why don't you grab it and I'll join you in a minute?"

Without a word, he did as she instructed. She

returned with a menu and handed it to him. He dropped it on the table without looking at it.

"I'll have two of those donut grilled cheeses and a black coffee."

"I'm sorry," Carly informed him, "but we haven't added those to the menu yet. If you look at the menu, you'll see we do have a great selection of—"

"Then a grilled cheese and tomato on white," he said tightly. "Skip the soup."

Great. He's starting off right away with an attitude.

Carly put in his order and returned with his coffee. She sat down and faced him.

Benoit fisted his hands on the table. "I know you were spying on us at the shower," he said, his expressive eyes darkening. Except for the brash demeanor, she could see why Dawn found him attractive.

Carly folded her arms on the table. "Who's us?"

"Cut the horse crap. You know what I'm talking about. You think I didn't notice your shadow when you were eavesdropping in that corner? There was an overhead light right next to you."

Darn. She hadn't realized she'd thrown a shadow.

"I knew you'd have to sneak out eventually, so I backtracked and peeked around the doorway. I saw you watching Tony bumble his way across the foyer."

Yikes. Caught in the act.

"First of all, I wasn't eavesdropping," Carly

defended. "I got trapped there after I fetched Rose Manous's coat for her. I was trying to be discreet so I wouldn't embarrass anyone."

"Aw, how magnanimous of you. The cops have already been to my studio twice to question me. Someone told them about me and Tony arguing that day, and they're trying to put the screws to me. They're saying I had a motive to off him." His face reddened with anger.

"I'm sure that's part of a standard investigation," Carly said in a quiet voice. "Why *were* you so angry with Tony? Was it about money?"

Benoit aimed a finger at her. "You're something else, you know that? Who are you to question me?" When Carly didn't respond, he lowered his voice. "Klarissa promised me Tony was going to invest in my startup. But every time I asked him about it, he told me he hadn't made up his mind yet. I was counting on that investment. I *needed* it."

"What did you need it for?"

He ticked off reasons on his fingers. "My editing software is out of date, I need a new tripod, and I need to invest in better lighting. None of that stuff is cheap. I know it looks like I'm only taking pictures, but videography is a lot more technical than that." He drank a long sip from his mug.

She waited for him to calm down, then asked, "Ron, that day at the shower, I assume you took a lot of footage. Did the police ask to see your videos?"

"They did, and I cooperated fully. Know what they found? *Nada*. Nothing. If anyone poisoned Tony, they didn't do it while I was videotaping. Duh."

Unless you poisoned him.

"If it's any consolation," Carly quipped, "I was questioned by the police too. And if you're here to ask if I told the police what I overheard that day, the answer is yes."

He lifted his mug to his lips. "That's what I figured. You're one of those goody-two-shoes types. Always doing the right thing," he added with a sneer.

"Ron, I'm curious about something. Why did you wait this long to ask me? The shower was on Saturday."

"No kidding. What are you, a human calendar?" He ran a hand through his hair. "I had other troubles to deal with. Investors breathing down my neck to get their money back. If Tony had come through like Klarissa promised, I wouldn't be in this mess. What I need now is a bank loan—which won't be easy, given the current state of my credit. My only other option is to look to private sources."

Carly's mouth opened.

"I didn't mean loan sharks," he snapped at her. "I meant credit companies that charge a king's ransom in interest."

He sat back when Suzanne came over with his

grilled cheese platter and a big smile. "There you go, sir. Need a coffee warm-up?"

"Uh, no thanks." He glared down at the sandwich, grilled to perfection and oozing with golden cheddar. "Shoot, this looks good."

Suzanne raised her eyebrows at Carly and then strode off.

"Why don't I leave you in peace to enjoy your lunch?" Carly said, sliding toward the edge of the bench seat.

Ron lifted a sandwich half and aimed a corner at his mouth. "Before you go, let me give you a clue. If you really want to know who had a motive to kill Tony, it was his own bestie, Adam Bushey."

Carly almost stumbled getting out of the booth. "Adam Bushey? Wasn't he Tony's best man? What motive did he have?"

Ron laughed. "The oldest one in the world. He's in love with my cousin Klarissa."

CHAPTER TWELVE

CARLY HURRIED THROUGH THE SWINGING DOOR into the kitchen, her mind in a whirl. Ron's declaration about Tony's best man was a verbal bombshell.

Ron hadn't elaborated further, even when Carly tried to pry additional details from him. He'd clearly enjoyed shocking her, as evidenced by the crafty grin he'd flashed her way. Carly had tried not to show her surprise, but she was sure her stunned expression betrayed her.

Nonetheless, she wondered: Was Ron only spinning a tale about the best man to misdirect the police? Or was Adam genuinely in love with Klarissa?

Carly poured herself a glass of ice water. She reeled her memory backward to the day of the shower. Adam Bushey had been coming in just as Carly was being allowed to leave. But why was he there? Had he already learned about Tony's demise?

She was trying to reconstruct the scene in her head when Valerie bumped through the swinging door with a pan of dirty dishes. "Man, these are heavy." She set them down next to the dishwasher and looked at Carly. "Taking a break?"

"Just for few minutes," Carly said. "You seem cheerier than you were this morning. Is everything okay?"

Valerie shrugged and began scraping food scraps into the compost bin. "I'm okay. I had a phone call late last night that upset me, but I'm not going to think about it anymore. What's done is done, right?"

Carly smiled. "I guess so. But if you ever need to vent, I'm available."

"I know you are. Hey, while I rinse the dishes, can you grab another container of soup and bring it out to Grant? His pot is getting low."

"You got it."

Carly set her water glass on the pine desk and returned to the dining room with a new container of soup. Her heart fluttered when she saw Ari sitting on his usual stool at the counter. He leaned over the counter as she approached.

"Hey, you," he said in his deep voice. "I've missed you the last few days."

"Ditto," Carly said. "Things have been crazy, haven't they?"

He nodded, a worried look creasing his brow. "More for you than for me. Shall we plan a date night for Friday?"

"Absolutely. And if the predicted snowstorm hits,

we can hunker down at my place with a giant pizza and watch old movies with Havarti." She leaned a bit closer. "Have you heard any more about...that person we talked about?"

Ari sighed. "Nothing. As far as I know, it's status quo."

Which meant Gretel Engstrom was still unaccounted for.

Carly suddenly remembered the raffle tickets. She wanted to tell Ari about her visit to Penny Harper, but it wasn't the time or place. She put in his order for a Sweddar Weather and said, "We'll talk later, okay? I have a few things to tell you."

By 3:00, when the dining room was quiet, Carly went into the kitchen. She googled Bushey's Pet Grooming on her cell phone and the web page came up instantly. It was a colorful, eye-pleasing site with photos of happy clients—both canine and feline alike. The prices were listed, as were the hours. She was happy to see over a dozen positive reviews from customers, as well as an A-plus rating from the Better Business Bureau. It made her feel better about entrusting Havarti with them. The address was only a short ride from her apartment. She called and made an appointment for Havarti to have a "bath and brush" the following day, with a drop off at 8:00 a.m.

Next Carly pulled the raffle tickets from her tote and dropped them onto the desk. While she was sure many of her customers would be happy to buy tickets, she didn't want them to feel pressured. She was mulling the best way to offer them when Suzanne came into the kitchen.

"Whatcha got there? Tickets?" Suzanne asked her, removing her apron.

Without mentioning Gretel Engstrom, Carly explained why she had them. "I'm trying to think of a way to offer them to customers without being pushy."

"Why don't you ask Gina to make a sign for you? Out of all of us, she's the artistic one. She can write 'raffle tickets are available from your server' or something like that. She can draw cute little doggie and kitty pictures on it."

"If you're implying my stick figures aren't a Van Gogh equivalent, I get the point," Carly joked. "But that's a good idea. I'll try to catch up with her later."

Suzanne grabbed her jacket from the closet and pulled her knitted hat over her head. "Okay, I'm outta here. See you guys tomorrow!"

~

Carly made a quick call to Gina, who agreed to stop by before the eatery closed. In her stationery shop she used cardboard stand-up signs to display her handcrafted greeting card styles, so she agreed to bring a few of them along.

Shortly after 4:00, Valerie left. She'd joined her

aunt's bridge club—a game Carly had never been able to fathom—and wanted to make an early supper for the two of them.

Carly returned to the dining room. A sole customer was seated at one of the booths near the front, his cell pressed to his ear.

"It's just you and me, kid," Grant said jovially, doing his best Bogie imitation. He was flipping over a Some Like it Hot.

"Yup. Kind of like the old days, before Valerie." She smiled at him. "How did we ever survive without her?"

"I don't know, but she's fantastic, isn't she?"

"The proverbial godsend," Carly agreed, "and I love the way the new schedule's working out. You're in a peppy mood today. Any special reason?"

He shrugged, but the sparkle in his eyes betrayed him. "I've got a da—appointment with the head of dietary at the elementary school this evening. She's very interested in my healthy lunch packets for kids. If she likes it, she'll write a proposal for the School Board. I'm kind of psyched."

"Grant, that's great! Let me know how it goes, okay?"

"You'll be the first to know—well, after Mom and Dad." He grinned and plated the sandwich. "Take this over to Detective Allard?"

Carly glanced over at the booth. "Um, sure. Is he state police or local?" she whispered.

"Local. I found out recently he and my dad know each other."

"Ah." Carly took the plate from Grant and went around the counter. "Detective Allard?" she said, setting his sandwich in front of him.

The full-faced fiftysomething with a heavily creased forehead sat back and nodded at Carly. He heaved a noisy sigh into his cell. "Will do, Chief. Let me gulp down my supper and I'll be right over."

Carly waited until he disconnected. "Anything else I can bring you?"

"Yes, thanks. I'd better have a coffee refill. It's gonna be a long night."

"Oh dear. Any particular reason?" Carly asked him, her antennae on full alert.

He hesitated, then said, "Well, since everyone's gonna hear about it soon enough, I might as well tell you. Our town manager, Gretel Engstrom, has been officially declared missing."

CHAPTER THIRTEEN

CARLY HURRIED INTO THE KITCHEN AND CALLED the chief.

"I know you're crazy busy and can't talk long, but is it true? Gretel's been officially declared missing?"

"It is," he said soberly. "A team went back to her house and found new evidence. They now believe she was taken against her will. They found scuff marks on the concrete floor in the garage leading to the start of the driveway. If someone took her in the middle of the night, they probably dragged her to their own car and stuffed her in the trunk."

"The neighbors saw nothing?" Carly asked anxiously.

"She only has a few neighbors close enough to see or hear anything, and they all claimed they hit the sack by ten. No one heard a sound." The chief sounded as frustrated as Carly was.

Carly tapped her fingers on the pine desk. "Chief, do you think this has anything to do with Tony Manous?"

He sighed into the phone. "I've been racking

my brain, but I can't see how. Carly, I gotta dash. I've got a couple of reporters in the lobby—word apparently traveled fast. I'm going to have to make a brief statement before I head over to Gretel's."

The fact that he was going there himself spoke volumes. She wished him luck and disconnected.

Although Carly didn't know Gretel personally, everything she'd heard about the woman had been glowing. Who would want to harm her?

Carly instantly thought of Penny Harper. The poor woman was probably tearing her hair out with worry. The thing Penny had feared most was coming true. Something had happened to her boss, and it wasn't looking good.

The remainder of the workday was busy, but not overly so. As Carly wiped down tables and put away perishables, Gretel's face at the shower that day kept jumping into her mind. Attractive. Serene but thoughtful, and a bit out of her element.

Which was odd for a professional, polished woman like Gretel. But the guests had grown tipsy, Carly recalled, and some were more than a little vulgar. Carly now wished she'd taken a moment to speak to Gretel that day, if for no other reason than to offer a friendly word or two.

Where are you, Gretel? What happened to you?

Carly was grateful for the distraction when Gina popped into the eatery around 6:30. She had three cardboard placards in hand.

"Which do you like best, the blue, the green, or the pink?" she asked Carly, plopping onto one of the stools.

Carly wiped her hands on a clean towel and examined the placards. She liked the pink—it was bright and eye-catching. But the green was more of a seafoam, muted and yet noticeable even from a distance. Grant heartily agreed, so green it was.

"Excellent choice," Gina said. "I'll take a pic of a raffle ticket, then enlarge it and tack it at the top. I'll add some enticing language below that, with sketches of cute dogs and cats. Sound like a plan?"

"You're the best," Carly said.

"So true. In the meantime, give me five tickets." Gina pulled a ten-spot out of her wallet.

"Yay. My first customer!" Carly gave her the tickets and collected the stubs from her. Then she gave her the news about Gretel.

Gina's mouth opened. "*Whaaat?* I hate to say it, but that sounds bad. Really bad."

"I know." Carly grimaced. "I can't help thinking it's connected to Tony Manous."

Gina chewed her lip, and her dark eyes blazed. She hopped off the stool and gathered up her placards. "Listen, stop up to my place after you close. I'll have a steaming pot of peppermint tea and some leftover lasagna waiting for you."

"Sounds perfect. I have a few other things to tell you too."

After Gina left, Carly made arrangements with Becca to check in on Havarti. She and Grant closed promptly at 7:00, and Carly scooted upstairs.

Although Gina's apartment was directly over the eatery, it could only be accessed by a separate door at the back of the building. From there, a staircase led to Gina's apartment and to a door that had once been painted flamingo pink. Thanks to Gina's handiwork, the door was now a dove gray, with a bit of delicate stenciling at the top.

"Smells so good in here," Carly said, the scent of peppermint tantalizing her senses. She threw her coat over Gina's sofa.

Gina's living room was an extension of the kitchen, styled somewhat like a studio apartment. The bedroom, however, was a separate room, with tall windows facing the street on one side and the parking lot on the other. Gina had dressed her bedroom windows with cocoa-colored Austrian shades, a feature Carly adored.

Carly rubbed her hands together and went over to the kitchen table. A bright blue teapot resembling Aladdin's lamp rested on a tile next to two pottery mugs. Over mugs of peppermint tea, she and Gina sat across from one another.

"I'll zap the lasagna in a little while," Gina promised, "but first tell me about Gretel."

Carly took a sip of her tea. "I found out about it yesterday, but I couldn't tell anyone except Ari.

The chief swore me to utter secrecy, which was killing me."

She told Gina everything she knew about Gretel's disappearance, including what she'd gleaned from her visit to Penny Harper. "The police have been hoping Gretel would show up or call, and then they could quietly drop the whole matter. Sadly, that hasn't happened, so now she's been declared officially missing."

Gina listened intently. Carly could almost see the wheels spinning in her head.

"While the police are following their leads," Gina said, "I think the first step for us is to check out Gretel's diploma. I'm so glad you thought to snap a photo while you were in her office!"

"I swear, you read my mind. That's exactly what I was thinking. Can we use your laptop?"

Gina reached behind her and slid her laptop off the countertop. She fired it up and asked Carly to pull up the photo on her cell.

"I'll have to enlarge it," Carly said, spreading her thumb and forefinger over the picture. "Ah, now I can see it." She read the name of the school to Gina—a small, prestigious college in Ohio. "Her full name is Gretel Laila Engstrom. She earned her Master of Business Administration in 2006."

Gina nodded as her fingers flew over the keyboard. "Okay, I think we're in luck. The college has online yearbooks going all the way back to 1952."

"Yay!" Carly said, crossing her fingers for luck.

She got off her chair and stood behind Gina to peek over her shoulder.

Gina plugged "2006" into the search bar, and a link to the yearbook came up instantly. She tapped a key to download it, humming the *Jeopardy* theme song as she waited.

"Here it is," Gina said, after the yearbook was downloaded. "Now we just have to find Gretel."

With Carly peering over her shoulder, Gina scrolled slowly through every page in the yearbook. Not a single student bore the name Gretel Engstrom, or Gretel *anything*.

"Darn," Carly said, blowing out a breath.

"Yeah, I'm bummed. I thought for sure we were on the right track." Gina made a face.

Carly squeezed Gina's shoulder. "Something just occurred to me. If Gretel got her master's in 2006, she'd have gotten her undergraduate degree earlier."

"Yes! See, I knew you were the smart one."

Carly batted her friend's arm playfully, and for the next fifteen minutes or so, they scrolled through the college's yearbooks from 2002 through 2005. Once again, there wasn't a "Gretel" to be found.

"Wait a minute," Carly said. "Gretel didn't necessarily earn her master's and her undergraduate degrees from the same college, right? In fact, she probably didn't. I'll bet we've been looking at yearbooks from the wrong college!"

Gina groaned. "You're right. We should have

thought of that before." She pushed her laptop to the side and headed for the fridge. "Let's have our lasagna, then we'll try to come up with another way to find her. I mean, she wasn't hatched from an egg, right? She has to be from *somewhere*." She removed a foil pan from the fridge. "Don't forget, you said you had other stuff to tell me."

While Gina carved two slabs of cheesy lasagna from the pan, Carly told her about Ron Benoit coming into the eatery, his attitude more than a little surly.

"He actually *said* Adam Bushey was in love with Klarissa?" Gina set the lasagna on a glass pie dish and shoved it into the microwave.

"Yep. He said Adam had the best motive of all to kill Tony." Carly pulled two plates from the cabinet above the sink and set the table.

"Well, ain't that a kick in the head." Gina pressed buttons on the microwave. "With friends like Ron Benoit, who needs enemies?"

"I'm not sure they are friends. Their only connection might have been through Tony. Anyway, guess who has an appointment for a 'bath and brush' at Adam's spa tomorrow?" She grinned at Gina.

Gina laughed. "Oh, you are a sneaky one. First you use an unsuspecting dog to worm your way into Penny Harper's good graces. Then you recruit him to help you solve a murder. If Adam only knew what he was in for."

"What?" Carly said innocently. She batted her eyes.

"I'm only going to ask Adam a few questions. Besides, Havarti loved every minute of his visit to Penny, and the spa has an A-plus rating from the BBB."

"Well, then. That seals the deal."

After they gobbled down a quick supper, Carly pulled the laptop over. She googled Gretel again, this time adding her middle name.

"I'm getting the same hits I got before," she said, disappointed.

Carly googled her again. This time she included the name of the college. Once again, nothing. She was almost ready to give up when another link caught her eye. Feeling her heart pound, she opened it. Her mouth dropped as she scanned the article. "Gina, I've got something. It's an obituary."

Gina gasped. "Gretel's dead?"

"No." Carly looked over the laptop at Gina. "But her mom is."

~

Carly had instantly forwarded the link to Chief Holloway with a quick note: *Gretel's mom deceased.* But later, on the drive home, she couldn't stop thinking about what she'd learned.

Gretel's mom, Anneli Carter Engstrom, had been living in a small Ohio town when she passed in 2014. That was before Gretel moved to Balsam Dell; before she landed the job as town manager.

Anneli's husband had passed back in the early 1990s, leaving her a widow for well over twenty years. As for siblings, Anneli had two brothers, both of whom predeceased her. If Gretel herself had any siblings, none were mentioned in the obit.

"Where are you, Gretel?" Carly murmured to herself in the car. "Are you in hiding, or are you in trouble?"

Some instinct deep inside Carly feared it was the latter.

Once inside her warm apartment, she hugged Havarti, gave him a few treats, then texted Becca to thank her for checking in on him. After that she called Ari, and the two had a long chat on the phone. When the subject of Tony's death came up, Ari's tone grew more fretful.

"Ari, I know what you're thinking, that I'm trying to solve a murder," Carly said.

"Are you?" His voice rose with concern.

She groaned. "Honestly, I am, sort of. Right now, I'm more worried about Gretel. Which is strange because I don't even know her."

After a pause that seemed to go on forever, Ari finally said, "Carly, I know you feel involved somehow because you were almost certainly in that house when Tony was poisoned. But keep in mind, if that's true, it means someone who was at that shower is a very dangerous person."

Carly couldn't deny anything he was saying.

The same scary thoughts had traveled through her own mind. "But we don't even know how he was poisoned, Ari. Until the police come up with an answer, we can't assume anything."

Ari sighed. "I know that. But honey, let's be frank. You *do* have a bit of a reputation for nailing killers. I'm worried that makes you a target."

Again, everything he said was true. "I know I've said this before, but I'm being so careful. And in the interest of full disclosure..." She told him about Havarti's appointment with Adam Bushey the following morning.

"Actually, I know Adam," Ari said. "When he bought the spa building last year, I did the electrical upgrade for him. He's a quiet guy, sort of low key. That's probably why he's good with animals, although I never saw him do any grooming. Hey," he said suddenly. "I have a thought. Why don't I go with you tomorrow to drop off Havarti?"

The plea in his voice squeezed Carly's heart. "Ari, that's sweet of you, but really, I'll be fine. Besides, aren't you heading to Williamstown tomorrow on a job?"

He sighed. "You're right, I am."

"What you need to do is stop worrying," she soothed. "I'll text you when I get to the restaurant, okay?"

After a few more minutes, they disconnected. Carly loved that Ari worried about her, but she hated that she *caused* him worry.

Shortly before 11:00, Carly dropped into bed, her body limp with fatigue. Unfortunately, her mind was working overtime. Sleep eluded her like a frisky little pup. She was eyeing her bedside clock when a realization struck her.

When Gretel applied for the position as town manager, she must have given her resume to the Select Board. Wouldn't her resume have listed a prior address, along with her employment and education history?

First stop in the morning: drop off Havarti at the pet spa. After that, it would be on to the town hall for another visit with Penny Harper.

With that thought in mind, Carly drifted off to sleep.

CHAPTER FOURTEEN

THE HAVARTI DROP-OFF DIDN'T GO AS CARLY planned.

She'd arrived at the spa promptly at 8:00 a.m., stepping inside a waiting area that was both spacious and welcoming. The tile floor was immaculate, the walls painted a soothing, celery green. A row of leatherette chairs faced the reception desk. Shelving along an adjacent wall held grooming products and pet accessories, which were apparently available for purchase.

A slender woman with salt-and-pepper hair came around the side of the reception desk. "Hello, there, I'm Paula," she said with a kindly smile.

Carly had barely introduced herself when Paula shifted her gaze downward. "And this must be Havarti! Look at that sweet little face!" She stooped down and held out her hand to the dog. Havarti licked Paula's fingers.

Carly smiled down at the pair, pleased that the woman so clearly loved dogs. Carly was asked to fill out a lengthy history for Havarti, after which Paula took charge of his leash. "We have you down for a 1:00 pickup?"

"Yes, that's fine," Carly said, "but is the groomer here? I was hoping to chat with him before he got started with Havarti."

"Adam is in, but he's prepping and sanitizing the grooming areas for the day. Is there a particular reason you need to speak to him?"

"I guess not," Carly said. "Please ask him to call me if he has any questions. Havarti's never had a professional bath before, so I'm a little nervous about leaving him with a stranger."

Paula touched Carly's arm. "I assure you, your precious darling couldn't be in better hands. Havarti will be fine."

With that, Carly thanked the woman and left. She texted Grant and Valerie to let them know she'd be delayed, but promised she'd get to the restaurant as soon as possible.

At 8:45, she pulled into the town hall parking lot. Luck was with her when she spotted Penny Harper. Penny was hurrying into the building, her coat collar snugged high around her neck, a coffee cup in one gloved hand.

Carly locked her car and headed into the building. By the time she reached the lobby, the elevator door was closing. Opting for the stairs, Carly reached Gretel's office in time to see Penny letting herself in with her key.

"Oh!" Penny jumped slightly when she saw Carly. Her face was pinched, her eyelids red. "You scared me. I wasn't expecting anyone this early."

"I'm sorry," Carly said. "I didn't have a chance to call first, but I would really like to speak to you."

Penny looked at her with an expression so hollow it made Carly ache. "This really isn't a good time. If it's about the raffle tickets, just do what you think best."

"It's not about the raffle. It's about your boss. Please, Penny, I want to help."

With a weary sigh, Penny ushered her through her boss's office and into her own, locking Gretel's door first. "I'm going to lie low today," she explained. "The last thing I need is any reporters trying to get in."

"I don't blame you there."

Penny set her coffee cup on her desk and hung her coat on the wooden rack behind her. "You already know, I'm sure, that Gretel has been declared missing," she said. "The police are pulling out all the stops to find her, so what is it you think you can do?" Her tone was sharp.

Without being asked, Carly sat down opposite Penny. "Well, first I have a confession. When I was here yesterday, I took a photo of Gretel's diploma."

Penny glared at her, her face blanching. "Why would you do something like that?"

Carly didn't want to reveal what Don Frasco had

told her or that the chief had previously alerted her to Gretel's disappearance. She skirted the question. "The thing is, I want to help. I saw Gretel briefly on Saturday, at the Taddeo shower, and something in her expression sort of got to me. She looked so out of place, almost as if she didn't know why she'd been invited."

"You were there?" Penny sagged in her chair. "I didn't know that. What a small world. But you're right. Gretel only went to that shower because of her friendship with the bride-to-be's aunt, Megan Gilbert. I sensed she'd have done anything to get out of it, but she didn't want to hurt Megan's feelings. Megan's such a sweet person."

Carly let that sink in for a moment. Then she said, "Last night I did some googling on Gretel. My friend Gina helped me. Penny, we couldn't find one iota of evidence that Gretel got her master's degree from that college."

"So what? Is everyone's life story supposed to be online?" The snip in her voice betrayed a touch of fear.

"No, but we searched the college's yearbooks for that year and for several years prior. No one with Gretel's name was in any of those classes. But then something occurred to me. She probably got her undergraduate degree from a different college."

"Yes, I agree, but where are you going with this? How is this helping?" Penny took a sip from her cup.

The room was growing warm. Carly loosened her coat collar. "Penny, I found something else when I was googling. I found the obituary for Gretel's mom."

"Oh." Penny pressed her fingers to her lips. "Then Gretel probably didn't send me that text, did she? Now I'm even more frightened."

"I forwarded the obituary link to Chief Holloway last night, but another thought popped into my head. When Gretel got the position as town manager, she must have given her resume to the Select Board, right?"

Penny's eyes widened. "Gosh, you're right. I never even thought about her resume. The problem is, personnel files are strictly confidential. I have no way to access it."

Carly was disappointed. "No way at all?"

"Let me think a minute." Penny closed her eyes and then opened them wide, as if a light bulb had switched on. She picked up her phone and pressed three numbers. "Lucille? Can you come into my office for a moment? I've locked Gretel's door, but I'll let you in."

A few minutes later, Lucille Webster, the human resources director, was sitting beside Carly. Penny briefly introduced the two but dispensed with pleasantries. "Lucille, is there any way you can get me a copy of Gretel Engstrom's resume?"

Lucille looked torn. "I suspect I know why you're asking," she said quietly, "but you know I don't have the authority to do that." She reached over and squeezed Penny's hand. "Honey, I'm worried sick about her too." And then she shot up straight in her chair. "Wait a minute. What am I thinking? I was on the Select Board when Gretel was appointed. I reviewed her resume!"

"My gosh, I'd forgotten that." Penny's eyes took on a hopeful gleam. "Can you remember anything at all from it?"

Lucille chuckled. "Not the details, but here's the kicker. Remember back when I broke my hip and was out of commission for several weeks?"

Penny nodded. "That was a terrible time."

"Well, that was right around the time we were on the hunt for a new town manager. My assistant used to forward proposals and such to me via email so I could work from home. I specifically remember her forwarding three resumes for me to review."

Carly felt a surge of excitement. "Are you saying Gretel's might be in your home computer?"

Lucille blew out a breath. "It should be. I'm using the same old dinosaur I've had for seven years."

"Lucille," Carly said, "would you have checked Gretel's references? Or called her colleges for verification?"

"The colleges, no," Lucille said. "But in that town where she worked—heck, I can't remember the name—I do recall speaking to one of the town council members about Gretel. He couldn't say enough good things about her. He said he hated to lose her, but he wished her well."

Penny folded her hands as if in prayer. "Lucille, would you be willing to share that resume with me? Gretel's life might be at stake."

"I...don't know," Lucille hedged. "Shouldn't I offer to share it with the police instead? This does seem to be an urgent matter."

"Yes, of course," Penny said, disappointment etching her features.

Lucille looked conflicted. She rose from her chair and leaned toward Penny. "You know I've always valued confidentiality, Penny. Giving you a copy of Gretel's resume would be a serious breach for which I could be terminated. Despite that, and against my better judgment, I'm going to forward it to you. I know how close you are to Gretel, and we all want the same thing—for her to come home safe and sound. And you"—she turned to Carly—"I recognized your name when Penny introduced us. You've helped the police round up some seriously bad folks, haven't you?"

"A few," Carly said, feeling her cheeks heat. "Is there any chance the email with Gretel's resume is in your phone?"

"No, it would be too old. But I'm sure it's still in my home computer. And now," Lucille said, with a meaningful wink at Carly, "I think I'll head home for a *very* early lunch."

Carly got the message. She was scooting home so she could email Gretel's resume to Penny.

~

When Carly arrived at the eatery, she discovered they had a surprise visitor. Chief Holloway was seated at a stool near the front, Valerie perched on the one beside him. They each had a mug of coffee in front of them, and Grant was preparing a cheesy biscuit, *sans* the bacon, for the chief.

"Hey, everyone," Carly greeted her crew. "Chief, you're here early."

His face reddened slightly. "Morning, Carly. After my biscuit's ready, can you and I have a chat?"

"Sure thing. Is that why you're here?"

After an uncomfortable silence, Valerie said, "Actually, I asked him if we could talk about a private matter, and he offered to come over here." She looked at Holloway with a question in her eyes, and he smiled at her.

"You can tell them, Val," the chief said. "In fact, I think it's a good idea for Carly to be aware of the situation."

Uh oh. "Aware of what situation?"

Valerie glanced down at her hands. "I…might need a restraining order," she said, "against my former boyfriend-slash-business partner."

Carly didn't know what to say. When she first

hired Valerie, she'd learned a few tidbits about her prior life, but Valerie had never filled in the details. But her work ethic was exceptional, and she'd already proven herself to be a dependable and hardworking employee. From Carly's standpoint, that was pretty much all that mattered.

Carly reached over and touched Valerie's shoulder. "I'm sorry to hear that, Val, but I'll do anything I can to help."

"Thanks. I really appreciate that."

After an awkward silence during which no one said a word, Grant slid the biscuit onto a plate and set it down in front of Holloway. "There you go, Chief."

"Thanks, Grant," the chief said. He turned to Valerie. "Val, I need to speak privately to Carly, but you and I will chat again later, okay? In the meantime, try not worry. You've got my cell number on your speed dial. Don't hesitate to use it."

Valerie gave him a timid smile, her eyes bright. "I won't. Thanks, Fred."

Carly tried not to gawk, but she couldn't help herself. What was going on between Valerie and the chief?

The chief picked up his biscuit and mug. "Carly, can we chat in the kitchen?"

"Um, sure. Of course. Let me just grab a coffee."

Grant slid a mug over to Carly, and the chief followed her into the kitchen. The moment the swinging door closed, Carly said, "Chief, now I'm worried about Valerie. Is she okay?"

They sat together at the pine desk.

"She'll explain it all to you, but it seems that when she and her ex—a guy named Luke—sold their mom-and-pop country store, Valerie got left with almost nothing. She always thought they owned the store together, but when she and Luke split, she found out otherwise."

"Oh no, that's terrible." Carly pressed her hand to her chest.

"Even worse, this Luke fellow had gotten embroiled in a romance with their assistant manager, a woman they hired just so Val and Luke could spend more quality time together."

"Yecch. That's even more awful. Cuts right to the quick, doesn't it? Val must have felt so betrayed."

"She'll explain the rest of it," the chief said. "She's been wanting to tell you the whole story, but she was worried you might think less of her." His voice softened. "She loves working here. She doesn't want anything to jeopardize that."

"Thank you for sharing that, Chief. My gosh, I would never think less of her for being duped by her boyfriend." She leaned toward him. "This Luke guy, is he dangerous?"

"My sense is that he's not, but he's been calling Val constantly and it's rattling her. Bottom line—the other woman left him, and now he wants Valerie back."

Carly felt her blood rise to a simmer. "What a jerk. The nerve! I'll have a talk with Val, let her know I'm fully supportive."

"Thank you, Carly." His eyes had a glow she'd never seen before. "You're a good person. And now, on to the next topic," he said, his voice tighter. "I got your message last evening. And while I appreciated learning Gretel's mom is deceased, I'm wondering why you were googling Gretel in the first place."

"Chief, you're the one who told me Gretel was missing. I was only trying to help." Carly sipped from her mug.

The chief sighed. "I did, and your impressions from Saturday were helpful. But why are you pursuing it? The police are handling it now, and we're doing everything in our power to locate her." He took a bite of his grilled biscuit.

"I know that, and I respect your position. I can't explain why Gretel got to me Saturday, but she did. The look on her face—" She shook her head.

"Wait a second. You said before she didn't look frightened," the chief reminded her. "Are you changing your story?"

"Good gravy on a grasshopper, of course I'm not changing my story!" Carly looped a finger through her mug handle. "Look, Chief, I know it sounds nutty, but I can't help thinking back to that brief encounter I had with her at the shower. It was only a moment in time, but she looked like she'd rather be anyplace else on earth than where she was. Scared? No. Anxious to bail? Definitely. If I had to guess, I'd say she was there solely for her friend Megan's sake."

The chief studied Carly for several seconds. Then, softly but firmly, he said, "Okay, I get it, sort of. I know you can't stop yourself from wanting to help people in trouble. Must be something in the genes, I don't know. But I want you to listen to me. I was at Gretel's house late yesterday, and I didn't like what I saw. Carly, you have to stop doing your Nancy Drew bit this time, and I am deadly serious when I say that. I didn't want to mention it earlier, but I'm now leaning toward Manous's death and Gretel's disappearance being connected."

Carly nearly leaped off her chair. "You found new evidence, didn't you?"

"There were things that looked out of place. Things I can't discuss. We've sealed off the house, so don't even think of going there."

Carly sat back, her thoughts jumping all over her head. "Um, no. I won't."

The chief polished off his biscuit and coffee. "Hey, I've gotta run. Remember what I said, okay?"

"I'll remember." *Remembering is easy. It's the doing that's hard.* "One last question, though. Did Gretel have a home computer?"

"A laptop, and we have it in custody." The chief rose and pushed in his chair. He picked up his plate and mug.

"Chief, before you go," Carly said, wincing, "I'd better tell you something else. You'll probably be hearing from Penny Harper this morning. She has some information for you." She squeezed her eyes shut, bracing for his reaction. When she opened them, his gaze was harder than granite.

"Tell me."

Carly gave him a short version of her conversations with Penny Harper and how they concluded that they needed to locate Gretel's resume.

"I don't know why I'm surprised that you sought out Penny Harper," Holloway said through clenched teeth. "But this is it, Carly. From this point on, you are prohibited from any further involvement in Gretel's disappearance. Is that clear?"

"Your statement is clear, yes," she said. *But I'm pretty sure you don't have the authority to prohibit me.*

"And for your edification," he added, "requesting Gretel's resume from the town's HR department was next on my agenda. Believe it or not, cops think of those things too. I'm heading over to the town hall the moment I leave here." He brought his dishes over to the sink and turned on the faucet.

"You don't have to rinse—"

"Already done," he said, wiping his hands on a paper towel. "Please thank Grant for the biscuit for me, will you? He refused to let me pay."

"I will." She smiled, hoping to diffuse his annoyance with her.

No such luck.

He left through the back door without another word, not even saying goodbye to Valerie.

CHAPTER FIFTEEN

Havarti's tags jingled as he trotted across the lobby of the grooming spa. The moment he spied Carly, he gave two short yips and then high-tailed over to her and began dancing around her legs.

"Hey, sweet boy!" She lifted him into her arms and kissed his head. "You smell wonderful. Did you have a good bath?"

Adam Bushey came toward them, a smile on his face and Havarti's leash in his hand. Now that Carly was seeing him up close, she realized how handsome he was. Wearing a light blue shirt with "Bushey's Pet Grooming" embroidered on the pocket, he handed the leash to Carly.

"Thanks," Carly said with a smile. "How did he do?"

"He did great, didn't you, little guy?" Adam cooed to Havarti. "He had a nice bath, a bit of a trim, and he even got his toenails clipped." He smiled and held up two pieces of fabric, one peach, one green. "Polar bear or snowman?"

"I'm sorry, what?" Carly asked him.

"His bath comes with a complimentary bandanna. Polar bear or snowman?"

Carly grinned. "Oh, I think we'll go for the snowman. Besides, I like the green."

"Excellent choice." Adam reached over and gently tied the green bandanna around Havarti's neck. When his eyes suddenly met Carly's full on, the warm smile he'd been sporting vanished. "I remember you. I saw you leaving the Chapin home when I was going in on Saturday. You must've been one of the guests."

"Not exactly," Carly said and explained why she'd been there. "I remember you too. What I'm wondering is why you went there in the first place. Had you already heard what'd happened to Tony?"

Adam swallowed. "Klar asked her aunt to text me with the bad news about Tony. After all, I *was* supposed to be his best man. I was so shocked I didn't know what to do. I kept thinking, no, no, this must be a mistake, so I drove over there immediately. When I saw all the police cars, I knew it must be true, that Tony was dead." His eyes narrowed with suspicion. "Why are you asking me about it? Why is it any of your business?"

Carly shifted Havarti to her other shoulder. "It turns out that in the process of narrowing down suspects, the police have put Dawn Chapin at the top of their list. I'm only trying to help her."

He shook his head. "But that's crazy. Dawn wouldn't hurt a fly." He licked his lips and blinked. "Last I heard, they don't even know how Tony died yet. Have you heard anything?"

"Not really," Carly said evasively, "although there's been talk of poison. Adam, can we talk for a few minutes? Privately?"

After a long hesitation, he dropped his shoulders in resignation. "Okay, but only for a few."

Carly clipped on Havarti's leash and set him down. They followed Adam to a small office off to the right. Adam closed the door and waved a hand at the only free chair opposite his desk. Instead of taking his own chair, he leaned against the front of the desk, arms folded over his chest.

Carly lifted Havarti and sat down with the dog in her lap. "Thank you. I won't keep you long."

"Then let's talk. You obviously think you know something about me, don't you?"

Wow, the claws came out pretty quickly, didn't they?

"The only thing I know," Carly said evenly, "or rather what I heard, is that you might be in love with Klarissa. Is there any truth to that?"

His mouth opened. "How dare you ask me that? Why would you say such a thing?" His broad shoulders sagged, and his voice trembled. "Listen to me. I care very much about Klarissa, but I'm not in love with her. Even if I were, I'd never do anything to hurt Tony."

Carly let that sink in for a moment. "Adam, how well do you know Tony's stepmom?"

He looked irritated at the question. "Why? What's she got to do with anything?"

"Probably nothing, except that I heard Klarissa never got along with her," Carly replied.

"Look," he said tightly, "I know everyone, including Klar, thinks Rose Manous is a gold digger. But Tony loved her. She takes good care of his dad—a cantankerous old coot if there ever was one. The old man's got a bad ticker, and Rose dotes on him like a mother hen."

"I only met Rose briefly," Carly said, "but she seems like a woman who cares about her family. By the way, how long had you and Tony known each other?"

"A long time," Adam said. "Before I started my grooming business, I worked for Tony in the Grounds and Recreation Department." He gave a slight smile. "I actually designed the landscaping for a lot of the town's public buildings. Didn't get any recognition for it, but—" He shrugged. "I'm not a glory hound, so I was happy to let Tony bask in the praise."

"Really? Was that before Tony landed the greenskeeper job in North Carolina?"

"It was. When Tony found out he got that job, he was so psyched. He didn't think he had a shot until they called him and told him he was hired. He couldn't stop crowing about it for days."

"He was obviously excited," Carly said with a smile. "He was starting a new phase of his life—new marriage, new job, new home."

"Yeah," Adam said, looking pensive. "After that, the idea he'd been toying with about becoming town manager flew right out the window." He made a flying motion with his hand.

Carly's pulse jumped. "Wait a minute. Tony wanted to be town manager?"

"He did, at one time. He thought he could do a better job, and he does...*did* have an MBA. He said it was time for fresh blood. 'Out with the old, in with the dynamic,' he used to say. Plus, it would've meant a hefty pay raise. That was a biggie, especially with marriage on the horizon. But mostly he wanted to make his dad proud. The old man was active in local politics way back when, and he'd always hoped Tony would follow his lead." Adam's eyes misted. "Every time I think about it, I can't believe he's gone. If someone really poisoned him, I'd like to know why. He was arrogant at times, but he was still a good guy."

"I guess if we knew why, we'd know who," Carly quietly pointed out. "Back to the town manager thing. Had the town been looking to replace the current one?"

"Not that I know of, but it's a pressure cooker job. Most of our town managers have lasted six, maybe seven years before they resign. Tony was hoping that would happen sooner rather than later with Gretel Engstrom."

Carly sat back and thought about that. It still didn't make sense.

"But even if she did resign, why was Tony so sure he'd be appointed to replace her? Isn't that a pretty competitive position?"

"It is, but believe me, Tony's dad has a lot of pull in this town. And despite his faults, Tony was a super likable guy. He knew how to work the system. My opinion? I think his dad was pushing him into it. As long as I've known Tony, he's always loved working outdoors. That's why he was so pumped about the greenskeeper job. Sitting at a desk all day would've driven him crazy." Adam shot her a look. "Why are you asking all these questions? Tell me again why you care."

Carly gave Havarti's chin a tickle. "As I explained, I don't want Dawn to be wrongly blamed for whatever happened to Tony."

"Interesting," he said, his tone riddled with doubt. "So, all of a sudden, you guys are buddy-buddy?"

"Not…so much," Carly replied. "But we've become friends, and I defend my friends."

It was a slight exaggeration, but it was close to the truth.

Adam leaned toward her and folded his hands. "Let me tell you something about Dawn. She's a good kid. I've always liked her. But she has a history of, well…mental instability. She can't function without Klar at her side. She's the Tweedledum to Klar's Tweedledee, if that makes any sense. She's had lousy luck with men, and you know why? Because she picks losers. I'm sure right about now she's rejoicing that Klar won't be moving to North Carolina. Not only rejoicing, but relieved."

Whoa.

After an awkward silence Carly said, "That was quite a speech, Adam. Why don't you tell me how you really feel?"

He shrugged. "It is what it is."

"Yes, but first you said Dawn wouldn't hurt a fly. In the next breath you say she's unstable. Which is it?"

His face flushed again. "It's both. I'm sorry, but I've watched her cling to Klar for so long…I guess it just came out that way."

"So you've known Klarissa a long time?"

His eyes clouded. "I have. I'm the one who introduced her to Tony. How dumb am I?" he added sullenly.

Another interesting tidbit. Carly filed it away on her mental notepad.

She stroked Havarti's fur. "How about you, Adam? Are you glad Klarissa won't be moving away?"

He looked sharply at her. "That's a loaded question, isn't it? If I say yes, then it's like saying I'm glad Tony's dead."

"And if you said no?"

"I want what's best for Klarissa," he murmured, his eyes taking on a glazed look. "We've been friends since junior college."

"I appreciate you being frank about all that," Carly said. She studied his expression long enough to make him fidget. "Adam," she said quietly, "you *do* love her, don't you?"

Adam's eyes flashed with anger. "You have a big fat nerve, you know that? Now I have clients to groom, and you've already made me run late. Pay your bill and get out before I call the police and have you physically removed."

Yikes, Carly thought. He'd gone from helpful to defensive in a heartbeat.

Carly nodded. "I'm leaving right now."

On her way out to the reception desk to pay her bill, something occurred to Carly. She hadn't talked to Klarissa since Saturday, since that horrible day of Tony's death.

Maybe it was time to pay a condolence call.

CHAPTER SIXTEEN

Once Carly was seated in her car with Havarti buckled safely in the back seat, she checked her phone for messages. She was dismayed to see she'd missed two text messages from Penny Harper, the second more urgent than the first.

Carly started her engine and called her.

"Carly, thank heaven you called!" Penny sounded tearful, almost frantic. "I...I have a problem. A dilemma, really, and I need your advice. I know you're busy, but is there a chance you can stop over at my office?"

"I just picked up Havarti from the groomer. Let me bring him home first, and I'll be right over."

Penny sighed with relief and thanked her. "See you soon."

After she disconnected, Carly grimaced. How was she going to justify her absence, yet again, from the restaurant?

On the other hand, she was the owner, the boss. And now that Valerie was on board, Carly's occasional treks out of the office shouldn't create a hardship. It was one of the reasons she'd hired an assistant manager—that, and to help with the workload.

She called Valerie and explained her plan.

"You go right ahead," Valerie told her, a smile in her voice. "The lunch crush is dwindling, and we're keeping up just fine."

"Thanks, Val. I'll try not to be too long. Maybe you and I can have a chat later?"

"Absolutely. Let's make it a plan. Oh, and wait till you see the poster Gina made for the raffle tickets! It's rad!"

Carly smiled to herself. Gina had come through for her again.

After bringing Havarti home, Carly headed to the town hall. Penny was pacing in front of Gretel's office, waiting for her. Her eyes were puffy and her cheeks pale. She looked as if she'd gotten zero sleep the night before. When she saw Carly, she opened Gretel's door quickly and nearly shoved her inside.

Without a word, Carly followed Penny across Gretel's office and through the side door into Penny's.

"I didn't mean to alarm you," Penny fretted, closing her office door, "but now that the police declared Gretel officially missing, I can't keep quiet any longer."

Carly sat down and loosened her scarf. For Penny to be this agitated, it had to be big.

Penny sat down and opened her lower desk drawer—the same one where she'd stored the raffle tickets. This time she pulled out a clear plastic bag. It was the same bag Carly had seen before.

Penny plopped the bag onto her desk and tore open the seal. "When Gretel first went missing," she explained, "I searched through her desk. I was looking for something, *anything* that might have her mom's address on it. Instead, I…found these." Her face reflected her misery as she pushed the bag toward Carly.

Carly held up one finger. "Hold on." She reached into her tote and dug out the vinyl gloves she always carried. They'd come in handy on more than one occasion, and she didn't want to risk leaving fingerprints. She slipped them on and reached inside the plastic bag, pulling out all the envelopes at once.

The envelopes, which were identical, were about the size of a greeting card. Each one bore a local postmark and was addressed to Gretel in care of the town hall. None had a return address.

Her heart thumping, Carly opened the first one. She pulled out a sheet of paper that was pale gray with a slim blue line across the top. On it was typed a simple message:

> You're a phony. Not what you claim. Resign and no one will ever know.

Carly felt her color drain. "This reads like a threat."

"That's only the first one," Penny said in a shaky voice. "It's postmarked way before the others. Go on, they get worse."

Penny was right. There were four more letters, mailed about two weeks apart, beginning at the end of the summer the prior year. Each one ramped up the threat a notch. The last one read:

> Phony girl, you have refused to heed my warnings. Pack your desk. You won't be working there much longer. Do you really want to endure the disgrace?

"Penny, exactly when did you find these?"

"Tuesday morning," Penny confessed. "When I still hadn't heard from Gretel after that odd text message, I knew something had to be wrong." Her eyes brimmed with tears. "Oh, Carly, she's in trouble, isn't she?"

Or worse, Carly thought, hating where her dark thoughts were taking her.

"I'm not sure, but why didn't you show these to the police right away?"

Penny sniffled. "At first, I…I thought Gretel had gone into hiding. If that was the case, I didn't want to jeopardize her future by giving the police these letters. I figured she'd eventually contact me, or better yet, just show up." She wrung her hands. "I was wrong, wasn't I? By holding out, I did the exact opposite!"

And suddenly, Carly got it. "Penny," she said softly, "you know what the letters mean, don't you?"

With that Penny burst into tears. She nodded miserably. "Yes," she choked out. She cried for at least a full minute, then blew her nose.

"Tell me, please," Carly begged.

Penny sucked in a long sniffle. "Gretel doesn't have an MBA. She created a phony diploma and a bloated resume so she could apply for the town manager position." She opened her desk drawer and pulled out Gretel's resume. "I didn't want to risk emailing you this, so I printed it. Lucille emailed it to me a few hours ago."

Carly skimmed Gretel's resume as Penny went on. "Gretel's from a small town in Ohio. After high school, she attended community college for a year, but money was tight so she postponed her education until she could save enough for tuition. In the meantime, she got a job working for the fiscal officer in one of the townships. Turned out her work was so precise, so efficient, her boss began trusting her with major fiscal decisions. Gretel relished the challenge, and within a year she'd saved the township several thousand dollars. She was a demon for cutting waste, and the township began to see more money in its coffers. Her boss took most of the credit, but she didn't care. She absolutely loved her job."

Carly could guess what happened next. "But it wasn't enough, was it? At some point, she wanted recognition for her work."

"Yes, that's exactly right," Penny said. "Keep in mind, she still hadn't gone back to school. At some point she started perusing jobs online. That's when she noticed the opening for a town manager in Balsam Dell. She'd never even set foot in New England, but she desperately wanted to apply. In the region where she was living, she didn't see a future for herself. The position required an MBA, so..." Gretel shrugged her shoulders.

"So she created her own," Carly murmured.

"For what it's worth," Penny said in defense of her boss, "she's been taking online and evening college classes. She'll have her BA within a year, and then she'll work toward earning her master's. She spends every evening studying, Carly. She doesn't even have a social life."

Carly forced a smile, but in the pit of her heart she feared for Gretel.

One thing about the letters had struck her, though. The threat to Gretel appeared to be one of exposure, not physical harm. The writer had asked if she wanted to "endure the disgrace." That suggested that her secret would be divulged, not that her life would be ended.

"She sounds like a dedicated woman. I'm sorry I was never introduced to her. Penny, you need to give these letters to Chief Holloway right away, okay?"

"I know. The moment you leave, I'm going to call him." Her expression wilted. "Do I…have to tell him everything I told you?"

"I would," Carly advised. "Gretel's safety is our top priority, right?"

"Of course," Penny said hoarsely. "Will I be in trouble?"

"I don't think so. The chief is a pretty fair guy." *Except when he thinks I'm meddling.* Carly slipped her cell phone out of her tote. "Before I leave, may I take pictures of the letters?"

"By all means—be my guest. In fact, Lucille tells me you're quite the detective." She graced Carly with a weak smile.

"Not true, but that's kind of her to say." Carly took photos of both the envelopes and the letters, and then snapped off her vinyl gloves. "I'm heading to the restaurant now, but call or text me if you think of anything else."

"I surely will," Penny said and escorted Carly out of her office. She clasped her hands nervously. "Carly, there's a chance Gretel's okay, isn't there?"

"I have high hopes," Carly said, giving her a quick hug. "Never give up, okay?"

Carly hopped onto the elevator and waved to

her. As the door slowly closed, she heard Penny crying.

~

"Oh my gosh, this is unbelievable!"

"Isn't it?" Valerie squealed. "Your friend is an *artiste extraordinaire*."

Carly moved closer to the poster, which had been propped on a small table next to the soda machine.

At the top of the poster board, a dog that resembled Havarti held a giant-sized raffle ticket between his teeth. Below that, Gina had sketched a line of cats and dogs gazing up and a newly improved shelter, complete with a tin roof and roomy dog runs. In a fun, readable font, she'd spelled out the details of the fundraiser, including colorful sketches of three baskets stuffed with prizes.

"We've already sold thirty tickets," Grant said, coming up next to Carly with a proud grin. "At this rate, you'll have to ask your friend for more."

"I'm afraid she has more serious things on her mind right now. Did Suzanne leave?"

"Yep. Ten minutes early," Valerie said. "Something at the school with Josh. Did you hear? Grant's going to give him violin lessons after hours."

Grant looked pleased. "Yeah, ever since Josh saw me play the cello at his school's holiday pageant, he's been thinking he might like to try the violin. I can give him some starting lessons, but if he really enjoys playing and wants to continue, I'm going to recommend a professional violinist to teach him."

Carly shrugged out of her coat sleeves. "I don't know how you juggle everything, Grant. You're like a magician."

"So, what's the story with your friend?" he said. "You said she had more serious things on her mind."

Carly glanced around. At that moment only two booths were occupied. "My friend is Ms. Engstrom's assistant," she said quietly. "You know, the woman who's missing?"

"Ah. Got it." The door opened and three women strolled in. They paused to read the poster. Valerie greeted them and seated them in a booth, while Grant went back behind the counter.

In the kitchen, Carly texted Gina to thank her for the poster. The moment she'd hung up her coat, her cell rang.

"Cool poster, isn't it?" Gina bragged playfully.

"Totally. You rocked it, lady. I'm going to text a picture of it to Mom. She already thinks you're the greatest artist since Georgia O'Keeffe."

"Thanks, but it's only a poster, and I'm not even really an artist. Speaking of your mom, have you heard from her lately?"

Carly smiled. "I got a text from her yesterday. She and Gary are on someone's yacht, cruising the

Gulf. She told me she's already gone through one package of Dramamine, and if her second one runs out, she's going to throw herself overboard. Either that or throw Gary overboard for making her go on the yacht in the first place."

"I love your mom," Gina said with a giggle.

"Yeah, me too. Hey, I've got a restaurant to run, and Valerie's waving at me from the kitchen door." Carly signaled to Valerie to come in.

"Later then!" Gina chirped.

Valerie stepped into the kitchen and scooted over to the closet. "I didn't want to burst in on your phone call," she said, snapping her jacket off its hanger.

"That's never a problem. You work here, and you're entitled to be in the kitchen."

"Thanks." Valerie sounded relieved. "I wanted to let you know I'll be leaving now. It's almost four." She laughed. "Can you believe I've joined a ladies' bowling team?"

"Hey, that's great," Carly said with an encouraging smile. "I think the last time I bowled I got about a nine, but I'm sure you'll do far better. How did you happen to join?"

"I saw a notice on the library's bulletin board, so I emailed the team leader. It's a great way to make new friends, don't you think?" Valerie eyes lit up at the prospect.

"A perfect way." Carly was genuinely happy for

her, although they still hadn't talked about Valerie's issues with her ex. "We'll chat tomorrow then, okay?"

"You betcha."

After Valerie left, Carly returned to the dining room. Only one booth, near the back, was occupied. Carly was learning that her business was more seasonal than she'd imagined. Although the days were growing longer, it was still dark by 5:30. It was the lunch hours, between 11:00 and 2:00, when they'd been serving the bulk of their customers.

She was clearing dishes off the tables and piling them onto a tray when a woman bundled up like an expeditioner to the North Pole came in. Something about her was familiar, but with her knitted hat pulled low and a scarf covering much of her face, it was impossible to see who she was.

The woman glanced around, as if trying to get her bearings. When she finally pulled off her hat and tugged her scarf below her chin, Carly smiled. It was Klarissa's aunt, Megan Gilbert.

AKA Auntie Meggs.

Carly set down her tray and went over to greet her. "Megan, I didn't recognize you at first. It's nice to see you."

"And I'm happy to see you too," Megan said, a hitch in her voice. Her gentle face radiated pain, and her eyes glistened. She gave Carly an impulsive hug.

"How have you been holding up?" Carly inquired.

"I'm hanging in there, I guess, but things are still pretty awful. But it sure is good to see you, Carly," she said, her voice breaking. "I swear, yours is the first friendly face I've seen since I left Julie's house on Saturday. You were so kind that day. I felt as if I'd known you forever."

Carly thought back to how helpful Megan had been when Dawn fainted on the stairs. While everyone else had been hovering over Tony's prone form, Megan had gathered Dawn into her arms and spoken soothingly to her until the EMTs arrived.

"I was grateful to you, as well," Carly said. "I was at a loss when Dawn fainted. No one else seemed to realize I needed help. You stepped right in and took over."

"Oh, well, I've known Dawn forever," she explained. "Julie and I have been friends since our early school days. I was the sister Julie never had."

"Come on over and sit down," Carly encouraged. "Can I get you a warm drink? Something to eat?"

"Something to drink would be wonderful. Thank you." Megan sniffled and gave her a tiny smile. "I know I shouldn't be barging in on you like this, but I was feeling desperate. Klar and Ursula are so steeped in mourning, I can't even talk to them. They hide in their rooms, and I can hear Klar crying." Her voice cracked and she let out a muffled sob. "I...didn't think it would be this bad."

Carly couldn't even imagine how Klarissa must be feeling. The heartbreak of losing the man she loved, and only a few weeks before her wedding, had to be the worst thing she'd ever experienced.

She led Megan to a booth near the front of the restaurant. "You're not barging in at all. It's warm in here, so why don't you take off your coat and I'll get you something hot. How about some orange-flavored tea? From my own private stash."

"Sounds lovely," Megan said with a weak smile. "I could use a pick-me-up."

A few minutes later, Carly was seated across the booth from Megan with a mugful of fragrant tea. Megan added three sugars to her own and stirred it with her spoon.

"I should actually apologize," Carly began. "I've been meaning to make a condolence call to Klarissa, but with one thing and another my schedule got away from me."

"No need for an apology," Megan said. "I'm sure everyone understands. Looking around this charming restaurant, it's obvious what takes up your time." Her gaze landed on Grant, and she flashed him a smile. He must've been observing them, because he returned her smile with a gracious one of his own.

"Klar and I will never forget your generosity," Megan continued, "in agreeing to cater her shower on such short notice. Everything you did was perfect." She linked her fingers together on the table. "Klar knows you refused to accept the rest of what you're owed, Carly. It was overly generous of you."

"Thanks, but I really do feel bad about the way it all worked out," Carly explained. "So Klarissa's been staying at her mom's?"

"She has. She couldn't bear to go back to her own apartment. The memories of Tony there are too overwhelming." Megan snatched a napkin from the metal dispenser and squashed it against her eyes.

It was so painful to watch, Carly didn't know what to say. She let Megan cry for a bit, then finally said, "I'm so sorry, Megan. I'm sure this is almost as hard on you as it is on her."

"You're right about that," Megan said bitterly. "It's horrible enough that my niece's fiancé was murdered, but now one of my best friends has disappeared. The police think she might be in trouble." Her eyes filled again. "Oh Carly, I think she is too."

Carly lowered her voice. "Are you referring to Gretel Engstrom?"

"Yes, I guess most people have heard about it by now. The last time I saw her was when I drove her home late Saturday."

Carly took a sip of her tea. "How did she seem to you?"

"Fine, I guess. We were both so shaken by Tony's death, we barely spoke on the way to her house. I dropped her off, she waved from the window, and that was the last I ever saw of her."

Carly knew Gretel had gone to the police station the following morning, so she was seen in public after that. Had Megan been aware of that?

"When the police contacted me and asked if I knew her whereabouts," Megan went on, "I was shocked. It was so unlike her to bail like that and not tell anyone, especially me. That's why I knew something wasn't right."

"Have you been friends long?" Carly asked her, careful to use the present tense.

"Not really, only about a year and a half." Megan smiled. "We met at a crafts fair, of all places. I'm kind of a serious crafter, and I had a display of my handmade dolls that day. Gretel loved them. She spent so much time browsing in my booth that eventually we got talking. We realized we had a lot in common. Single gals, no boyfriends to speak of. She said my dolls reminded her of the raggedy doll her mom made her when she was a kid. Anyway, she bought one, and the next day we met for lunch. Dopey me, I didn't even know she was the town manager."

Carly toyed with the idea of mentioning the town contract Gretel and Tony had been at odds over. But Megan looked so morose, she decided not to bring up the subject. As the witch from a famous movie said, *I'll bide my time.*

"You've had a lot to cope with over the past week," Carly said. "Is there anything I can do?"

"Actually," Megan said, "that's one of the reasons I came to see you. I've been trying to coax Klar into coming over to my house for a visit. You know, just to get out of Ursula's place and clear her head. She keeps saying, 'I will, Auntie Meggs, I promise, but right now I just want to stay here and cry.'" Megan shrugged and her eyes misted again.

"Sounds like she's really struggling. Has she seen her doctor?"

Megan sighed. "She has, and he prescribed some anxiety medication. If it's helping, I haven't seen any sign of it yet." She sat up straighter and her eyes widened. "Carly, that's where you come in. I thought if you could join us for a luncheon at my house, maybe she'd agree to come too. She needs a change of scenery and some good old Vermont fresh air. She admires you so much. I'm hoping you might be the catalyst, so to speak." She gave her a hopeful smile.

Carly wasn't so sure Klarissa admired her. It was more a case of being grateful that she'd saved her from having to cancel or postpone her shower.

Still, she jumped at the idea. It would give her the chance to learn more about Tony and to gauge Klarissa's feelings about the debacle that'd been her shower.

"I'll be glad to accept, if I can," Carly said. "What day were you thinking?"

Megan wrinkled her nose. "Tomorrow? I know it's short notice, but with Klar, short notice works best. I don't want to give her time to back out."

Carly pushed aside her empty mug. "You and Klarissa are very close, aren't you?"

Megan nodded. "We have been since she was a toddler. Back then, Ursula was one of those makeup consultants that called on customers in their homes. She was on the go all day, sometimes in the evening. Her then husband was on the road a lot for his sales position, so when Klar was little I babysat her a lot." Her expression softened. "Oh, Carly, she was the sweetest child you ever saw. She almost never cried, and she was such a love bug. I can't bear seeing her suffer like this." She pressed her fingers to her lips to stifle a sob.

Carly's throat clogged. Megan's devotion to her niece was so genuine that she was suffering along with her.

"It's obvious she adores you too," Carly said. "You didn't have a job at the time?"

Megan pulled in a breath. "I'd been working for a local florist, but I gave it up to help Ursula. It was time for me to leave, anyway—the florist owner didn't appreciate creativity. You had to arrange flowers *their* way, like a robot. It turned out to be a blessing in disguise because that's when I started making my specialty dolls. While little Klarissa slept, I sewed. Once I began selling them, I was amazed at how in demand they became. I consigned with some of the local gift shops, and that's when I started making serious money. These days, the internet sales keep me hopping."

"That's a great story of entrepreneurship," Carly said with a smile, although she wanted to get Megan back on track. "So what time were you thinking tomorrow?"

"Yes, tomorrow," Megan said, as if she'd temporarily lost the thread. "I was hoping for something like two o'clock? By then Klar is usually starving, although she's barely eaten all week. I'm hoping to entice her with all her favorites."

Tomorrow was Carly's day to leave at four, and she and Ari had made plans to get together. They'd both been so busy all week, they'd barely had a chance to catch up. Plus, she missed him!

"Megan, I think I can juggle it, but can I get back to you? I want to be sure there's enough coverage here."

"Absolutely," Megan said. "If you can let me know by this evening, it'll give me time to prepare. If Klar knows you're going to be there, I'm sure she'll make an extra effort." She started gathering her gloves and hat.

"Megan, before you go," Carly said, "has Klarissa been in touch with Tony's mom? I'm sure his death must have devastated her."

"Tony's stepmom, you mean." Megan set her

gloves on the table and released a sigh. "Yes, Rose has called the house several times. I know the poor woman is shattered over Tony's death, but Klar really doesn't want to talk to her, and my sister treats Rose like she's invisible."

"That's a shame," Carly said.

Megan's face reddened slightly. "Truth be told? The only time in my life I ever argued with Klar was over her mother-in-law to be. Klar firmly believes Rose is a money-grubber, that she only married Tony's dad for his money. I tried to make her see that if they were going to be family, she had to try to get along. Rose has so many good qualities, even if Klar is blind to them." Her voice had grown so soft it was a near whisper. "And Rose loved Tony dearly. That much I'm sure of."

Megan's words reminded Carly of what Adam Bushey had said, that Rose was a devoted caretaker to Tony's dad.

"I really do have to go," Megan said, shooting an anxious glance at the front window. "I hate driving in the dark." She gave Carly her cell number. "Will you text me or call me later to let me know?"

"I will. I promise." Carly waited until Megan had bundled up and then walked her to the door.

By the time Megan had left, it was pitch dark outside. Their sole customer had left, although Grant was working on a few takeout orders.

"Hey," he said, when Carly joined him behind

the grill. "Gotta admit, it's so quiet in here, I was sort of eavesdropping. Did I hear you say that was the bride-to-be's aunt?"

"Yes. Megan Gilbert." Carly started putting away some of the condiments in the fridge below the counter.

"Poor woman looked as sad as I've ever seen," Grant commented. "I almost wanted to give her a hug myself." He slid a Some Like it Hot into a takeout container, next to a sealed container of tomato soup.

Carly was only half listening. She tapped her fingers absently on the counter.

"Earth to Carly. Over," Grant joked.

"I was just thinking," she said. "What do you think about having shorter winter hours? We'd still open at eleven, but we'd close at six instead of seven."

Grant shrugged. "I don't have to think. I'm all for it. But how are you defining *winter*?"

"The three months it gets dark earliest—December, January, and February. On March first, we go back to regular hours." She held out her hands. "Easy cheesy."

Grant laughed. "That's actually a smart idea. Lately we've had only a smattering of customers after four. If you calculate what it costs to stay open that last hour of the day, I'll bet it would work out in your favor. Earnings wise, that is."

"One drawback," Carly noted. "Cutting back

your and Valerie's working hours would affect *your* earnings."

"Yeah, but not by much, and it's already the end of January. By March we'll be back to regular hours. If Val's on board, I am." His dark eyes lit up.

"You're looking a bit cryptic all of a sudden," Carly said with a sly smile. "Anything you'd like to share?"

He took a breath. "Okay, here goes. If everything falls into place, I'll be signing a contract with the school for my healthy lunch packets."

"Grant, that's fantastic!" Carly squealed.

"Don't cheer yet," he cautioned. "I still have to work with dietary to calculate the nutritional value of each packet. Plus, the School Board has to vote on it, which is a biggie. Approving it will mean taking a *bite* out of their annual budget."

Carly giggled. "Very amusing, but we're lucky enough to live in a progressive town, so I think they'll approve."

The door opened, and the takeout customer came in. Carly rang up the order and bagged his sandwich container, thanking him for his business.

By the time she finished, Grant's cheerful mood had evaporated. Lines of worry furrowed his brow as he scraped down the grill. "I'm worried, Carly. Even though you've been silent about it, I know you've been talking to people. Asking questions, I should say."

Carly went over and stood beside him. "It's only talking, Grant, and always with other people around," she assured him. "Will you stop worrying?"

He shook his head with frustration. "Do you still carry pepper spray?"

"I do," she confirmed. Ari had given it to her after her first encounter with a desperate killer. "It's in my tote as we speak."

"Then will you do me a favor, please, and move it to your coat pocket?" He grabbed a clean cloth and poured a small amount of water on the grill.

"I will, I promise," Carly said.

The remainder of the day was quiet, so they closed at around 6:45. As always, Grant walked Carly out to her car behind the building. He made sure she was buckled inside before waving and heading off to his own car.

Sitting in her Corolla as it warmed up, Carly shivered. She couldn't help thinking of Gretel, missing now for four days. Was she safe and warm somewhere, hunkered down to avoid being found? Or was she, as Megan feared, in some kind of trouble?

There was a worst-case scenario, but Carly didn't want to think about that.

At that moment, she wanted to be home, where a freshly bathed, adorable little dog was eagerly awaiting her arrival.

CHAPTER SEVENTEEN

Havarti hadn't been the only one anticipating her arrival.

When Carly pulled into her driveway, Ari's pickup was there. He'd brought along her favorite Chinese food, along with a bouquet of flowers. It was the best surprise she'd had in a very long time.

Unfortunately, it came with a catch.

After Carly arranged the flowers in the vintage vase she'd inherited from her grandmother, Ari took her aside on the sofa.

"Honey, when we were making plans for tomorrow night," he said, "I totally forgot something. One of the contractors on the Williamstown job is an old classmate of mine. I'm supposed to go to his bachelor party tomorrow night at the VFW hall."

"In Balsam Dell?" she asked.

"Yup. I'll get out of it if you want, but he's kind of a good guy so I hate to let him down."

"Ari, I'm totally fine with you going." Carly smiled at him. "Why would you even apologize?"

He kissed her lightly. "Because I should have

mentioned it before. And I shouldn't have forgotten about it in the first place."

"Like they say, stuff happens." She gave him a longer kiss.

After that they enjoyed a leisurely dinner. Strange as it felt, they'd managed to avoid all talk of murder. Hours later, by the time Ari left, Carly felt better about everything—despite knowing that Tony's poisoning and Gretel's disappearance were still unresolved.

Before she turned in, Carly checked with Grant and Valerie about leaving around 1:00 on Friday instead of waiting until 4:00. Both gave their hearty approval, which meant Carly could attend Megan's luncheon.

On Friday morning, she got another, even bigger surprise. Grant, Valerie, and Suzanne had conspired with each other to give Carly the entire day off. Suzanne was saving for a trip to Disney World, so she was happy to work the extra hours instead of leaving at 3:00. They strongly suggested a spa day but told her to do whatever she pleased.

The spa day sounded tempting, but Carly had other ideas. Although Tony's body hadn't yet been released for burial, his family was nonetheless grieving.

With that in mind, Carly drove straight to the local deli. There she bought a platter of veggies and cold meats, complete with condiments. She added a small condolence card to the top. Since she'd already looked up the Manous's address, she headed there next.

The Manous family lived in a stately brick residence in a neighborhood of similar homes. The wide driveway was plowed and sanded. Only three cars were parked there.

Carly climbed the steps and rang the bell. She was mildly surprised when a uniformed nurse answered the door.

The nurse smiled. "May I help you?"

"Hello, I'm Carly Hale. I wanted to deliver this to Tony's family," she explained.

The nurse, a fiftysomething woman wearing an old-fashioned white uniform, gave her a kind smile. "I'm Doris, and that is so sweet. I'm sure Rose and Gordon will appreciate it." She reached for the platter, but Carly held it tight.

"Is Rose home?" Carly asked. "I'd like to offer my condolences, if she's up to having a visitor."

"She's been with her husband all morning," the nurse said solemnly. "But I'll check to see if she can see you for a few minutes. Why don't you come on in?"

Carly stepped inside, welcoming the warmth. The nurse took the tray and asked her to make herself comfortable in the parlor, then disappeared through a doorway.

Glancing all around, Carly saw floral arrangements covering nearly every surface, each with a tiny card poking up from a plastic stick. She chose an elegant wing chair and made herself comfortable.

After several minutes, Rose finally came into the room. She looked pale and shaky. Dark lines underscored her bloodshot eyes. Her melancholy expression made Carly's heart want to burst.

"Oh, goodness," Rose said when she saw Carly. Her short legs wobbled for a moment. Carly ran over and helped her over to the plush sofa, then sat down beside her.

Rose immediately started to cry.

"Rose, I'm so sorry about Tony, about everything," Carly said. "And I'm sorry it's taken me this long to call on you."

"What a kind, lovely lady you are," Rose said tearfully, "to even think of me after everything that's happened. You can't imagine how glad I am to see you again. We don't have much family left, and I'm sick of the police. All they do is ask questions, and not very nice ones." Her words ended on a sour note.

"I'm sure they're doing their jobs as best they can," Carly soothed, though she didn't expect Rose to agree. "Looking at all these flowers, I can see you have a lot of people who care about you."

Rose waved a hand and scowled. "Those are mostly from Gordon's old cronies. Not one of them has even stopped by. What kind of friends are those?"

Carly wondered at that. Were the circumstances of Tony's death keeping mourners away?

"The worst part," Rose went on, "is that Tony's fiancée won't talk to me. I've called her several times, but she won't come to the phone. I tried her cell and her mother's home phone." She pulled a tissue from the pocket of her black slacks and dabbed her eyes.

Carly lightly rubbed Rose's back. "Remember, Rose, she's grieving too. Give her time to come to terms with the loss. This is so hard on both of you."

"Time. *Phhttt.* Like that's going to help." Rose grasped Carly's wrist in a vise. "That family, the Taddeos—they're heartless. Even the mother, Ursula, never gave me the time of day. I heard the names they call me. They say I married Gordon for money, but it's not true!"

"People say things they don't mean," Carly said, though she suspected Klarissa and her mom weren't among those.

"That day," Rose went on with a sniffle, "I was so proud of my pastries. I spent so much time baking and decorating them. I wanted them to look beautiful enough to please that thankless woman. And what does she do? She sends a message that she doesn't want my homemade baked goods on the table with the special cake she ordered from Sissy's."

No wonder Rose had felt crushed. "I'm sorry, Rose. I can't justify Klarissa's reasons, but it sounds as if the cake meant something special to her."

Rose loosened her grip on Carly. "You're being kind, but I know the truth. She was always trying to twist Tony's mind against me. When it didn't work, she did everything she could to hurt me."

Carly remembered seeing Rose's cell phone on the table next to the pastries. "Is that why you called Tony that day? To tell him what Klarissa had done to you?"

"Yes, that's exactly why. He was angry and told me he would be coming right over to speak to her. He said he wasn't going to put up with her nonsense any longer."

Timing wise, Carly tried to pin down the order of when everything happened.

After she'd seen Rose crying in the breakfast nook, she'd escorted her to the cloakroom to fetch her coat. Once Rose had left, Carly started to head back to the kitchen when she heard Dawn talking to someone—who she now knew was Tony—in the dining room. Carly had hidden in the foyer to avoid interrupting them, and that's when Ron Benoit came into the dining room from the other doorway. After a kerfuffle over investment money, Dawn and Ron went back toward the kitchen, but Tony left the room through the foyer.

So when had Tony been poisoned?

"Rose," Carly said carefully, "when I found you sitting in the breakfast nook that day, how long had you been there?"

The question clearly unsettled Rose. "I don't know. It seemed like quite a while. I had called Tony, who said he was coming right over, so at first I was going to wait. But then I thought, *no*, I should leave, in case he and the fiancée get into a big fight. I didn't want to be in the middle of that!" Her eyelids fluttered, and she pressed her fingers to her lips. "It's all my fault, isn't it? If I hadn't called him—"

"It's not your fault, Rose," Carly soothed. Unless you poisoned him yourself, she thought. "When you were leaving, do you recall seeing his car?"

Rose stared at Carly, then slowly shook her head. "No, but I wasn't looking for it, either. I just wanted to go home, away from those cackling women."

"I don't blame you for that," Carly said, then thought of another question. "What about Klarissa's aunt Megan? Has she been in touch with you since Tony's death?"

Rose's fierce gaze softened. "No, but at least she never treated me like dirt. Of that bunch, she's the only good one. I'll tell you who did call—the maid of honor. She wanted to say how sad she was about Tony. I was surprised. She has such a snooty mother."

Snooty mother. "Mrs. Chapin?"

Rose gave a sharp nod of her head. "She looked at me like I wasn't good enough to set foot in her fancy house. I know I'm too sensitive, but it hurt my feelings." She held up one finger. "Will you excuse me for a minute?"

Rose left the room and returned a few minutes later carrying a sealed plastic container. "Please take these home with you, Carly. Ever since Tony died, no one trusts my baking anymore, but I know my cookies are delicious."

Intrigued but apprehensive, Carly peeled off the lid. Inside the container were at least two dozen star-shaped cookies. They resembled shortbread but had an odd purple tint to them.

"These look delicious." Carly tried to sound enthused. "Thank you. I can't wait to try one when I get home."

"Try one now, please, before you go," Rose insisted. "I want to know how they taste to you."

Carly hesitated. Surely Rose wouldn't poison her. Would she?

Omigosh, why am I thinking that? Do I think Rose might have poisoned Tony?

She was saved from taste testing by the sound of someone coughing violently in the adjoining hallway. Moments later, nurse Doris came around the corner, her wheelchaired patient leading the way.

"There you go," the nurse singsonged. "Gordon, this is Carly Hale. She came to pay her respects." She wheeled him over so that he faced Carly and Rose, then tucked a fleece throw over his shoulders.

Gordon Manous's snow-white hair was uncombed, his eyes raw with anguish. Garbed in flannel pajamas too large for his shriveled frame, he clutched a hankie to his mouth. "What's your name again?" he rasped.

"I'm Carly Hale, Mr. Manous. I came to offer my condolences over the passing of your son."

"You knew my Tony?" he said, reaching a thickly veined hand toward her.

Carly took his fingers and squeezed them gently. "Not personally, but I knew his fiancée, Klarissa, and I met Rose on Saturday. I'm so very sorry for your loss."

Doris touched his shoulder. "Carly brought you a *lovely* tray of cold cuts and cheeses, Gordon. It even has some of those olives you like."

His eyes watered. The grief etched into his features was so profound it made Carly's stomach throb. Slowly, he released her hand. "Thank you."

Rose stared at her husband with a worried expression, then reached over and cupped his knee. He placed his hand loosely over hers and then his tears began to flow.

"He was the light of my life," Gordon rattled out. "Why didn't the Lord take me, instead? What use am I, an old man with a bad ticker!"

Carly had no answer for him. Nothing she said was going to offer any comfort.

The nurse rubbed his shoulders in a soothing gesture. She looked at Carly and shook her head.

Gordon's filmy gaze shifted to the cookie container in Carly's lap. "Don't eat those," he advised her, then looked directly at his wife.

Rose's face crumpled. "Gordon, why would you say that?"

"It's time for your medication now, Gordon," Doris said abruptly. "Say goodbye to Carly." She turned his chair around, and before Gordon could form a response, she wheeled him out of the room.

"Poor Gordon." Rose's voice quivered. "He's out of his head with grief. I can't bear to watch him like that."

Gordon Manous's suffering was undeniable. "His nurse is helpful, though, isn't she?" Carly asked her.

"Yes, she's very much a help," Rose said. "But she's only here in the morning. The rest of the day his care is in my hands. When I was younger, I was strong. But now, it's so hard..."

Carly paused. "Rose, can you hire another private nurse to help out, maybe in the evening?"

"I've tried," Rose said, "but the agency is stretched too thin. Private nursing is at a premium these days." She crushed her tissue in her hand. "I'm sorry, Carly, but I need to check on Gordon. Thank you for visiting us. It means so much."

Carly knew she was being dismissed, but in this case she was grateful. With each moment that passed in the Manous home, her comfort level went down.

At least she'd delivered her tray of food. If nothing else, she'd made her condolence call.

She hurried out to her car, her box of cookies in hand. It was only 10:30, she realized. And since she didn't have to be at Megan's until 2:00, she had the entire day to do whatever she pleased.

Spa day, she thought with a chuckle. More like a *spy* day.

Having a Friday off was so out of the ordinary, Carly was determined to make the most of her free time. She'd worn out her welcome with Adam Bushey, although he'd done a great job with Havarti's bath. But there was another, even grumpier fellow whose actions she hadn't fully explored.

After grabbing a large coffee at the nearest drive-through donut shop, Carly pulled into a parking slot. She looked up the website for Ron Benoit's studio. Before making a note of his address, she checked out a few of his customer reviews. They all ran along the same lines.

Benoit's a great videographer but an ogre to work with.

Just when I thought he couldn't get any more arrogant, he proved me wrong.

Don't waste your money on this annoying jerk.

Ten minutes later, Carly was pulling into the strip mall that housed "R. Benoit Videography." A plain stucco building, it boasted three other businesses. Ron's was tucked between a tax preparation service and a pizza parlor. The lights were on inside, so at least she hadn't wasted a trip.

How much he'd be willing to share with her was another thing altogether.

As she approached the door to his studio, she saw a large television screen in the glass front window. She paused for a moment and watched samples of Ron's videography sweeping across the screen. The video was an amalgam of different weddings, shifting smoothly from one to the next in a tasteful display. Carly had to admit—she was impressed with his work. After watching for a few minutes, she opened the door and stepped inside.

A bell above the door jingled. After only a few seconds, Ron came out of a room at the back of the studio. When he saw her, the automatic smile he no doubt pasted on for customers was replaced instantly with a glower. "What are you doing here?" he snarled at Carly.

Carly took in a slow, calming breath. If she wanted Ron's help, she was going to have to sweeten her attitude and play nice with him.

She forced her own smile to look genuine. "I was admiring your display in the window. You do some very nice work."

He bit down on one side of his lip and scrutinized her for a moment. "I can't tell if you're joking or not, so why don't you tell me why you're here. If it's to ask me if I offed Tony, you can leave now."

"I wasn't going to ask that at all," Carly said. She

looked over at a desk that sat off to one side. "Is it okay if we sit?"

"People normally make appointments to see me," he said, a slight swagger in his gait as he moved toward her. He glanced at his watch. "I can spare fifteen minutes. Less if I decide I want you out of here."

It was obvious Ron wasn't going to make her feel welcome, so she dispensed with any more small talk. "I'll accept that."

Ron plunked down onto his desk chair. Carly sat in the chair adjacent to the desk and set her tote on the carpeted floor.

"I'll be as brief as I can," Carly promised. "Ron, you took a lot of videos at the shower on Saturday. Did the police confiscate them, or do you have copies?"

"My camcorder stores my footage to the cloud, but I also transfer each one to a hard disk. That's a short version of a complex process, but to answer your question, yes, I have copies."

"Have you reviewed them yourself? I mean, after you got home that day did you watch any of it?"

He narrowed his eyes. "Why do you care?"

Carly tried not to sound exasperated. "Because if someone in that house poisoned Tony," she said evenly, "maybe, just maybe, there's something on one of those videos that will help us identify the person."

He laughed and swung his feet up on his desk. "Help *us*? Man, you are something else, lady. So now you know more than the cops, is that it?"

"I never said that," Carly defended. "I'm sure the police have reviewed your footage thoroughly. But they weren't at the shower like I was. I was there from the beginning—even if most of my time was spent in the kitchen." She refrained from mentioning Gretel, though she was hoping the town manager might appear in some of the videos.

He studied her face, as if trying to decide whether she was serious or not. After several excruciating moments during which Carly felt his eyes drilling through her, he plopped his feet on the floor.

"You know what, Nancy Drew? I'll bite. I'm gonna let you see the footage I have, just to get you out of my hair—and my life. But I need something in return." He waggled his eyebrows. "Any ideas?"

Ignoring the obvious suggestion, she offered him an innocent smile. "How about a twenty-five-dollar gift certificate to my eatery?"

He pointed a finger at her. "Done."

A few minutes later, Carly was seated before a computer screen. She'd hoped to view the footage alone, but Ron insisted on running the show.

The video began with the guests happily enjoying their meals. Amid the chatter, there was some good-natured bickering—nothing that would send up any alarms. Klarissa had played the role of bride-to-be to the hilt, reveling in being the center of attention. As the wine in the bottles dwindled, a few of the women grew rowdier.

After watching for several minutes, Carly caught only one glimpse of Gretel Engstrom. Gretel had smiled politely at everyone as she ate a grilled cheese, but her expression betrayed her discomfort. No one attempted to include her in conversations. Carly wondered why Megan hadn't sat with her friend, then realized she'd been seated at the "table of honor" with the bride-to-be, Dawn, and their moms.

"That's about as far as I got before—oh, wait." Ron said suddenly. "When I went into that fancy dining room and caught Dawn pretending to flirt with Tony, I took about half a minute of video in her grandfather's so-called smoking sanctuary." He made air quotes around the phrase.

Carly sat back and looked at him. "But why? No one was in there, right?"

"Right, but the first time I ever saw that room, I was fascinated by it. With those thick curtains blocking most of the natural light, it has an eerie ambiance—like something you'd see in a noir movie from the thirties or forties." Ron's eyes had grown animated.

With a few clicks of his computer mouse, the room in question appeared on the screen. Ron's camcorder had panned the walls slowly, taking in the brocade curtains, the framed photos of jet planes, the painted vases flanking the stone fireplace like porcelain sentinels. With the dim overhead chandelier providing the only light source, the room had a shadowy quality.

Ron paused the video. "When I dated Dawn, which thankfully wasn't for long, she said she always felt the presence of her dead grandfather in there."

Carly had to admit—as portrayed in the video, the room *was* a bit ghostly. If she tweaked her imagination, she could almost see the smoke from Grandfather Stone's cigar as it curled toward the sculptured ceiling.

As for Ron's crack about Dawn, she decided not to comment. *Yet.*

"Is that the end?" she asked him.

"Yup. That's all she wrote." He grinned. "Remember, I'd already caught on that you were hiding in that corner in the foyer. I almost sneaked over to scare you—my camcorder was on—but at the last second I decided to act like a gentleman."

"For a change?" she said dryly, tempering her words with a smile.

He laughed. "Touché, Nancy Drew. You—"

"Ron!" Carly said suddenly, "Go back. I want to see that video again."

"What? Why?" He stared at her as if she'd grown a third arm. "Your fifteen minutes is almost—"

"Ron, please, just play it again, okay?" Carly begged.

With a roll of his eyes, Ron replayed the short video. When the camcorder moved over the stone fireplace, she yelled, "Stop!"

He paused the video.

"Look, right there." She pointed to one of the porcelain vases. "That shadow doesn't look right. The vase is curved, but the shadow isn't. Something else is there. Something *behind* the vase. It almost looks like someone's crouched behind it."

He stared at it and shook his head, "No, you're... wait a minute." He used the mouse to zoom in on the shadow. "Well, I'll be darned," he said quietly. "You've got one heck of an eagle eye, Nancy Drew. It doesn't look like much of anything, though. Someone could have stuck an umbrella back there, or a tennis racket."

"But it's there," Carly murmured, almost to herself. *And it's shaped vaguely like a person.* "Are you going to show the police?"

Ron barked out a laugh. "Will you listen to yourself? If I show them this shadow, they'll think I'm even nuttier than Dawn is."

Carly sat back and folded her hands in her lap. "Ron, why do you put her down that way?"

"That's easy. Because I can't stand her. She follows my cousin around like a stray puppy. I swear, if Klar didn't lead her around by the nose, she wouldn't know which direction to turn." He shook his head with disgust.

"She's an intelligent woman, Ron, and she has feelings," Carly chided him. "Could you make an effort to be a little kinder to her?"

"I could, but it's easier if I just stay out of her orbit."

"Why did you date her in the first place?"

"Because my cousin begged me to. She said, 'Will you please give me a break from that clinging vine and ask her out?' Klar still owes me for that one."

Clinging vine. Is that how Klarissa spoke about her loyal, longtime friend?

"Anything else?" he said abruptly.

He started to shut off the screen when Carly stopped him. "Ron, before you do that, can you print out a still shot of that shadow for me?"

Ron huffed out a breath and clicked the mouse a few times. "I suppose. Anything to get rid of you. Just don't tell anyone where it came from." He rolled his chair backward over the floor to where his printer rested on a table. "What'll you give me for it?"

"You're already getting the gift certificate," she reminded him.

He snatched the printout out of the tray. "Then how about investing in my company?"

Yikes. He caught her by surprise with that one.

"Invest? Ron, I'm a small business owner just like you are. I don't have funds to invest in others."

He rolled his chair toward her and gave her the printout. "That's what I figured you'd say. I have work to do now, so it's time for you to go. Where's my gift certificate?"

Now Carly was getting irritated. "I don't carry them with me. The next time you stop in for lunch, just ask for me or my assistant, Valerie. I promise it will be there for you."

She left with the printout, and he disappeared into a back room. Something occurred to her as she was getting into her car. Ron had been quick to notice her shadow at the shower that day as she was attempting to remain hidden in the foyer.

So why did a shadow that looked so obvious to Carly totally escape his notice?

CHAPTER EIGHTEEN

SHORTLY BEFORE NOON, CARLY STOPPED AT HER apartment. Havarti looked both surprised and ecstatic to see her, since it was Becca who usually gave him his midday bathroom break.

Carly's luncheon at Megan Gilbert's was at 2:00, so she freshened up and changed. She chose a white sweater embroidered with hearts, and a pair of maroon pants. Ari had given her the sweater for Christmas, and it quickly became one of her favorites.

Before she headed for Megan's, Carly popped in downstairs to say a quick hello to her landlady, Joyce Katso. Joyce, who suffered from MS, had made huge strides in her therapy since the day Becca took over as her caretaker. She'd graduated from a wheelchair to a walker and was getting out of the house far more often.

Carly had one more stop to make—Sissy's Bakery. She'd asked if she could bring dessert, and Megan had welcomed the offer. The bakery made individual rum cakes with sweet orange frosting, which supposedly Klarissa loved. Carly picked up a half dozen. After that, it was on to Megan's.

Megan's house was on one of those country roads that seemed to go on forever. The only clue that Carly had found the correct address was the name "Gilbert" painted on the mailbox. Two other cars were parked in the driveway. Carly recognized one of them as Dawn's.

The home itself was a white bungalow with green trim that made Carly think of a cottage out of a fairy tale. Stained glass wind chimes hung on both sides of the front porch, their colors capturing the sunlight as they danced in the winter breeze.

Megan opened the door before Carly even rang the bell. "Carly, I saw you drive in. I'm so happy you could make it!" Her eyes sparkled, and her auburn hair shone. It was a far cry from her droopy persona of only the day before. She gave Carly a quick squeeze and beckoned her inside.

"I'm so pleased you invited me," Carly said, handing Megan her coat. "I love your house."

Carly took a moment to absorb the eclectic décor in Megan's living room. Most of the wooden furnishings—coffee table, end tables, and hutch—were painted in pastel colors and intricately stenciled. Handmade dolls and fabric creatures filled nearly every space. Tucked among those were plants of every kind, some so unusual Carly didn't have a clue what they were. Her own experiment with owning a plant had failed miserably. Even a succulent that required little watering had perished in her care. She was amazed at how vibrant Megan's varieties were.

"Now I see why you call yourself crafty," Carly said, following Megan into the dining room. "Your...décor is amazing."

"Thank you! The girls are all here, so we can relax and have our lunch. Do you like fruit punch?"

"I do, thanks."

Carly followed Megan into the dining room, where the theme appeared to be lace. The tablecloth, the curtains—even the linen napkins at each place setting were trimmed with creamy lace. A cheesy, savory scent wafted from the kitchen, jump-starting Carly's taste buds.

At the head of the table, Klarissa sat with her eyes cast downward, her red hair limp and unwashed. She wore an oversized gray sweatshirt that her thin form swam in. When she saw Carly, her eyes filled with tears.

"Carly." She rose and gave Carly a hug. "It's really good to see you."

"How are you holding up?" Carly asked her, aware of how lame that sounded. How would anyone be holding up only days after their beloved fiancé was poisoned?

"Not great. I feel...broken." Klarissa plucked at her sweatshirt. "This was Tony's."

Dawn saved Carly from responding by coming around the table and hugging her. "I'm really glad you could make it."

Ursula Taddeo, seated adjacent to her daughter, nodded politely at her. "We're all grateful you could be here, Carly. Needless to say, we owe you a lot." Her voice was toneless, her expression blank.

"Mrs. Taddeo, you don't owe me anything," Carly assured her.

Megan handed her a glass of punch. "Why don't you have a seat. I'm sure we're all starving, aren't we?" She looked over at her niece, no doubt hoping to see a spark of interest. The desperation in her eyes was so intense it almost made Carly want to cry.

Dawn helped Megan bring out the food—a cheesy bacon and cheddar quiche, whole wheat rolls, and a salad of arugula and pears that looked mouthwatering. Most everyone was hungry, and before long their plates were clean. The only one who picked at her food was Klarissa, who ate about a third of her quiche and a few leaves of her salad.

Throughout the meal, no one mentioned Tony. It was almost as if nothing had happened to him, or worse—that he'd never existed. Carly wanted to bring Tony's family into the conversation, but how?

When they were all through eating, Megan scooted into the kitchen. She returned with a lovely porcelain teapot shaped like a birdcage, with a tiny bird at the top. Dawn helped her set out teacups and saucers. While Dawn poured tea for everyone, Megan brought out the rum cakes, which she'd arranged on a platter.

"Klar, look what Carly brought," Megan warbled, as if her niece were four years old. She waved the plate in front of her. "Your favorite rum cakes from Sissy's!"

Klarissa wrinkled her nose at the dessert. "I'll take mine home for later."

Megan sagged visibly. "Well, I'll give everyone their own. You can eat them now or later." With a defeated look, she passed around the rum cakes.

For Megan's sake, Carly wanted to dive into her own. But after the heavy lunch she'd eaten, she could barely manage a bite. What she really wanted was to ease the conversation into the events of Saturday. Tragic as Tony's death was, she felt sure someone knew more than they were saying.

Carly forked a small portion of rum cake into her mouth. After she swallowed, she said, "Yesterday I brought my little dog, Havarti, for a bath at Adam Bushey's grooming spa."

Klarissa's snapped her head toward her. "You went to Adam's?"

"I did," Carly said. "I noticed the sign on his car the other day, so I gave the spa a call. It was Havarti's first time having a professional bath. He loved it."

"What possessed you to call Adam, of all people?" Klarissa looked incensed.

"As I said," Carly explained, feeling her cheeks heat, "I saw the sign on his car. He was very good with my dog." *Snarky with me, but great with Havarti.*

"Never mind. I don't want to talk about Adam." Klarissa swiped a finger over the frosting on her rum cake and stuck it into her mouth.

Ursula glared at her daughter but said nothing.

"What I want to know," Klarissa said acidly, "is when are the police going to start looking harder at that sniveling gold digger Rose Manous. I mean, who else had a real motive? It's always been about money with her, and with Tony gone, she'll be rolling in Gordon's soon enough. How's that for a motive?" She picked up her fork and threw it on the table.

"Klarissa, that's enough," Ursula said tightly. "Where are your manners?"

"You know it's true, Mom. You said it yourself."

"I said she married for money. I didn't say she murdered for it."

With that, a hush fell over the room. Dawn's mouth dropped open, and Megan looked stricken.

Ursula slipped her hand into her purse, which was looped over the back of her chair. Carly heard the pop of a cap, and in the next instant Ursula placed a tiny pill next to Klarissa's cake plate.

Klarissa looked at her mother, then popped the pill into her mouth. She swallowed it with a swig of tea.

Something for anxiety? Carly wondered.

After what felt like an eternity, Megan rose partway off her chair and held up the teapot. “More tea, anyone?”

Carly held up her cup. “Yes, thank you, Megan.”

While everyone had their cups refilled, Klarissa retrieved her fork and took a bite of her cake. “It’s delicious,” she said, smiling at Carly. “Thank you for bringing these.”

It was the first smile Carly had seen from Klarissa since she arrived. “Oh, you’re very welcome. Sissy’s is my number one go-to place for sweet treats.” She thought about the purple cookies Rose had given her. They were still in her car.

Klarissa looked over at her aunt and smiled, her eyes a bit glassy. “Auntie Meggs, don’t forget about the gift you made for Carly.”

Megan grinned. “Shall I bring it out now?”

Everyone nodded, and Megan hopped off her chair. She returned a minute later with the most beautiful handmade doll Carly had ever seen.

About a foot tall, the doll was crafted primarily from fabric and yarn. Its eyes and lips were expertly stitched to create a sweet, girlish face. The hair, also made from yarn, was almost a perfect match to Carly’s short locks—right down to the light chestnut color.

But it was the outfit that blew Carly away. The doll’s winter hat, scarf, and leg warmers were knitted in a rich raspberry color. A matching sweater peeked out from underneath a pale green sweatshirt, over which was a rose-toned, cross-body purse with a single jeweled clasp. She looked ready for a day of shopping or maybe lunch with friends.

Carly couldn't stop staring at it. "Megan, this is positively gorgeous. Is this mine?"

"It sure is." Megan beamed. "Do you like it?"

"Oh my gosh, I love it." Carly ran her finger over the wraparound scarf. "Such tiny accessories. I can't imagine having the patience to create this."

"Well, what can I say? I love what I do. Right now, I'm backed up with orders. I've got to start getting my act together or my customers will be screaming."

Klarissa got up from her chair. Stumbling slightly, she went over and wrapped her arms around her aunt. "Isn't my auntie the best?" She kissed Megan on the cheek and said, "I gotta hit the bathroom."

While Klarissa went off in the direction of the kitchen, Megan and Dawn began clearing the table. Half-eaten rum cakes sat on everyone's plates. "I'll wrap up everyone's dessert so they can take them home," Dawn offered.

Dawn and Megan both went into the kitchen, leaving Carly alone with Ursula.

"Carly," Ursula said quietly, "I know you saw me slip my daughter a pill, and I wanted to explain. Even before Tony's death, Klarissa suffered from anxiety. She has since she was a young girl. It was triggered by a traumatic experience that still haunts her. Before that, she was a sweet, loving child without a care in the world." Ursula's eyes watered. "Forgive me. I hate getting emotional."

"Please, there's nothing to forgive," Carly said, touching Ursula's arm. "Klarissa's dealing with a lot right now. I can't even imagine how I'd feel if someone I loved suddenly passed, and in such a tragic way." When Ursula didn't respond, she added, "Mrs. Taddeo, I paid a condolence call this morning on the Manous family. They're both devastated over all this. Tony's dad looked extremely unwell."

"You went over there?" Ursula gave her an odd look.

"I did. I'd met Rose at the shower, and I wanted to offer my sympathies. I know it's not my place, but I want you to know—they're both hurting too. A lot."

Ursula's eyes clouded. "I'm sure they are," she whispered. "I…I think Klar and I had better go. She needs to rest."

When Klarissa returned from the bathroom, she all but fell against her mom. She yawned. "I'm tired."

"I know you are, honey. Let's get you home," Ursula said.

Klarissa rested her head on her mother's

shoulder and reached for Carly's hand. "Thank you for coming to my luncheon," she said in a childlike voice.

"I was happy to be invited." Carly cupped Klarissa's fingers, which felt icy. "Call me if I can help you with anything, okay?"

Megan came out and helped her sister and niece on with their coats. She handed Ursula a brown paper bag and wrapped Klarissa in a hug. "You know I'm always here for you, sweetie. Have the rest of your rum cake when you get home."

With Megan's parting words, mother and daughter left. But Klarissa's sudden change in character worried Carly—she'd looked almost in a daze. Could one tiny pill have caused it? Was her mom overmedicating her?

Dawn returned to the dining room, this time smiling. The tension lines in her face had relaxed. It was almost as if she was relieved that the other two were gone.

"Okay, Auntie Meggs," Dawn announced, "everything's cleaned up and put away. And now you *have* to show Carly your workroom."

Megan held out an arm. "Twist it," she said with a sly smile, and Dawn pretended to do so.

"I can't wait to see it." Carly grinned and set her doll on her chair. "Lead the way."

Megan led them into a room at the back of the house. She flipped on the overhead light. "This used to be a spare bedroom, but when Klarissa got into her teen years I made it into my workspace."

"Wow." Carly looked all around, awed at what she was seeing.

Shelves lined every wall, each boasting dolls of different shapes and styles and colors. Several were garbed in outfits trimmed with delicate lace and the absolute tiniest of buttons.

A few of the shelves held animal shapes—dogs, cats, cows. On the floor, large plastic containers held stacks of basic doll forms—bodies waiting to be made into adorable, huggable friends.

"My friend Gina—she owns What a Card," Carly said, "would be ecstatic if she saw all this. She's designing a line of three-dimensional Victorian-style cards. She's been trying to buy those teeny-tiny buttons, but she hasn't been able to find the quality she wants."

"Say no more. A local woman makes them for me—her work is amazing. I'll give you her contact info before you leave, okay?"

"Thanks, Megan. She'll appreciate that."

"And this"—Megan pointed to a high-tech sewing machine—"is my real baby. I couldn't work all this magic without it."

"Megan, this is so impressive," Carly said. "I can't even repair a hem, so this boggles my mind."

"Thank you." A shadow crossed Megan's features. She went over to a corner shelf and removed a black-and-white fabric cat. It had big green eyes and a quizzical face, and wore a brooch like the one Gretel wore, with tiny colored jewels forming a miniature cat.

"I made this for my friend Gretel," Megan said in a ragged voice. "I called it Glamour Puss, which is what she always called her kitty when she wanted to tease her."

Carly took the cat from her. "It's very sweet, Megan. She has such a curious expression."

"It only needs a few finishing touches," Megan said, "but I never got to them before—" She broke off and choked out a cry.

"You don't have to say it, Auntie Meggs. We know," Dawn said softly.

"How, *how* can it be that Gretel vanished into thin air?" Megan cried. "Why can't the police find her?"

Carly blew out a sigh. "I'm sure they're doing everything possible. If there's anything you can remember, anything at all, be sure to tell Chief Holloway. Sometimes even the smallest thing can help."

"I know. That's what the police told me." She sniffled. "But that last day I saw Gretel was so chaotic, I can barely remember what I said to her or what she said to me."

Carly felt so helpless, she didn't know how to comfort the woman. First Tony's death, then her dear friend's disappearance. It had to be weighing on her.

She glanced through the window that faced the back of Megan's property. The yard was small, but beyond that was a snow-covered field that stretched for some distance to a dense forest of maple trees.

Megan noticed her peering outside. "It's a fabulous view, isn't it? You can't see it now with all the snow, but there's a brook that trickles along the edge of the field. The neighboring farm owner had a few cows that used to drink from it. There was a barn too, but it's gone now."

"It must be so peaceful," Carly offered, "to be able to gaze out at such unspoiled beauty. Have you owned this house long?"

Megan smiled over at Dawn. "My gosh, Dawn, what is it—well over twenty-five years, right?"

"At least," Dawn agreed. "Klar and I used to have sleepovers here. Auntie Meggs would make us brownies and popcorn and hot chocolate, and we'd watch TV *way* later than we were supposed to."

"When the girls got older," Megan went on, "they didn't care as much about sleepovers. I missed those times, but I knew they were growing up. They both became beautiful young women, didn't they?" She turned her gaze to the window and stared into the distance.

Since the question seemed somewhat rhetorical, Carly wasn't sure if she was expected to answer.

"Yes, they did, both of them," she agreed. She realized she was still holding Glamour Puss. She went over and returned it to its original place on the shelf.

"Auntie Meggs, I should really be going," Dawn said, "but thanks so much for having this luncheon. At least Klar got out of the house for a few hours. I hope it did her some good."

"I hope so too, though I have my doubts. I'll call my sister in a bit to see how she's feeling. So where are you headed now?" Megan asked.

Dawn made a face. "My attorney wants to see me in his office *after* five this afternoon." She lowered her voice. "He doesn't know it yet, but...I'm going to fire him."

"What?" Megan looked puzzled. "Why?"

"We don't see eye to eye," Dawn said, sounding frustrated. "He coaches me on what I should say to the police, even if it stretches the truth. I also think"—she looked down at her boots, a blush tingeing her cheeks—"I think he's been hitting on me, but in a sneaky way. Like asking if we can talk about the case over drinks."

Carly was incensed. "Dawn, that is so unprofessional. The *case* represents your future, your well-being. Do you need help finding a different lawyer?"

Dawn shrugged. "I don't know. Do I even need one? I mean, I know I'm innocent."

At this stage of the investigation, Carly had no

idea if she needed one. But she'd known more than one innocent person who'd almost gone to prison for a crime they didn't commit. "I'm not sure what to tell you, Dawn. Are the police still treating you as a suspect?"

"I guess so, but for the past two days they've left me alone."

Maybe you're in the eye of the hurricane, Carly thought morbidly.

They all ambled back to the dining room. Megan twisted her hands. "Honey, I don't like you being unrepresented. Let Carly help you, okay? I really feel you should have a lawyer. Problem is, I don't have a clue who to recommend."

Dawn looked from one woman to the other. "Do you, Carly?"

"I can give you the name of an excellent one. She has a connection to Chief Holloway, so she'll want to be sure there's no conflict of interest before she takes you on as a client."

"Oh, thank you," Dawn breathed. "Now I can ditch my idiot lawyer for good."

Carly wondered why Megan had been so insistent about the lawyer. Did she suspect Dawn was in more trouble than she realized? Or did she know something about Dawn that no one else knew?

Like maybe Dawn actually *did* poison Tony?

One thing had become clear to Carly today. Megan was as protective of Dawn as she was of Klarissa.

"I should be going along too," Carly said. "Megan, this has been a lovely afternoon. Thank you for inviting me—and for the beautiful doll. I'll treasure it."

"I'm so glad you like it." Her eyes sparkled.

When Megan went off to retrieve their coats, Carly said quietly to Dawn, "It's been almost a week since the shower. Do the police know how Tony was poisoned yet?"

Dawn puffed out her cheeks. "The state forensics division is still doing testing, but they've determined one thing—the poison was organic. And whatever it was, it's not terribly common."

Organic. Derived from living things?

Megan returned with their coats and scarves. "Now you girls bundle up," she instructed. "It'll be dark soon, and it's going to drop into the teens tonight. Thank heaven the snow hasn't started, but it'll be coming down later so be careful."

Like obedient children, Carly and Dawn did as she instructed. Megan gave them each a bag with their rum cakes, and then handed Carly her doll and her tote.

"Oh, wait!" Megan dashed off and returned a minute later with a folded slip of paper. She tucked it into Carly's coat pocket. "Give that to your friend. It's got the phone number, email address, and website for my button lady. She won't be sorry she called."

"I think I hit the jackpot," Carly joked. "I'm leaving with all sorts of goodies."

After a final round of goodbyes, Carly and Dawn headed outside. The sky was beginning to darken. The feel of snow was in the air. Megan watched them from the porch for a few moments, then finally waved and went inside.

"I actually told Auntie Meggs a fib," Dawn confessed as they picked their way toward their cars. "I don't have to meet my lawyer. I already fired him this morning."

"You did?" Carly was surprised.

"Yup. I know he has a good reputation, but the creep definitely came on to me." She paused. "Carly, do you have time to have a cup of coffee with me? I know we're both really full from our late lunch, but I...kind of dread going home. The second I walk in, Mother's going to rip into me for dumping that stupid lawyer. I'm sure he's already called her and given her an earful about me firing him. She's going to be livid."

Carly's heart went out to Dawn. Why did she remain living in that house with a mother who verbally abused her? Was it possible she couldn't afford to live on her own?

There was one more place Carly had hoped to check out before she went home, but Dawn looked so needy she couldn't refuse her. "Sure, where would you like to go?"

"How about your place?" Dawn said, a slight hesitation in her voice. "It's so comfy and relaxing there."

Carly hadn't anticipated that. The last time Dawn had come over, Gina had been there too. This time Carly would be alone with Dawn. The thought made her slightly nervous.

What am I thinking? That I now think Dawn might really be guilty?

"Um, okay, sure. I want to stop at my restaurant first to be sure everything's okay. Can you meet me at my apartment in about forty-five minutes?"

"Will do." Even in the faint glow of the porch light, Dawn's face looked visibly relieved.

"See you in a bit, then." Carly started to go to her car when she noticed something glinting on the pavement. When she bent and picked it up, she saw that it was a tiny gemstone. It looked like the ones Megan used on her dolls.

She climbed the porch steps and knocked on Megan's door. Megan was surprised to see her. "Hey, did you forget something?"

"No, but I found this in the driveway." Carly showed her the gem. "I thought it might have come off one of your dolls."

"Gee, thank you," Megan said, taking it from her. "It probably fell out of one of my bags from the crafts store. Drive carefully."

After warming up her car for a minute, Carly

backed out of Megan's driveway and headed for the eatery. Memories of a killer who got too close for comfort rolled through her mind.

But Dawn wasn't a killer. She was a sad young woman who needed help—and who also needed a friend.

As for Carly, today's luncheon at Megan's had raised a lot more questions.

What she needed now were more answers.

CHAPTER NINETEEN

Her gang at the eatery squealed when they saw her come in through the back entrance. Even one of their regular customers turned and gave her a wave.

"What are you doing here?" Valerie chided with a grin. "You're supposed to be lounging at a spa somewhere, getting all sorts of delicious things done to your face."

"Or your body," Suzanne tossed in with a wicked giggle.

"Oh, you guys," Carly scoffed. "I'm not even going to take my coat off. I just wanted to see how you're all doing."

"Super." Valerie clasped her hands. "Carly, wait till you hear this. A group of book clubbers came in earlier this afternoon. Four women and a man, right?"

Suzanne nodded. "They didn't get sandwiches, but they ordered a ton of cheesy dippers. They couldn't stop raving about them! Course a few of them had their eyes on Grant too, but we won't even *go* there," she joked.

"Here's the best part," Valerie said, her voice rising. "Their book club is sort of new, and they've been looking for the ideal place to meet every week. And they decided...they want to meet here every two weeks at three! Isn't that fab?"

Carly smiled. "Wow, that *is* fab. It kind of makes my day. Did they all squish into one booth?"

"I brought a folding chair," Suzanne went on, "which worked well. Maybe in the future we can extend the size of the booth with a small table?"

"Yup. I can see that," Carly said.

"Carly, tell us about your day," Valerie urged. "Did you do anything fun? Did you at least treat yourself to a facial?"

"Not quite." Carly gave them a watered-down version of her visits to Ron Benoit, the Manous family, and Megan. "Ari has a bachelor party tonight, so after I leave here, I'm going home. Dawn Chapin is meeting me there."

"Again?" Grant had come from behind the grill to join them.

"Yes, again." Carly was annoyed at having to defend her decision. "She's feeling kind of needy. I didn't want to say no."

Grant's brow wrinkled. Carly knew he was thinking of another time, another killer.

"I'm letting Dawn know that you're all aware of her visit so please, all of you, stop worrying about me." She gave each of them a fast hug. "And thank you for giving me a whole day off. It made me realize how much I miss this place when I'm not here!"

With that, Carly headed home. By then it was pitch dark outside, and tiny snowflakes were beginning to drift down. So far it wasn't sticking, but driving later on might get dicey. If it reached the point where it coated the roads, Carly would urge Dawn to go home.

About five minutes later, Carly pulled into her driveway. Dawn's car was already there. She'd parked behind Becca's old Lincoln, leaving Carly's space free. They trotted up the front steps together and into Carly's apartment.

"Why don't you take off your coat," she told Dawn, as Havarti danced around her feet. "I need to give my dog a bathroom break, then I'll be right back."

"Take your time," Dawn said, settling onto the sofa.

Carly escorted her dog outside, hurried him through his business, then rushed back upstairs. Not that she thought Dawn would snoop, but she didn't want to leave her alone in the apartment any longer than she had to.

"Shall I put on some coffee?" Carly asked her guest.

"That would be great." Dawn rose from the sofa and followed her into the kitchen, Havarti at their heels. A few minutes later they were seated at the kitchen table, steaming mugs of coffee before them.

After a few minutes of small talk about the weather, Carly asked, "Dawn, what's really the story with Klarissa? I don't mean to tattle, but her mom slipped her a pill today. After that she looked a little dazed."

Dawn nodded grimly. "I'm not surprised. Ursula means well, but Tony died almost a week ago. Klarissa needs to start dealing with the loss, not keep numbing it with medication." Her lips twisted. "That's my opinion, anyway. I actually think she should see a grief counselor, don't you?"

Those two words, *grief counselor,* triggered an unwelcome memory—the death of Carly's own husband almost two years ago to the day.

Daniel was killed when his pickup truck skidded off an icy bridge and rolled down an embankment. He'd been delivering wood to a family in dire need, but he never made it there. After months of anguish, Carly had returned to Balsam Dell, where she made plans to open her grilled cheese eatery. It turned out to be the balm that helped heal her grief.

Although grief counseling had been helpful, Carly knew her strength would have to come from within if she were to get past Daniel's death. She told all this to Dawn, whose jaw dropped.

"My gosh, I knew your husband died in an accident, but I didn't know all those details. I'm so sorry for your loss."

"Thank you," Carly said, "but I'm in a good

place now. But speaking about it reminds of something Mrs. Taddeo mentioned to me earlier. She told me Klarissa's been suffering from anxiety since she was a young girl. Something to do with a traumatic experience. Do you know what she was referring to?"

Dawn rolled her eyes. "Yeah, I do, but don't listen to Ursula. She's been using that as an excuse for Klar's behavior since…like, forever. My opinion? I don't think Klar's anxiety has anything to do with what happened."

"So, what *did* happen?" Carly asked.

Dawn let out a breath. "Not long after Auntie Meggs bought her house, the woman who lived in the farm next door dropped dead on her kitchen floor, right in front of Klar."

"On Megan's kitchen floor?"

"Exactly. She was a sweet lady, somewhere in her sixties, I think, and she was super fond of Klar. Her name was Nan, and I don't think she ever had kids. She kept a few cows and chickens—it was more of a hobby farm than a real one. I was only a kid, but I remember how kindhearted she was. When one of her cows got sick and almost died, she was beside herself over it. But anyway, whenever Klar was visiting Auntie Meggs, Nan would bring over cookies and treats, sometimes a book or puzzle. And then one day, Nan had a heart attack and dropped dead, right there in Auntie Meggs's kitchen."

"Oh, the poor woman," Carly sympathized. "Were you there when it happened?"

Dawn stared at Carly for a moment, then her voice grew soft. "I was, but I was in the bathroom when Nan dropped. I remember hearing Klar scream, and I ran into the kitchen. Nan was on the floor with her eyes open, clutching at her heart and saying something about a cow. And Klar, she was crying so hard she could barely breathe. She was like, hyperventilating, you know?" Dawn shook her head, and her brow furrowed. "Thinking back, maybe that experience *did* scar Klar. I mean, if I can recall it with that much detail, it's probably burned in Klar's mind."

"That could well be." Carly added a drop of milk to her coffee. "How old were you both when it happened?"

"About eight, I think. At the time I didn't know people took pills for anxiety, or even what anxiety meant."

At eight, Carly wouldn't have known much about anxiety, either. At least not the kind medication was prescribed for. Her dad, who died when she was seven, was much older than her mom and a Vietnam vet. Carly'd been too young to understand his bouts of depression. The few memories she had of him were of a quiet, loving dad.

"Dawn, can I ask you another question? And please don't answer if you think I'm being too nosy."

"Sure." Dawn toyed with her spoon.

"Why are you still living at home? It's obvious you and your mom don't get along. Forgive me, but... she seems to find fault with everything you do."

Dawn's face flushed. "Is it that noticeable?"

"I only saw you together for a short time, but it sure seemed that way," Carly said gently.

"My father calls it inertia," Dawn said sharply. "He says it's easier for me to stay where I am and block out everything around me than it is to find a place to move to. He says I'm addicted to luxury, even if I'm miserable in my personal life." She stirred her coffee absently.

That's quite an observation coming from a dad who's not around much, Carly thought.

"Does he think you should move?"

"Oh, totally," Dawn said. "The thing is, I'm not even sure what I could afford. I have no idea what rents are like these days."

"You'd have to look around, but I'll bet you could find something decent in your price range. You do okay as a wedding planner, don't you?"

Dawn took a sip from her mug. "As I said, it wasn't my first career choice, but I've done pretty well. I always have bookings on my agenda. Klarissa's wedding was an anomaly. It was like...she fought me every step of the way. Carly, I'd swear she purposely turned that deposit check in late so she could do battle with the Balsam Dell Inn." She looked befuddled by her friend's actions.

Carly remembered what Ron Benoit had said earlier—that Klarissa had called Dawn a "clinging vine." Could Klarissa have sabotaged her own shower to make her best friend look bad? What would she have gained by that?

Carly chose her words carefully. "Dawn, go back to before Tony came into the picture. Were you and Klarissa pretty tight?"

Dawn stared at Carly, as if that was an odd question. "Well, sure. We've been best friends since we were kids. You heard what Auntie Meggs said, didn't you? We had sleepovers there almost every weekend."

"I know, and it's obvious she adores both of you." Carly smiled. "But you were both much younger then. You're adults, now, and past that magic twenty-nine mark." She said it with a teasing smile so Dawn wouldn't take offense.

Dawn seemed to mull that. "That's true, but neither of us ever moved away, so we've always been there for each other. Klar is the outgoing one, and I'm the quiet one." She frowned and looked away. "At least that's what everyone says."

"Your mom and...Auntie Meggs," Carly pressed on, "have they been friends since they were kids? I only ask because they don't seem to have much in common."

"Yeah, pretty much. They're the same age, and they attended elementary school together. After sixth grade, Mother went to private school and later to a women's college. But whenever she came home, she always gravitated back to Megan. At least that's how Auntie Meggs tells it."

Carly still found it strange. Megan was both domestic and industrious. She'd built a home-based business for herself that provided her with a good living—one that she loved. She was also like a second mom to Klarissa, and often even to Dawn.

Then there was Julie, who was almost the polar opposite of Megan. Raised in a wealthy household with parents who doted on her and a father she almost worshipped, she'd grown up expecting everyone to do her bidding. And if Dawn was telling the truth, she was overly fond of male attention and had no problem attracting it.

"I'm honestly not sure what Mother sees in someone as sweet as Auntie Meggs," Dawn went on. "Mother's other friends are a lot like herself. Cold fish, I call them. But Mother does adore being fawned over and Auntie Meggs fits the bill, so maybe that's the attraction." Dawn shrugged and took another sip of her coffee. "Plus, like I said, they've been friends since they were kids."

"Those flower arrangements at your home—did you say Megan makes those for your mom?"

"Yes. Oh, you never got to see it!" Dawn set down her mug. "Auntie Meggs has a sort of solarium on the back side of her house. It's on the basement level, but it faces east and has that curved kind of glass that attracts sunlight. In her younger days she worked for a florist, so she's pretty good with arranging flowers. It's sort of a side gig, but she only does it for friends."

"She a woman of many talents, for sure," Carly said, remembering the handcrafted dolls. "The doll she gave me is so detailed, it almost looks like a real child. In fact—" She held up a finger and left the kitchen. She returned with the doll, running a finger over its sweet face before setting it on the table where they could both admire it.

Dawn grinned. "Auntie Meggs is so artistic, isn't she?"

"She sure is. It's no wonder her work is in such demand. I'll have to find the perfect spot for this little darling, where everyone can see her." Carly fluffed the doll's knitted skirt.

"You'd never know it because she's always so bubbly," Dawn said, "but Auntie Meggs suffers from a severe travel phobia. It's even got a name—hodophobia. She rarely ever leaves the Balsam Dell area, and she won't set foot on a bus or a train, or, heaven forbid, a plane."

"Gee, that's kind of sad." Carly frowned slightly. "So she never takes a vacation?"

Dawn shook her head. "Never. But on the other hand, she claims she's happy staying close to home. I think she's accepted her disorder as part of who she is."

"I guess that part is good," Carly said. "What about your mom and Ursula Taddeo. Are they pretty friendly with each other?" She knew the answer but wanted to hear Dawn's take on it.

Dawn laughed. "Not a chance of that. It's weird, the way they've always disliked each other."

"Did something happen between them?" Carly topped off each of their coffee mugs.

"If it did, it must've happened way back. As kids, Klar and I always had Auntie Meggs to rely on, so we just tuned both of our mothers out. As you probably guessed, my mother isn't exactly the nurturing type. Another thing I always wondered is whether Ursula was jealous of her younger sister's friendship with Mother."

Or if Ursula was bitter because Julie had a fling with her husband, Carly mused.

"This one day, when I was young," Dawn said, her eyes clouding, "I came home after a day of summer camp—a place I loathed, by the way—and found Mother lounging out by the pool. I started to show her the ugly birdhouse I made when I noticed a man lying on a chair *very* close to her. At first I thought Dad had gotten home early from his business trip, until he lifted his head. The man was way younger than Dad, with dark hair and lots of muscles. Mother's face went red as a beet, and she ranted at me for sneaking up on her." Dawn's eyes hardened, just as her words softened to a whisper. "Mother always liked them young."

Carly felt something tumble inside her. What an awful experience for a child.

Almost as terrible as seeing a woman drop dead in front of you.

"I'm sorry," Dawn said softly. "I shouldn't have told you that story. You're so easy to talk to, I guess it just came out."

It struck Carly that both Klarissa and Dawn had been lugging around a lot of emotional baggage since childhood.

The soothing image of Rhonda Hale Clark appeared in Carly's mind. Loving, nurturing, protective—everything a mom should be. If she'd been raised by a mom like Julie Chapin, would she be the same person? Or would she be resentful and brooding, like Dawn?

"Dawn, you don't have to apologize. I'm only sorry that happened to you. I can only imagine how unpleasant that was."

Havarti, who'd been snoozing next to Carly's chair, suddenly lifted his head. He got up and went over to Dawn, then curled up at her feet, his nose resting on his paws.

"He's so sweet," Dawn said, reaching down to caress his head. "I'll bet he brings you a lot of comfort, doesn't he?"

"He sure does." Carly peeked through the window. The snowflakes were beginning to fall faster. "Dawn, I'm worried about you driving home.

While I'm enjoying your company, I'm wondering if you should head out before the snow sticks to the roads."

Dawn blew out a sigh. "You're right. I should." She took a long sip and drained her mug. "You were going to suggest a lawyer for me?"

"Oh, right," Carly said. "Chief Holloway's daughter Anne is Havarti's veterinarian. Her partner, Erika Swanson, is a lawyer, and a darned good one from what I hear."

Dawn's face brightened. "After that creep of a lawyer I had, a woman would be so welcome." Her shoulders sagged. "Oh shoot, tomorrow's Saturday, though."

"Give her a call anyway and leave a message," Carly suggested. "She probably checks them even on weekends." She texted the lawyer's name to Dawn. "If she has a conflict of interest, I'm sure she'll let you know, but I'm hoping it works out for you."

"Thanks, Carly. This is so helpful." Dawn turned to stare out the window. "The police haven't haunted me in a few days." She crossed her fingers. "I can't help hoping they're looking at someone else as Tony's killer."

Either that, or they're hoping you'll get complacent and trip yourself up.

Dawn rose and carried both mugs over to the sink. When she turned, Carly took Dawn's arms in her hands and spoke quietly. "Tell me, in the pit of your heart, do you suspect anyone in particular?"

Dawn's gaze dropped. She shook her head, but her face had paled considerably. "No. No one in particular."

Carly nodded, but something had flickered in Dawn's eyes.

Something that frightened her more than she was willing to admit.

Later, watching through the window as Dawn backed her car out of the driveway, Carly couldn't help feeling a sense of déjà vu.

It was a feeling she couldn't shake.

When Dawn told Carly about finding her mother lounging by the pool with that young man, a thought had sneaked into her mind.

Mother always liked them young.

Had Julie ever tried to lure Tony into her web? If so, had she succeeded?

A myriad of scenarios slithered around her brain, like worms after a heavy rain. All were terrible to contemplate, but one in particular stuck firmly in Carly's head.

What if Tony and Julie had once had a fling? And what if Julie became enraged when Tony broke it off because he'd fallen in love with Klarissa? Could Julie have seethed over it, concealed her wrath until she had the chance to do away with him?

It was the stuff of B movies, but it happened.

Although the possibility was remote, Carly couldn't seem to evict it from her mind.

CHAPTER TWENTY

Ari called shortly after 10:30 to let Carly know he'd made it home safely. He told her the roads were icing over and cautioned her to be extra careful in the morning.

"Have you heard any word on Gretel?" Carly asked him, removing her hot chocolate from the microwave.

"No, nothing," he said. "But I'm not in that loop, so there could be news that hasn't reached us yet."

Disappointed, Carly told him about her visit with Dawn, keeping the personal details to herself. It wasn't her place to divulge any of Dawn's private issues.

"She's a troubled woman, isn't she?" Ari offered. He sounded worried for Carly's sake.

Carly had a lot more to tell him but decided it could wait. It was getting late, and he sounded drowsy. There'd be plenty of time to catch him up on everything when they saw each other on Saturday.

Before he could express any additional concern

about Dawn, Carly piped in with, "Hey, I missed our date tonight. Are we on for tomorrow?"

"You bet we are." His throaty voice gave Carly a delicious shiver.

By the time they disconnected, Carly had finished her hot chocolate. Havarti had already had his nighttime visit to the backyard, so they both dropped into bed.

For a long time, Carly lay awake. She'd visited with so many different people during the day that her mind was on overload.

Rose Manous and her grieving husband.

The crabby Ron Benoit.

Megan and her guests—Klarissa, Dawn, and Ursula.

Dawn's revelations had topped off the evening by leaving Carly with even more questions, and little in the way of answers.

After tossing and turning for close to an hour, she finally drifted off. Despite the jumble of faces that haunted her dreams, it was Gretel's that invaded them the most. Over and over, Gretel's worried face popped into Carly's mind. Carly barely knew the woman, and yet she felt as if Gretel had been trying to tell her something.

It sounded crazy, she knew, but she had to follow her instincts.

~

After jolting awake at 6:30 a.m., Carly hurried through her morning routine. Overnight, a light snow had fallen. Becca, bless her, had shoveled the driveway *and* cleaned the snow off Carly's Corolla. Carly would return her kindness later with a container of Grant's delicious tomato soup for both Becca and Joyce to enjoy.

Though it was still early, a weak January sun was peeking above the horizon. Ice sparkled off the trees, where the branches hung like snowy brushes ready to sweep the landscape.

As Carly made her way across town, she was careful to avoid icy spots. Even when roads looked clear, a stray patch of invisible ice could be treacherous. On mornings like this one, accidents weren't uncommon.

She recalled the chief saying that Gretel lived in a pretty Cape Cod on Western Avenue. It wasn't much to go on, but she took her time, perusing names on snow-topped mailboxes as she made her way slowly along the road. She'd driven only a few miles when she spotted it—a silver mailbox with the name ENGSTROM posted on the side. White with black shutters, the house was straight out of a calendar of quaint New England scenes. On either side of the front steps, the house was flanked by thick rhododendrons, their leaves curled and huddled against the cold. An evergreen wreath adorned with fat pine cones hung from the front door.

Carly pulled her car over to the side of the road and shut off the engine. She'd come prepared—boots, hat, scarf, heavy coat. She'd even remembered to bring her slip-on cleats to give her purchase on slippery surfaces. Whether she walked along the driveway or trekked across Gretel's yard, she was going to leave prints in the snow. The chief had warned her against checking out Gretel's residence, but the absence of any yellow tape told her the police were probably done with their investigation. If her tracks in the snow were later traced back to her and she was called on the carpet for it, so be it. It was a risk she was willing to take.

Carly tugged her rubber cleats over her boots, then slid her cell phone into her jacket pocket. Her pepper spray was there too, she realized with a tiny smile. She'd kept her promise to Grant and moved it from her tote to her coat pocket.

She shot a quick glance around. The nearest neighbor was at least a football field away, and she didn't see any signs of life. A dog barked in the distance. Otherwise, all was silent.

Carly had to admit—she had no idea what she was looking for. But she knew her mind wouldn't rest until she'd checked out Gretel's abode.

Acting as if she belonged there, Carly picked

her way slowly up the driveway, her cleats making crunching noises in the snow. She climbed the front steps and rang the bell—just in case anyone was watching. After a minute or so, she turned and looked around, then moved over to one of the windows. The ground was icier than she'd thought. She was thankful she'd attached the cleats.

Carly leaned over the window box, which was capped with snow. She cupped her hands around her eyes and peered through the window. She was looking into a dining room. An oval table surrounded by four chairs occupied the center of the room, atop a colorful braided rug. In the far corner was an old-fashioned hutch. On the adjacent wall was a low bookcase lined with hardcover volumes.

Carly looked back at the table. A thick book resembling a textbook rested there. She'd been so intent on studying the dining room that she didn't realize someone had stolen up behind her until she heard the crackle of frozen snow.

"What are you doing?" The voice was feminine, sharp as a blade.

Carly whirled around with a gasp, and in spite of her cleats she went down. Plopped in the frozen snow, she found herself face-to-face with a massive German shepherd. At the end of his leash was his owner—a tall woman with a questioning gaze wearing a furry brown hat.

"I—sorry," Carly mumbled, struggling to get up.

Her heart pounding wildly, she took the woman's outstretched hand and stumbled to her feet. The dog watched them curiously, as if they were merely doing a dance.

"Who are you?" the woman demanded, now that Carly was upright.

Carly explained who she was and how she knew Penny Harper, Gretel's assistant.

A smile slipped out from beneath the woman's austere gaze. "So, you're Carly Hale." She stuck out a mittened hand. "I'm Olga Posner, and this is Blossom. I've read about you."

Carly hoped it was because of her restaurant, but she suspected it wasn't. After shaking Olga's hand, she held her own out to Blossom, who licked her glove.

"So," Olga repeated, "what are you doing here?"

Carly brushed snow off her coat. "I'm not sure myself. Penny is so worried about Gretel, and a lot of other people are too. I guess I just wanted to poke around. In my defense, I sometimes notice things other people don't—"

"Say no more." Olga swiveled her head around, then pulled a sizable key ring from the pocket of her parka. "Would you like to go inside?"

Carly swallowed. *She has a key!* "I would."

Olga tied Blossom's leash to the porch railing. "You stay here and be the lookout, okay?" She kissed her dog on the snout.

"The police cordoned off the house a few days ago, but late yesterday they removed the tape," Olga explained. She slid her key into the lock.

Moments later, they were inside Gretel's home. The first word that came to Carly's mind was *spotless*.

Not a single item looked out of place—at least not that Carly could see. Then again, she wasn't familiar with the layout or what Gretel's "normal" looked like.

Carly followed Olga through the kitchen and past a small bathroom. Gretel's bedroom was at the end of the short hallway, at the rear corner of the house.

"Lovely room," Carly commented. The walls were painted a pale yellow, with a paisley border at the top. A folded patchwork quilt rested along the bottom of Gretel's double bed. On her nightstand was an old-style radio alarm clock and a framed photo of her cat.

"This is where the police found Buttercup," Olga said with a guttural sigh. "I'd have offered to take her, but she's terrified of Blossom, who wouldn't hurt a flea. Anyway, there's no way Gretel left her cat closed in this room. *No way.* If she needed someone to look in on her kitty, she always called me. That's why I have a key. I've been collecting her mail and her newspapers too. I'm saving them for when...when she comes home."

The sadness in Olga's eyes made Carly's heart wrench. "Did she go away often?"

"No, almost never. She was a real homebody." Olga walked over to Gretel's bureau and straightened the crocheted dresser scarf. "I'm not even sure she's used up all her vacation time. Last summer? When she took a few weeks off? I'd see her out in the yard with a cool drink and a book. Every few days I'd join her, and we'd chat for a while. But she always seemed antsy to get back to her reading."

"Did she ever talk about her family?" Carly wondered if Olga knew more than Penny did about Gretel's origins.

"No, never. She had a few gal pals. Mostly quiet types like herself. And me." She smiled ruefully.

Was Megan Gilbert one of the quiet types? Carly wondered.

"Olga, did you ever meet Gretel's friend Megan?"

"Megan Gilbert? Oh, for sure. She's a super nice lady, and a talented one. I bought three of her dolls for my nieces."

Carly smiled at that. "How about friends that *weren't* gals? Did Gretel have anyone like that in her orbit?"

Olga slowly shook her head. "As far as I know, there were no men in her life. Her job as town manager was her first priority. She put it before all else."

Carly skimmed her gaze around the bedroom. Gretel's extreme tidiness put her in mind of something her mom used to say. *A place for everything, and everything in its place.* To which her sister Norah would always accuse their mom of being a neat freak—which in Norah's mind was equivalent to being an ax murderer.

She ambled over to where Buttercup's litter box had been pushed into a corner. A plastic scoop was attached to the side of the box.

Olga noticed Carly staring at it. "That's another thing," she said, going over to stand beside Carly. "Gretel kept the litter box in the bathroom, never the bedroom. I know it seems like a small thing, but it bugs me. Why would she do something so out of character?"

"My guess is that she didn't," Carly offered grimly. "Olga, have the police questioned you?"

"Yeah, they questioned me twice about whether I'd seen or heard anything. I only wish I had." Olga sighed and bent over the litter box. "While I'm here, I might as well scoop that." She tossed her mittens on the floor and reached into the pocket of her parka. She pulled out a roll of clear plastic bags and tore one off. As she began to scoop, something in the litter caught Carly's eye. Tinier than a pea, it looked like a shard of blue plastic.

"Olga, what's that?" Carly pointed at the object.

Olga bent over and peered at it. "Huh. Beats me. Part of something Buttercup was playing with, I suppose, like maybe a toy."

"Or something someone might have dropped when they grabbed Gretel?" Carly said in a shaky voice.

Olga looked at Carly, and her face paled. She scooped the blue shard into the plastic bag and tied the bag in a knot. "I'm taking this to the police. If they ask what I was doing in Gretel's house, I'll tell them I was doing what the police should've done. If you spotted that, why didn't they?" Her jaw tightened with resolve.

"Thank you, Olga. Be sure Chief Holloway gets it, okay? And can I snap of picture of it first? I want to enlarge it and see if I can make out where it might've come from."

Olga held up the bag. "Be my guest."

Carly took a few photos with her phone, then Olga retrieved her mittens, and together they locked up the house. Outside, Blossom's tail was wagging like a flag in a stiff wind.

"She's so pretty," Carly commented. "I have a little Morkie. His name's Havarti."

"Aw, that's sweet." Olga untied her dog's leash from the railing. "Maybe we should exchange contact info. Just in case one of us hears something about Gretel?"

"Excellent idea."

After they exchanged cell numbers, Olga said, "Gretel's done so much for this town, Carly, and she's such a good-hearted person. If I find out someone's harmed her, believe me, I'm gonna want a few minutes alone with them."

Carly started to respond when somewhere across town, a siren wailed.

~

It was a little after 8:45 when Carly arrived at the restaurant. She'd left the cookies Rose Taddeo had given her in the car overnight, so she grabbed them and headed inside.

Grant was preparing his morning biscuit. The scent of bacon made Carly suddenly ravenous.

"Hey," Grant greeted her. "Everything okay? You're later than usual."

"Everything's fine." She plunked the cookie container and her tote on the counter. "Is Val here yet?" It was unusual not to see Valerie perched on a stool around this time, sipping a cup of coffee at the counter.

"Not yet." He opened the fridge under the counter. "Biscuit?"

"Yes, I'm starving. I'm worried about Val, though. The roads are still pretty slick in spots." Carly tugged off her jacket and checked her phone.

No message from Valerie.

She didn't want to be a nag, but she sent off a quick text to her assistant manager: Everything okay?

Carly was halfway through her cheesy bacon biscuit when Valerie let herself in through the front door. Her face was drawn, her usual perky smile absent.

"Val, what's wrong?" Carly hurried over to her.

Her face blotchy, and her eyes red, Valerie unbuttoned her wool coat. Instead of responding to Carly's question, she said, "Oh, Carly, I don't know what to do. I'm so happy here. I love all you guys. But...my ex showed up at my aunt's last night, and..." She hitched in a breath.

"He didn't hurt you, did he?" Grant raced around from behind the counter.

Valerie held up both hands. "No, no. Nothing like that. Luke's a first-class manipulator, but he's not violent. No, he wants to talk about a reconciliation. He wants me to forgive him for the terrible mistake he made." She sniffled. "Let me hang my coat and get my coffee and I'll tell you the whole story. If nothing else, you guys deserve an explanation for the way I've been acting lately."

Carly knew bits of the story from what the chief had told her, but she wanted to hear it straight from Valerie.

A few minutes later, the three were seated in a booth. Valerie declined having a biscuit but eagerly wrapped her hands around a mug of coffee. She cleared her throat.

"Luke and I owned a little country store just

outside of Rutland. It had a counter where we served breakfast and lunch till four in the afternoon. I was the grill cook. Luke did the hiring and the accounting, but I did pretty much everything else. I made sure the store was always spotless, that we never ran out of inventory." She gave up a regretful smile. "My counter was super popular. There was almost never an empty stool."

Grant smiled at her. "That's easy to believe."

"Anyway," Valerie said, pulling in a breath, "over time, we realized the store was consuming us. We almost never took a day off. When Luke suggested hiring an assistant manager, I leaped at the idea. Our income could support it, although we had to tighten our own belts a tad. But I was happy to do that to have some real help."

Carly knew where the story was going, but she didn't interrupt.

Valerie's lip curled. "Enter Jasmine Elrod, a thirtysomething with bleached blond hair and a perfect hourglass figure. She was clever, wicked smart, and a hard worker. She'd also set her sights on Luke, who caved like a paper tent."

"Oh, Val, I'm so sorry," Carly said.

A text pinged from Carly's tote, which she'd left on the counter. Whoever it was, she'd check it later.

"Next thing I know," Valerie spat out, "after seventeen years together, Luke's dumping me for her. She persuaded him to sell our country store and use the proceeds to invest in an organic food shop. Which promptly bit the dust eight months later, by the way."

Carly was appalled. "But didn't you own half the country store?"

"I thought I did," Valerie said miserably. "It turned out Luke had put everything in his name, including the deed to the property. I was young. I was in love. I'd grown up with a grandmother who wasn't very nurturing, so I'd never really had anyone care about me before. Not the way Luke did. Anyway, I never questioned the paperwork or his business decisions. I…I just assumed my name was on everything. How's that for being dumb?" she groaned.

"You're not dumb, not by a long shot," Carly assured her. "He took advantage of your trusting nature, that's all."

Grant pushed aside the remains of his biscuit. "That's just awful. How could anyone do that?" He shook his head with disgust.

"Since we weren't married, I didn't even have the benefit of a divorce settlement. I could have hired a lawyer and fought Luke for my rightful share. But I was so humiliated, so beaten down, I just wanted to get as far away as I could. It didn't take long for all our customers to find out what happened. Their pity was more than I could face."

"If it's any comfort," Carly assured her, "I'm immensely grateful that you found us."

Valerie swiped at her eyes. "Thank you. I'm forty-six years old, and you didn't flinch at hiring me. Do you know how much that means to me?" She tapped her fist to her chest.

Carly smiled. "Val, I'd have hired you if you were seventy-six. I knew from the get-go you were a perfect fit for us, and it didn't take long for you to prove that." She folded her hands on the table. "So, what are your thoughts about Luke trying to win you back?"

Valerie's cheeks went pink. "I…I'm not sure. Even though I told him I never wanted to see him again, there was this part of me that actually felt sorry for him. I mean, he looked so pitiful, you know? Almost tearful."

All part of the manipulation, Carly suspected. "The way you felt after he sold the store out from under you?" she said quietly.

"Yes! That's right," Valerie went on, anger now flaring in her eyes. "He lost all the money he got from selling *our* store. The store I devoted myself to for a good chunk of my earning years. All because of his dumb infatuation with that slick chick." She flicked her hand. "Jasmine's long gone, by the way. No more money, no more use for Luke."

Carly didn't know what to say. If she were Valerie, she'd want nothing more to do with Luke. But then her emotions weren't invested in all the years they'd spent together.

"Did you ever apply for that restraining order?" Carly asked, her ear catching the ping of a text again.

"No. Fred and I talked about it. Since there's no threat of physical violence, it wasn't the route to take." Valerie sat up straighter. "I need to be strong; that's the real solution."

"Does he know where you work?" Grant looked worried.

"Unfortunately, yes. My aunt got all flustered and let it slip out. It's not her fault." Valerie sighed.

Grant's dark brown eyes flared. "Well, if he shows up here and you want my help *escorting* him to the door, just say the word. I can be persuasive when I need to be."

"I'm sure you can." Valerie finished the few dregs in her mug. "Hey, thank you both for listening. Not to sound like a suck-up, but I definitely have the best boss and coworkers on the planet." She batted her eyes playfully, which made them all laugh.

Grant stretched his arms above his head. "I'm betting we'll have record business today. Even with only a dusting of snow, the skiers will be hitting the slopes in droves. And what'll they want after a day of skiing?"

"Grilled cheese!" the three chimed in unison.

"Oh hey, before we start working," Grant said, "I have something to give you guys. And I want your honest opinions, okay?"

Carly looked at Valerie and they both shrugged. "Bring it on," Valerie said.

Grant went over to the fridge beneath the counter. He returned with two animal-shaped dishes filled with veggies, fruits, cheeses, and grainy crackers. He handed one to each of them.

"Mine's a dog," Carly said with a grin. "The ears are strawberries and the whiskers are pretzels!"

"And mine's a kitty," Valerie squealed, "with a blueberry nose. And it's pawing at a piece of cheese shaped like a mouse!"

"Grant, these are amazing," Carly praised. "Where did you get these plates?"

"I special ordered them...well, with the help of a small loan from my dad. The clear covering is recyclable, and the plates are compostable. The cookie cutters were inexpensive, and the trial run we did at the school showed that kids gravitate toward foods cut into fun shapes."

"I can see kids absolutely loving these," Valerie gushed. "But they must be pricey to make, right?"

"Right now, yes. I'm working on finding different suppliers to get the prices down. The school is looking closely at the cost, so that might be a deal breaker. What we want is to get parents on board so they'll pressure the school to offer these."

"When you say *we*, you mean..."

"Um, me and the head of dietary at the elementary school." He didn't offer her name, so

Carly didn't press. She peeled back a corner of the dog's ear and popped a bite of strawberry into her mouth. "Delicious. I can't wait to show this to Ari." She resealed her plate so she could save it for later.

When Carly looked over at Grant, her heart almost burst. She wanted to tell him how impressed she was and what a bright future he had to look forward to. But if she did, she might cry, and Grant would hate that.

Valerie was already picking at her culinary kitty, breaking off a piece of the cheddar mouse. When she popped it into her mouth along with a whole grain cracker, it triggered a sudden memory in Carly's mind.

"Grant, I can't believe I forgot this, but I've been meaning to show you the cookies Rose Manous insisted on giving me yesterday. They're a strange shade of purple, but I'm sure it's not food coloring. And they have a weird smell."

Carly started to fetch the cookie container when her cell rang in her tote. She fished it out, surprised to see Gina calling so early. "Hey, good morning. What's happening?"

"Didn't you get my text messages?" Gina was almost breathless. "Gordon Manous was rushed to the hospital a short while ago. They think he overdosed on his heart medication."

Stunned, Carly dropped onto a stool. "Oh my..."

gosh. That's terrible. Is he..." Carly asked, sucking in a breath.

"He's in grave condition," Gina said bleakly. "His wife found him early this morning, and she immediately called 911. Evidently some of the pills were missing from his bottle, and Mrs. Manous thought he took them on purpose."

Carly closed her eyes. "What kind of pills?"

"They're heart pills, beta-blockers like the ones my dad takes."

Carly's head swam. *First Tony is poisoned, and now Gordon is near death.*

"How did you find out?"

"My aunt Lil at the beauty parlor, bless her gossipy little heart," Gina said. "One of the stylists at the salon has a daughter who works in the ER. Gave everyone in the salon the whole scoop."

Rose Manous's face flashed in Carly's mind. A devoted caretaker, burdened with a sick husband while still grieving for Tony. She already had one sad death to cope with. Was she about to have another?

Carly told Gina about her visit to the Manous home the day before and how feeble Gordon had looked.

"So you saw him yesterday?" Gina sounded astonished.

"Yesterday morning," Carly confirmed. Gordon's words suddenly came back to her. *Why didn't the Lord take me, instead?*

"How did he seem to you?" Gina questioned.

"Devastated over his son's death. Frankly, I'm not surprised he overdosed, if that's what happened. He spoke as if he didn't want to live anymore. It was heartbreaking to see."

Gina sighed. "Carly, Gordon Manous might not have taken those pills voluntarily. The police are looking into possible foul play."

An icy chill tickled Carly's spine. "What do you mean?"

"They think his wife might have given him the overdose. I know you said Rose seemed like a devoted woman, but face it—you don't really know her, do you?"

Carly groaned. "No, not really." She rubbed her forehead. "Do you know where Rose is now?"

"I'm not sure." Gina shuffled papers in the background. "Maybe if you call your pal the chief, he'll fill you in."

Not likely, Carly thought dolefully. "Gina, thanks for letting me know. Call me if you get an update on Mr. Manous, okay?"

"You betcha. I'll try to stop in later."

Carly found Grant in the kitchen, prepping enough salad to get them through a busy day. Valerie, who'd been wiping down the tables in the dining room, came in behind her.

Carly set the container of cookies next to the sink, then gave them both the grim news about Gordon Manous.

"Oh, those poor people." Valerie pressed her fingers to her lips. "It's like the family is cursed or something."

Grant set down the bag of field greens he was rinsing. "That's, like, terrible. And you were just there yesterday."

"I know, and that's why I have something to show you." Carly peeled back the lid on the cookie container and exposed the contents. "These are the cookies I was telling you about—the ones Rose gave me. Don't they look strange to you?"

Grant peered at the cookies, then picked one up and sniffed it. "They're icy cold, but they're also loaded with lavender—which, by the way, is a member of the mint family. Culinary lavender needs to be used sparingly, not dumped in like it was sugar."

"That purple stuff is lavender?"

He nodded and broke off a chunk of the cookie. "Whoa. There's enough lavender in here to choke an elephant. No one would add this much on purpose. She must've spilled it or something."

"Or something." Carly gripped his arm, her stomach churning.

"Before we jump to conclusions," Grant said, "it looks to me like she also added some food coloring gel. It's entirely possible she just loves the color lavender."

"Maybe," Carly said, "But right before I left there

yesterday, the last thing Gordon Manous said to me was, 'Don't eat those.'"

Grant wrapped the cookie pieces in a paper towel. "He probably realized what she'd done," he reasoned, "and was trying to warn you. Unless—" He looked at Carly and swallowed. "I think you should bring these over to Chief Holloway. They're probably fine, but just in case..."

"I agree," Valerie said, nodding vigorously. She found a paper bag for Carly to drop the container into.

"Okay, thanks guys. I'll be back as soon as I can."

~

Chief Holloway scrubbed his forehead with his fingers, then dropped his elbows to his desk blotter and folded his hands under his chin. Carly had given him a summary of her visit to the Manous home the day before, then presented him with the container of cookies.

"I'll pass the cookies along to the lead investigator," he said stiffly, "but now I have a question for you. What in tarnation were you doing at Gretel Engstrom's home this morning? I mean, what possessed you to go poking around there after I specifically told you not to?"

Seated opposite the chief, her hands in her lap, Carly flinched from his tone. She felt like she did all those years ago, when she and Gina got chastised by the high school principal for sneaking frogs out of the science lab and releasing them into a pond.

"You said it yourself," Carly sputtered in her own defense. "I notice things other people don't. I was only going to peek through the windows and walk around for a bit. I didn't think a neighbor would come along. A neighbor with a key," she mumbled.

"So you lucked out, didn't you?" He glared at her. "Carly, I am not the least bit amused by any of this. I can't fault you for paying a condolence call to the Manous family, but this time you've gone too far. Butting into an official investigation is not going to be tolerated. If you continue along these lines, there will be ramifications."

Carly felt sure it was an idle threat, but the reprimand stung. She was tempted to remind him how she'd helped the police put away bad people in the past but decided it would only antagonize him.

Holloway sighed gustily. "All that said, Gretel's neighbor came over a short while ago with that... whatever it was she scooped out of Buttercup's litter box. Set it down next to my coffee," he grumbled.

Biting her lip to stifle a giggle, Carly silently commended Olga for acting so quickly.

"I gave the bag to one of the investigating officers," he continued, "and it's on its way to forensics. He thought it looked like part of a small button, but we're not making any assumptions."

Carly had thought the same thing. While she was waiting for the chief to summon her into his office, she'd enlarged the picture on her phone. The object was curved on one side, flat on the other, with a tiny crescent carved out on the flat side.

"I'm thinking out loud now," Carly said, trying to sound humble. "Assuming someone *did* take Gretel against her will—maybe when they locked her cat in the bedroom, the cat struggled and snagged the button off his shirt. Or her shirt."

"We've already thought of that, Carly." He sounded exasperated, but then he softened his tone. "By the way, Penny Harper paid us a visit yesterday. We know all about Gretel's phony diploma. One of the department's young detectives already delved into her background and had come to the same conclusion. But Penny's information, and those letters Gretel received, confirmed it for us. I only wish she'd brought them to us sooner. To say the least, I'm...saddened."

Carly was too—but right then she was more scared for Gretel than disappointed in her. "Do you think it has anything to do with her disappearance?"

"Unfortunately, yes," Holloway said. "Someone clearly wanted Gretel to quit her job. When she didn't do that—" He held out his hands, as if unwilling to verbalize the thought.

"Chief, I don't even know the woman, but I'm scared for her." Carly heard the tremor in her voice.

He nodded distractedly. "I can't disagree with that."

"What happens next?"

The chief swiveled his chair around and stared out the window, as if the answer was in the snow-covered trees. "There's a wooded area behind her home that goes quite a ways back. A search party is headed out there this morning. We don't expect to find anything, but we need to eliminate the possibility that someone—" He broke off abruptly.

Dumped her there. That's what he started to say.

After letting that sink in, Carly said quietly, "Chief, I know you're less than happy with me right now. But if the search party does find anything—anything at all—will you please let me know?"

"I will, as soon as it becomes official. As for Gordon Manous's situation, from this point on you are not to contact anyone or speak to anyone in that family, especially his wife. Are we clear on that?"

"As clear as crystal," Carly murmured. "But I have one more question. Have they identified the poison that killed Tony?"

"Actually, yes. The report landed on my desk late yesterday, but we're keeping the information tightly under wraps. If we make it public, whoever poisoned Tony will no doubt work quickly to destroy the evidence."

"If they haven't already. Can you tell me anything

about it? Remember, I was at that shower, and I tend to be observant."

Holloway's smile was flat. "I might've used a different word, but yes, you are observant." His face darkened. "Against my better judgment, I'm going to tell you the name of the poison. If you share it with anyone, or ask anyone questions about it, I will personally lock you in our holding cell and throw the key down a sewer grate. Is that also clear?"

"Totally." Carly raised her hand. "I swear I will not share it with anyone or ask anyone questions about it."

The chief spoke quietly. "Tony Manous was poisoned with a toxin derived from water hemlock. It's one of the deadliest poisons in the world."

Water hemlock. Carly made a mental note, then grabbed her tote and got up to leave. "Do they know where it came from?"

"At this point, no. It grows wild in wet areas, but during a Vermont winter it wouldn't be very accessible. The Chapin property borders a small pond, but it's frozen over now."

"So, what's next? A search warrant for the Chapin mansion?"

"That's being discussed, along with other scenarios. And now I want you to forget I told you all this and go make grilled cheese sandwiches."

From anyone else, Carly would have considered his words patronizing. But she knew the chief well enough to read between the lines. He was telling her not to put herself at risk.

He walked her out to the lobby. "So, how are your mom and Dr. Clark doing in Florida?" he asked her, nimbly switching topics. "Living it up in balmy, eighty-degree weather?" His faint smile broke the tension that had sprung up between them.

She laughed. "Last I knew they were on someone's yacht, but Mom's been deathly seasick. I think she'll be glad to get home to a nice cold Vermont winter."

Holloway grimaced. "I feel her pain. I'm not much for the ocean myself. Give me a serene Vermont lake in the mountains any time." His face flushed slightly. "Um, how's Valerie doing?" He tried to sound casual, but Carly saw right through him.

"From my perspective, she's doing great," Carly said. "We all love working with her." She was tempted to ask him if he'd developed an interest in her, but she suspected she knew the answer.

"Tell her to call me if she needs help with that… matter," he said.

"I will. Later, Chief!"

Carly sailed out the door, the image of the chief and Valerie as a couple dancing merrily in her mind.

CHAPTER TWENTY-ONE

GRANT HAD BEEN RIGHT ABOUT THE SKIERS. BY one in the afternoon every booth was filled, mostly with folks who'd spent a morning on the slopes, their cheeks rosy and their moods jovial.

Ari occupied his favorite stool near the front—the one closest to the grill. Today he'd opted for a Smoky Steals the Bacon—a grilled cheese on Asiago bread stuffed with smoked Gouda and crispy bacon. After Grant plated his lunch, Carly set it down in front of him and freshened his coffee.

"You've been giving up chips in favor of greens, I see," she teased him.

"Can't help it." He grinned at Carly. "Grant's salad is too awesome to pass up."

"I totally agree. Hey, I meant to tell you. Starting on Monday, we're only staying open until six."

"Really?" Ari sounded surprised. "How come?"

"We don't get enough customers during the winter months to justify staying open till seven. Once March first rolls along, we'll go back to our regular hours. By the way, did you buy a raffle ticket for the animal shelter?"

Ari jabbed a fork into his salad greens. "I saw the sign. I'll grab five before I leave."

Carly left him to finish his lunch, then helped Valerie seat customers and clean up tables. Suzanne had taken a rare Saturday off to go sledding with her husband and son, so things stayed extremely busy.

Before Ari left, they made plans to meet at Carly's shortly after 7:00. Then they'd decide where to have dinner.

By 2:30, the lunch crush was mostly over. Carly was ringing up a takeout order when a slightly built man with a shock of blond hair came in. Clad in a black parka and brown leather boots, he clutched a cellophane-wrapped bouquet of flowers in both hands, as if they were so weighty he was afraid of dropping them. When his gaze bounced over the dining room, Carly's internal antennae zinged skyward.

Finished with her takeout customer, Carly moved toward the man. In the next moment the *thud* of something smacking the floor behind her diverted her attention.

Near the restroom, a spray bottle of cleaning fluid had slipped from Valerie's hands and was rolling across the floor. Valerie's face had gone pale, and she was frozen in place.

A customer scooped up the bottle, and Carly quickly retrieved it from him. "Thanks," she said and touched Valerie's arm. "That's Luke, isn't it?" she whispered.

Valerie gave an anxious nod. "I don't want to talk to him, Carly. He shouldn't be here."

"Then you don't have to. Let's go in the kitchen, and I'll come back out and have a little chat with him." She slid her arm through Valerie's, but suddenly Luke was right behind Carly, pushing around her to reach Valerie.

"Go away, Luke," Valerie ordered. "I told you not to come here, and I meant it."

Luke licked his lips and held out the bouquet. "I only want to talk, Val. Can't you at least do that much for me?" His voice was squeaky, not the forceful tone Carly had expected.

"For *you*? No, I cannot." Valerie folded her arms over her chest. "Take those away and take yourself with them." Her gaze flickered over to Carly, who was still holding the spray bottle. "Otherwise, I'll be forced to call the police."

Luke blinked furiously. "Geez, Val, come on," he whined. "That's not like you. Can't we just, like, talk? The way we used to?"

"Actually," Valerie said with an upward tilt of her chin, "it is like me. The *new* me. The me that refuses to be lied to and cheated and tricked. Goodbye, Luke. Do not come in here again. Ever."

Luke's mouth dropped open, and he swallowed hard. "Have it your way, then," he snorted in a childish tone. He tossed the flowers on the floor, turned on his booted heel, and stalked out the door.

For a few awkward seconds, the eatery fell silent. Carly was picking up the flowers off the floor when the clapping started. Lightly at first—then every customer in the dining room was cheering.

"You go, girl!" a woman shouted from a rear booth.

"That's telling him," an elderly gent called out, nodding his approval over his coffee.

Grant came over, his smile wide. "Val, you were awesome. I was prepared to boot him out of here, but you were fantastic."

Valerie's face lightened, and a smile touched her lips. "Thanks, Grant. My heart was pounding like a rabbit's, but it sure felt good." She glanced around and mouthed *thank you* to everyone, then scowled at the bouquet. "Figures there's roses in there. You'd think by now he'd remember how much I hate the smell of roses."

Carly looked at the flowers—a winter bouquet of white roses, blue delphinium, and evergreens, accented with sprigs of baby's breath. "Shall I toss them?"

"Be my guest." Valerie grinned. "And now, if no one objects, I'd like to get back to work."

They dispersed, and Carly went into the kitchen.

She started to dump the flowers into the compost bin, but something stopped her.

She stared at the bouquet, and a memory tiptoed around the rim of her brain. It was something from the day of the shower. Something that had looked out of place.

She needed to see Ron Benoit's video again. The one he'd taken of the "smoking" room at the Chapin home.

Would Ron be in his studio this late on a Saturday?

She made a quick phone call and was surprised when he answered. "Ron, this is Carly Hale. Is this a good time for me to deliver your gift certificate? I'd like to issue it before month's end. It's a bookkeeping thing."

It was a total fabrication, but it worked. Since today was Grant's day to leave at four, she didn't have time to waste. Without going into details, she explained her mission to Grant and Valerie, promising to return in under an hour.

Barely ten minutes later, she was swinging into a parking spot in front of Ron's place of business. Ron opened the door and locked it behind her, flipping his OPEN sign to CLOSED.

Carly's stomach twisted. "Why're you locking the door?"

"Because technically I close at three, and I don't need any pains in the butt seeing the lights on and thinking I'm open. I only left the door unlocked so you could bring over my gift certificate."

She gave him the gift certificate, and he slipped it into a drawer. "Thanks. I have to lock up now." His coat was on his desk. He'd apparently been preparing to leave.

"Ron, I do have another favor," Carly said quickly. "But it's a fast one. I promise."

"What now?" He threw up his arms. "You are one pain in the—"

"I need to see that video again. The one you took in the smoking sanctuary. *Please.* It's important."

"I was just on my way outta here," he groused. "What's the big yank about the video?"

"Because I think someone switched the flowers in the vase on the mantel, and I need to check it out."

CHAPTER TWENTY-TWO

BEFORE SHE DROVE OVER TO RON'S, CARLY HAD googled "water hemlock" on her cell phone. A photo of a plant with small white flowers jumped onto the screen. If it hadn't been for the caption, she might have thought it was baby's breath or Queen Anne's lace.

It was anything but.

She sat once again before the desktop screen where Ron had previously shown her the video. As the scene of the room emerged into view, Carly leaned closer for a better look. "Okay, pause right there," she said suddenly. "Can you enlarge the vase on the mantel?"

With an exasperated roll of his eyes, he zoomed in on the vase. "I don't get what you're trying to prove, but there you go."

Carly's heart jumped in her chest.

"Thank you, Ron. Will you print a screenshot of that?"

His lips pressed tightly together, he clicked the mouse a few times, then rolled his chair over to the printer. "This is the last favor I'm doing for you." He gave her the printout.

Carly knew she was taking a risk by asking Ron for more help. It was exactly the sort of thing the chief had cautioned her against doing. If Ron had been the one who poisoned Tony, then she was probably toast.

But when she analyzed it, Ron's potential motive evaporated like so much smoke. Killing Tony wouldn't have gotten him the funds he needed to save his business—only a possible murder rap. And Ron was too self-absorbed to risk decades in prison simply to exact revenge against Tony.

No. Another, more insidious motive had been in play.

What she didn't know was how Gretel Engstrom fit into the picture. She was the odd-shaped piece that refused to squeeze into the puzzle, no matter which way it turned.

One thing Carly felt sure of—Gretel's disappearance was not a coincidence. Even more chilling, she had a sinking feeling in the pit of her gut that time was running out.

Then she remembered something. "Ron, didn't you say you started videotaping when you were trying to catch me hiding in the foyer?"

He smirked. "Yeah, I was gonna sneak around the corner and yell 'gotcha' while I caught you on camera. Would've been a total hoot to scare you, but I decided not to."

"By any chance, would you have saved that section of video? The part where you walked through the dining room?"

He frowned. "Possibly, but I'd have to go back and check through my edits and I'm not going to do it now. I'm meeting Ad—I mean, a friend at the pub in like, five minutes. Thanks to you, I'm already running late."

"Were you going to say Adam?"

He flushed under his beard stubble. "Maybe, but what's it to you?" He shut off the computer screen. "Seriously, Carly, why are you doing this? It's getting freakin' annoying."

Carly ignored his rant. "Will you check tomorrow then, and let me know?" She folded the copy of the screenshot and slipped it into her tote.

"No, I don't work on Sunday. I'll think about doing it Monday, *if* the mood strikes me. Which it probably won't." He shoved his arms through his coat sleeves and practically pushed her out the door.

Carly hurried out to her car, tossing a wave and a smile at Ron as he locked up his studio. He returned neither gesture.

Moments later, his sedan tore out of the parking lot.

Carly realized it was almost 4:00. She needed to hustle back to the restaurant so Grant could leave, and then she needed to get in touch with the chief, ASAP.

She strode through the eatery's back door at exactly 4:09. "Sorry I'm late. I didn't mean to hold you up, Grant."

"I don't care about that, but we were getting worried about you," he said, concern lacing his tone. "Is everything okay? I feel like I ask you that ten times a day."

She laughed. "Everything's fine. I had to deliver a gift certificate and I got a little delayed."

"Who was the gift certificate for?" Valerie queried her. "You never said."

Avoiding eye contact with both of her employees, Carly tugged off her gloves. "It was for Ron Benoit, the videographer from last Saturday."

Before they could fling any more questions at her, she hurried into the kitchen. She dug out her cell and texted the chief: I have urgent info to share re our convo. Pls call me!

All she could do now was wait.

Grant left to prepare dinner for his folks. With their anniversary only two days away, he wanted to be sure they celebrated in style with all their favorite seafoods.

By 6:45, Valerie and Carly had the dining room and kitchen tidied up, and everything put away. Carly still hadn't heard from the chief, which she thought was odd—especially since she'd told him it was urgent.

"Carly, thanks for your help today," Valerie said as they were putting on their coats. "I'm sorry you had to witness that altercation with Luke, but at least he's out of my life for good. I hope," she added with a brittle laugh.

"You handled the situation perfectly," Carly told her. "I think he got the message."

They walked outside together. The temps had dropped into the twenties, but the sky was clear and studded with stars, illuminated by a near full moon.

"Need a ride to your car?" Carly asked her.

"Nah. A little fresh air won't kill me. Have fun with Ari tonight!"

"I plan to," Carly said with a grin, unlocking her car.

She was giving her engine a minute to warm up when she remembered something. She'd left the dog-shaped plate with the healthy treats Grant had given her in the kitchen fridge. She wanted to show it to Ari, plus they could sample the goodies as an hors d'oeuvre tray before they left her apartment to have dinner.

Carly shut off her engine, dashed inside, and retrieved the sealed plate. She slid it into her tote, then reached into her coat pocket for her keys. Something touched her fingers—a slip of paper. Stymied, she pulled it out.

Ah yes—Megan had given her the name of the

button lady for Gina. Carly's hands had been full as she was leaving, so Megan had tucked it into her pocket.

Carly started to drop the paper on the pine desk when her throat seized.

The paper.

It was pale gray, with a slim blue line across the top.

Oh no. No no no. It can't be…

Unless her eyes were playing tricks on her, it was the same paper that was used to send the threatening notes to Gretel Engstrom.

Her pulse racing, Carly slipped the paper into her tote and shot a quick text to Ari. She let him know she'd be delayed and that she was taking a detour to the police station.

Heart in her stomach, she locked up again. When she went back out to her car, something was different.

Her nerves tingling, her senses on high alert, she moved her gaze all around. Several feet away, behind her car, a misshapen lump rested on the pavement. Whatever it was, it lay there, unmoving, until it emitted a tiny, pitiful cry.

Someone or something is hurt!

Carly raced over, dropping to her knees when she realized the shape was human. She was fishing out her cell to call 911 when something solid smacked her from behind.

After that she slipped away into a cold, lightless world.

CHAPTER TWENTY-THREE

THE PAIN WAS A LIVING, BREATHING THING.

It drilled into the back of Carly's skull, as if someone was chiseling her initials into her brain cavity.

After several tries, she forced her eyes open. Darkness swirled above her in a dizzying circle—a kaleidoscope devoid of color. Wherever she was, she was lying on the floor, some sort of thin carpeting beneath her. Her coat had been removed and she was shivering all over.

Agony ripped through her head as she pushed herself to her elbows. The darkness wasn't as profound now. Shapes were coming into view. To her right, a plastic cup with a straw through the top rested just out of reach.

Water.

Desperately thirsty, Carly reached out her fingers. In the next instant, a weak voice cried out, "No! Don't...drink..."

Carly sucked in a loud gasp and swerved her head toward the sound. About four feet to her left, a woman lay on the floor. The woman stretched her fingers toward Carly and rasped out, "Who... are you?"

Ignoring her throbbing head, Carly inched closer to her. Her eyes beginning to adjust to the dark, Carly saw a thin, gaunt face framed by lank blond hair.

"I'm Carly Hale. You're Gretel, aren't you?"

Gretel nodded weakly. "Don't...drink from that cup. Pretty sure...she's adding poison."

Bile rose in Carly's throat. "Who's adding poison? Gretel, who brought you here? Was it Megan?"

Gretel winced. "Y...yes. This is...her cellar."

Megan Gilbert. Auntie Meggs.

Kind, caring, devoted...murderous Auntie Meggs.

Horror filled Carly. It threatened to bubble over and choke her.

"Please, what...day is it?" Gretel mumbled.

"It's Saturday. Which means...you've been here about six days." Carly moved closer to Gretel and stroked her face. Her skin felt dry and lifeless. "Have you had any water at all? Any food?"

Gretel's eyes closed. "S-some water. From the... toilet tank. But then she added something, so I stopped. Started...faucet water, but she turned it off. Only food...a few power bars."

Anger flooded Carly, giving her a burst of adrenaline. She pushed herself upward again, this time sitting up all the way. She looked all around, trying to acclimate herself to her surroundings.

Gretel was right. They were in a cellar. The bathroom Gretel mentioned was off to the left, a sliver of light illuminating the edge of the slightly open door. Against the far wall, beneath a long row of shaded windows, two large sinks sat side by side.

Carly got to her knees, then crawled over to the sinks. Using every ounce of energy she could force into her muscles, she pulled herself up, gripping the edge of the closest one. She tried both faucets, but nothing came out.

Her strength beginning to return, Carly reached over and lifted one of the shades. She peered into the darkness, trying to get her bearings. She couldn't be sure, but she thought they were facing the rear of the property and not the street side.

Gretel spoke up, her words coming out like sand being strained through a filter. "Your…coat. Over in the…corner." She lifted a finger about an inch off the floor and pointed toward the bathroom.

Carly looked to where Gretel was pointing. A bright moment of hope surged through her when she spotted her coat, lying in a crumpled mass against the concrete wall.

She hobbled over to where her coat rested and dropped to her knees. She shoved her fingers inside both pockets, feeling around for the one thing that could help them.

But the pepper spray was gone. Megan had obviously found it and removed it.

Then she realized something else. Her tote was there too—lying underneath her coat.

My tote. My cell is in my tote!

"Hang on, Gretel," Carly said, her voice rising. "My tote's here with my cell phone inside. I'm going to call for help."

Gretel started to cry—a dry, horrible sound that wrenched Carly's heart. "Cell's…gone. She… found it."

"No!"

Undaunted, Carly opened her tote and fished frantically around with both hands. But Gretel was right. The cell phone was missing.

With a cry of frustration, she continued rummaging through the tote. Maybe Gretel was wrong. Maybe Megan had missed the cell phone.

Then her fingers landed on something, and she let out a squeak of triumph. The dog-shaped plate with Grant's healthy snacks was still there. Megan hadn't found it! A laugh escaped her, and she began to cough. Gina always teased her about things getting lost in her oversized tote bags. Wouldn't Carly have a great tale to tell her now?

If they ever got out of there.

Carly dragged her coat and her tote bag over to Gretel, then turned around and sat up beside her. She felt her strength beginning to return, fueled by anger at a ruthless killer.

"Gretel, I have food. And it's safe."

She lifted Gretel's head gently and propped up her coat behind it. She gave her a section of tangerine, and then another. Gretel sucked out the juice first and then hungrily ate the rest. Carly knew Gretel should eat slowly, but the poor woman was literally starving. It was hard not to give her the entire plate.

Carly stroked Gretel's hair away from her face. "Gretel, do you know why she did this?"

Gretel's nod was almost imperceptible. "I...figured out she killed Tony. That night...she drove me home, she stopped for gas. I...needed a tissue, so I looked in her purse." She tried to swallow, but it came out as a dry cough. "I saw...letters. Same... stationery as...threatening notes I received. I...I always thought they were...from Tony, but I knew then...she...was behind it all. She must have... realized I figured it out. That's why she came back the next night..."

Megan poisoned Tony.

Carly's insides rolled as Megan's fiendish plan became clear in her mind.

Desperate to keep her precious niece close to her, Megan would've done anything to prevent her from moving away. Flying, or even driving to North Carolina to visit Klarissa, would never have been possible for Megan. Her severe travel phobia kept her rooted where she lived. North Carolina might as well have been a distant planet.

"Bu…Buttercup," Gretel whimpered. "Is—"

"Your cat's fine," Carly assured her. "Doctor Anne is taking care of her till you return."

Gretel lolled her head back. "Thank…God."

Upstairs, the cellar door squeaked open. Carly's heart lurched.

An overhead light snapped on, and Carly blinked from the sudden flash. After several agonizing seconds Megan descended the stairs, her footsteps loud against the wooden risers. She paused and gaped at the pair huddled on the cellar floor, a gun perched in her hand.

"Well, isn't this a kick in the pants. Now I have two of you to deal with." Her face was haggard, her eyes opaque with fury as she moved toward them.

"You need to let us go, Megan." Carly's voice quavered. "Gretel is dehydrated and in serious condition. She needs to get to the hospital."

Megan's laugh was harsh, so unlike her usual delicate titter. She waved the gun like it was a toy. "You think you're going somewhere, do you?" She flung a mouthful of obscenities at Carly, then stormed over and gaped down at Gretel. "Where did that food come from?"

"From me," Carly sniped at her. "Now get my cell so I can call for help."

Ignoring the command, Megan hissed, "You just had to butt in, didn't you? Klar's idiot cousin Ron called her a little while ago, screaming at her to get you to stop bugging him about his videos. He said you were obsessed with the vase in the smoking room. He wanted you out of his hair."

Oh glory. Ron Benoit triggered this nightmare.

Megan's gaze drifted sideways, then back to Carly. "And that's when I knew—you'd put it all together. I'd heard about you, but I thought people were exaggerating. Now that I know they weren't, I won't be safe until I get rid of you too."

"Is that why you attacked me in the parking lot?" Carly moved closer to Gretel, prepared to shield her if necessary.

"I had to. Don't you see?" Megan's voice grew agitated. "You put me in a terrible spot!"

Carly swallowed. "It's too late, Megan. I already called the chief of police. It won't be long before they find us. Do yourself a favor and get help for Gretel now."

"You're lying!"

Carly stared her down, then said, "How did you get Tony to meet you at the mansion while the shower was still going on?"

"Not that it's your business, but I brought a burner phone with me—one of those untraceable throwaways. My original plan was to text Tony a cryptic message saying he needed to get to the shower right away. I knew he'd be home watching sports, so if I timed it right, I could meet him at the door and whisk him into the smoking room without anyone seeing us. But when I saw Rose Manous setting out her pastries, an idea struck me. I pulled her into the breakfast nook. I told her Klarissa didn't want her pastries there because it would detract from the gorgeous cake from Sissy's Bakery. Rose cried, and I commiserated with her, hinted that maybe Tony should come over and talk sense into Klar. She hesitated at first, but with a little prodding she latched onto the idea. I left her alone, and the next thing I knew, I heard her sobbing over the phone to Tony."

"You tricked her, and Tony fell for it. He blamed Klarissa for not letting Rose put out the pastries, but all the time it was you." Carly's throat was parched, her voice growing ragged. "How did you persuade him to have a drink? Wasn't he there to confront Klarissa?"

"You really underestimate me, Carly. You should know by now I'm quite the actress. When Tony got there, I waylaid him at the door. I insisted he calm himself with a drink before I'd allow him to see Klar. He grumbled, but I tugged his arm and led him straight into the smoking room. I plied him with aged whiskey—laced with poison, of course. I made sure I didn't leave any prints on his glass." She laughed. "When he said he needed the bathroom, I told him to use the one upstairs. I promised I'd have Klarissa waiting in the foyer when he came back down." Her lip curled. "The fool. He was so pliable. I knew he wouldn't last long with all the poison in him. I was almost home free when Dawn and that idiot Ron came into the dining room right when Tony was heading upstairs. Poor Dawn, trying to use Tony to make Ron jealous. Anyway, when they started arguing, I crouched behind one of the tall vases. Thankfully their little tiff didn't last long. They all left, although I saw Ron linger to shoot some video of the smoking room. It was a miracle he didn't see me hiding behind that vase."

"You were gone from the shower quite a while," Carly pointed out. "Didn't anyone question where you'd gone off to?"

"Easily explained." Megan patted her abdomen. "I've always been plagued with tummy troubles. They made a great excuse for why I took so long in the bathroom." She made air quotes around the last word, and then her eyes darkened. "I swear, I don't know how that boy made it upstairs to the bathroom, but somehow, he did. Although his trip back downstairs wasn't quite as smooth, was it?" Her lips curved into a demented smile.

Carly forced back a gag. *She had to think.*

By now, Ari must be frantic. Had he read her text message? If so, he'd know she'd been on her way to the police station. He'd have started there, but when he realized she never arrived, he'd have checked her apartment and then the restaurant. Finding her car in the lot, the restaurant locked up and dark, he'd have known something was very wrong.

"By the way," Megan taunted, as if tuning in to her thoughts, "your cell phone is *incommunicado*. Not only is it turned off, but it's buried in the bottom of one of my plants, where no one will ever find it."

Plants.

"Those tiny flowers in the vases," Carly said, "the ones I foolishly mistook for baby's breath—they were water hemlock, weren't they?"

Megan's smile, once so sweet, became the predatory grin of a piranha. "A lovely flower, really, if it weren't so deadly. I used the water from the vase in the smoking room to make Tony's drink."

The flower arrangements in both vases had initially borne clusters of water hemlock. After Megan poisoned Tony's drink, she must have switched the water hemlock for baby's breath.

Which explained the drop of water Carly noticed on the dining room table while she was waiting to be questioned.

"What did you do with the water hemlock after you poisoned the vase water?"

Megan's eyes took on a manic glow. "I'd left some baby's breath in the private bathroom off the smoking room. Unless you knew that house the way I do, you'd never guess one of the closet doors led to a luxuriously appointed bathroom. After I poisoned

Tony's drink, I changed the water and switched the flowers. The water hemlock? I tore it into pieces and flushed it. Thanks to Julie's persnickety father, that bathroom has commercial grade plumbing. He always insisted on the best."

Carly felt Gretel stir beside her. "Well, you certainly were prepared, weren't you, Megan?" Loathing filled Carly. "Did you grow the deadly plants yourself? In your solarium?"

"Bingo! Give the girl a prize."

Megan began pacing back and forth, like a teacher giving a lecture. "It's used for medicinal purposes, you know—for migraines, cramps, et cetera. You can even send away for the seeds. But I harvested mine during the summer where the stream runs along the edge of the field. The younger the plants, the more toxic the poison." She wiggled her fingers. "I always handle them with gloves. Just to be safe."

Carly came close to retching. She took a deep breath and forced it back.

"What did you ever have against Gretel? She was your friend!"

Megan glared down coldly at Gretel. "None of this would've been necessary if she'd quit her job like she was supposed to. I sent her the first letter when Tony was bucking for extra funding for the playground project. In a way, it was a test to see how she'd react. When she caved on the funding, I knew I was golden. All I needed was to plant the seeds—how's that for a pun?—in Tony's head to aim for the town manager's position. With some pressure from Tony's dad, the Select Board would've appointed him in a heartbeat—so long as Gretel was out of the picture."

"Not true. Those jobs have to be posted," Carly snapped at her.

"So what? Tony already headed one of the town departments, plus he had an MBA in business. With Gordon Manous's influence, he'd have been a shoo-in."

"Didn't Tony wonder why Gretel's position had suddenly become available? How did you explain that?"

She laughed. "He knew Gretel and I were good friends, so I made up a little secret. I told him Gretel would be giving her notice soon, that she had family problems back in whatever one-horse town she came from and was leaving Vermont for good. It was a lie, but he totally fell for it. Men are so gullible. Anyway, he glommed right on to the idea of being town manager. He wanted desperately to please his dying father. I encouraged him, nudged him. Told him Klarissa would be so proud of him. He was totally on board with it, excited even."

"So you started a harassment campaign," Carly flung at her. "You sent Gretel letter after letter, convinced she'd panic and quit. I saw your blackmail letters. How did you even find out about Gretel's… past?"

Megan looked down at Gretel and made a cruel face at her. "Poor Gretel. You were so trusting, weren't you, sweetie?" she taunted.

Gretel flinched but said nothing.

Megan straightened and glared at Carly. "I couldn't believe my luck when she confided her *real* secret in me. It was like a sign from above, you know?" She raised her hands to the heavens, then lowered them again. "I knew, right then, I had all the tools I needed to get Tony that position as town manager."

"But she fooled you, didn't she? She refused to resign."

Megan's eyes took on a frightening glow. "Even when my notes got scarier, more threatening, she still didn't quit. What was weird was that she never confided in me about them. *Me,* her close friend." She sounded incredulous. "If only she had, I'd have insisted she quit. I'd have convinced her it was dangerous to stay on. But she never said a word. Even when I kept asking her if something was wrong, she still didn't spill her guts." She began pacing the floor in short sweeps.

"That must've been frustrating," Carly tsked. "And what a blow it must've been when Tony's dream job came through. Accepting it meant he and Klarissa could embark on a new life together—a married life. A life that didn't include *you.*"

Megan recoiled as if she'd been slapped. "Shut up. Klarissa never wanted to leave me."

"The wedding was getting closer," Carly continued, "and you were running out of options. Is that when you decided to poison him?" She shot Megan a baleful look.

Megan jabbed a finger down at Gretel. "If she'd only cooperated and quit her job, Tony would be the town manager by now. Gretel could've moved on with her life—she had other options. And my Klarissa would have stayed right here, with me, where she belongs!"

In that single, horrifying moment, Carly saw the extent of Megan's obsession.

Klarissa was her world.

Her life.

Living without her would've been unimaginable.

"You won't get away with this, Megan. Tell me, why did you drag Gretel over here?"

Megan licked her lips. "That night I went to her house, I thought I could surprise her and kill her quickly. But even after I smacked her hard in the head, she put up a struggle. She was a lot stronger than I realized. I panicked. I knew the longer I stayed, the better the chance of someone seeing my car in the driveway. So I slapped duct tape over her mouth and wrapped it around her hands and ankles. It was a miracle I managed to drag her to my car without anyone driving by and seeing us. I figured once I got to my place, I could dispose of her more efficiently."

Dispose of her. The words made Carly's insides flip over.

"Buttercup tried to stop you that night, didn't she?"

Megan rolled her eyes. "Yes! She kept trying to get between us. I finally carried her into Gretel's bedroom, but she clawed like crazy at me." Her lip curled into a pout. "She tore off one of my vintage buttons. I'm not sure I can forgive her for that."

"Even so," Carly said gently, seeing the depth of Megan's insanity, "you locked her in the bedroom with plenty of food and water, didn't you? Because you'd never hurt a cat, would you?"

"Of course not!"

"Then why not get help for Gretel? Please, Megan. She needs help urgently. And she'll remember how much you cared about Buttercup, won't you, Gretel?" She nudged her slightly with her hand.

Gretel looked at Megan with fading eyes. She nodded weakly and grated out, "Yes. I...I'll remember."

"But I...I can't." Megan stomped her foot. "Don't you see? This...all got away from me."

"Tell me, Megan," Carly said, more firmly now, "if I hadn't gotten here, what were you planning to do with Gretel?"

Megan swallowed, her desperate gaze darting

from Carly to the ill woman on the floor. "I... there's an abandoned well on the farm property next door. I..." She shook her head. "I never wanted it to end like this. But she didn't quit, like she was supposed to. And then she wouldn't drink the poison. This is all her fault!"

Carly closed her eyes, her insides forming knots of sheer rage. She reached down and wrapped her fingers around Gretel's hand, surprised when something was pressed into her own.

"Megan, listen to me," Carly begged. "If you call an ambulance now, you can reverse this terrible mistake and save Gretel. She's your friend, remember? If you let her die, you'll be charged with *two* counts of premeditated murder." *Three if you kill me.* "That means life in prison, Megan. Is that what you really want?"

Megan's gun wavered slightly. She covered her ears with her hands and began to shake all over. A piercing wail, like a wounded animal's, emanated from her lips.

She was unraveling, fast.

Carly was contemplating the fastest way to bring Megan down when muffled footfalls on the cellar staircase snatched her attention. She looked up, shocked to see Klarissa Taddeo slowly descending the stairs.

"Klarissa, go back up and call for an ambulance!" Carly cried out.

Ignoring her, Klarissa came all the way down. She sauntered over to where they stood. Beneath the stark light of the overhead bulb, her face was a sickly yellow.

"Two counts of murder, Auntie Meggs?" Her voice was raw with pain. "No, I don't think so. If Gretel dies because of what you did to her, it should really be *three* counts of murder, shouldn't it?"

CHAPTER TWENTY-FOUR

"KLAR!" MEGAN RUSHED TO EMBRACE HER NIECE, but Klarissa shoved her aside with her elbow. Megan gaped at her with a shocked expression, her gun flailing wildly. "Honey, listen I can explain—"

Keeping her eyes trained on Megan's gun, Carly repeated, "Klarissa, I am begging you, please call for an ambulance."

Still ignoring Carly, Klarissa said quietly, "I'd pushed it so far back in my memory that for a while, I'd convinced myself it never happened." She shook her head.

"Wha..." Megan swallowed, and then it seemed a light suddenly dawned in her mind. "Oh...no. You've got that all wrong, honey."

"Cowbane," Klarissa said through bared teeth. "That was the last word Nan spoke that day. I'll never forget the look in her eyes. She knew what you did, and she was trying to tell me. But I was only a little girl. I thought she was rambling. Because that's what you told me, Auntie Meggs! You said the heart attack gave her delusions!"

"Oh no, sweetie, listen to me. Nan did have a heart condition. That's why she collapsed—"

"She collapsed because you poisoned her! And why? Because she doted on the cute little girl with the curly red hair who loved her chocolate chip cookies!"

Somewhere upstairs, a door crashed open. Megan stumbled backward, toward the staircase. When she saw a man clomping down the stairs, she raised her gun.

Ari!

"No!" Carly lunged at Megan. She shoved the business end of Gretel's cat-shaped brooch deep into Megan's thigh.

Megan shrieked, and in the next moment she dove at the floor. Before Carly realized what was happening, Megan tore the lid off the cup with the straw and gulped down its contents.

Chief Holloway came pounding down the stairs, two uniformed officers in his wake. For several long moments, confusion reigned. Two EMTs strapped Gretel onto a stretcher, while Ari grabbed Carly and pulled her into his arms.

The chief retrieved the gun, which had skittered across the floor, then crouched down beside Megan. By that time, she was writhing on the floor, her lips stretched in pain.

Carly pulled back slightly from Ari, although he still held her hand. "Chief, Megan just swallowed her own poison. She needs to get to the ER too."

Holloway cursed under his breath. "There's another ambulance on the way. Carly, are you okay?"

"Aside from a slight bump on the head, I'm fine."

"Call for another ambulance," he ordered the closest patrolman.

Carly groaned. "I don't need one."

And then she looked over and saw Klarissa, huddled beside a female officer who spoke soothingly to her. The haunted look in those once sparkling blue eyes made Carly's heart almost crack in half.

Carly released Ari's hand and went over to her. "You'd already called for help, hadn't you? How did you know?"

Klarissa nodded, then pulled in a long, shuddering breath. "Auntie Meggs was with me at Mom's house when my cousin called to complain about you. When I told her what Ron said, she got this, like, weird look on her face. Then she ran out of the house like her hair was on fire. The more I put the pieces together, the more I realized she'd done something truly awful. When I got here, I knew immediately something was off. I sneaked over quietly and listened at the top of the stairs. I didn't have to listen long before I called 911."

"Thank you, and I'm so sorry, Klarissa. You don't deserve any of this."

Klarissa nodded. Her hair was a tangled mess, her face the color of flour. She stared down blankly at her aunt, at the woman who loved her so deeply she was willing to kill to keep her close.

The second stretcher arrived, and as they lifted Megan off the floor, Klarissa whimpered, "Please… don't hurt her."

Carly gathered Klarissa in her arms and hugged her for a long time. After that Klarissa left with a police escort.

By that time, two more EMTs had come in. "Oh boy, another one?"

With a sigh, Carly allowed them to shift her onto the stretcher. Carly held Ari's hand until they rolled her into the ambulance. His smile, that jaunty, teasing grin that had captured her heart so many months earlier, now turned her insides into a puddle.

"Meet you at the hospital?" she asked him.

"If I didn't need my wheels, I'd ride along with you guys. But since I do, I'll be right on your tail end all the way there." He took her outstretched hand and kissed each of her fingers. "I'll say one thing for you, Carly Hale. You sure know how to liven up a Saturday night."

~

At 2:30 in the morning, Carly was released from the hospital. She didn't have a concussion, only a bad bump to the head. Ari drove her home and stayed with her until morning, ensuring that she rested and drank plenty of fluids.

Carly was expected to show up at the police station on Sunday morning for yet another interview, but this time she didn't dread it. She wasn't fully rested, but she was anxious to tell her story. She needed to put the whole horrible night behind her.

In the meantime, Ari had been texting with the chief during the night. He'd learned a number of things.

Megan had survived the attempt to poison herself but was currently on a ventilator. Fluids and antiseizure medication had helped stabilize her, but she still floated in and out of consciousness. During her few periods of lucidity, the nurses reported that she uttered the same word over and over: *Klarissa*.

Gretel had also been admitted to the hospital. She was expected to remain there for at least a few more days. Dehydration had severely weakened her, and she was being pumped with fluids and nutrition. She insisted on keeping what was left of Grant's dog-shaped goody plate, so the nurses were storing it in their private fridge for her. One of the nurses said that Gretel was anxious to meet Grant so she could thank him for it in person.

As for Carly, Gretel couldn't stop praising her, but she also had a few complimentary words for the irascible Ron Benoit. In his own irritating way, he'd started the "rescue" ball rolling with that angry phone call to his cousin. If it hadn't been for that, Gretel might well have perished in that cellar.

After a light breakfast of oatmeal and coffee, Ari drove Carly to the police station. Chief Holloway looked as if he'd aged ten years. He ushered them into his office, where hot coffee awaited.

"I don't even know where to begin," Holloway said gruffly, scrubbing the bags under his eyes with his fingers. "You did precisely what I ordered you *not* to do and nearly got yourself killed. *Again.*"

Carly fidgeted in her chair, then met the chief's glare head on. "With all due respect, Chief, I'm not really required to take orders from anyone. Not unless I'm breaking the law, which I wasn't. Besides, I was on my way to see you when I was hit from behind, remember?"

A sly smile slipped from Ari's lips, but he hid it by sipping from his coffee cup.

"Which wouldn't have happened if you hadn't bothered the beans out of Ron Benoit." He heaved a long-suffering sigh. "On the other hand, if you hadn't been attacked and dragged off to Megan Gilbert's house last evening, Gretel might not have survived the night. I don't think I need to repeat how grateful she is. That goes for me, as well," he said grudgingly.

Carly shuddered when she remembered how close to death Gretel had looked. Despite that, she'd had the presence of mind to arm Carly with her cat-shaped brooch. Carly had used the wickedly sharp pin to stab Megan, which deflected her from firing at Ari.

"What happens to Megan now?" Carly asked.

Holloway puffed out his cheeks and released a breath. "After she's well enough to be discharged from the hospital, she'll be sent for a psych eval. My guess? She's going to stand trial for the murder of Tony Manous. As for the poison, the forensics team got to work early this morning. They went back over the all the items they collected at the Chapin house. It appears that both vases—the one in the so-called smoking room and the one in the dining room—bore remnants of water hemlock. After Megan made Tony's drink, she must've ditched the stems that were poisonous and added Queen Anne's lace, which is harmless."

"That's pretty much what she told me." Carly explained what Megan had said about flushing the poison stems down the toilet. Then she thought of something else. "Chief, what about the neighbor named Nan? The woman Klarissa thinks was poisoned by Megan?"

"That's another issue entirely. The DA will have to decide whether she wants to seek an exhumation of the body. I'm relieved to say—that's not my department."

They wrapped up the meeting, and Carly met

with Lieutenant Granger. After another taxing interview, she and Ari went out for brunch at the Balsam Dell Inn.

After they returned home, Carly called her mom. By the time she'd finished telling her the entire story, Rhonda was threatening never to leave her side again, even if she had to handcuff the two of them together.

Carly slept better that night than she had in over a week.

By Monday morning, she was ready for another busy day at Carly's Grilled Cheese Eatery.

CHAPTER TWENTY-FIVE

On Tuesday afternoon, Carly swung her car into Ursula Taddeo's driveway. She'd been invited to have coffee with her, Klarissa, and Dawn. She'd been pleased to accept.

Ursula met her at the door and took her coat. "We're so glad you could be here, Carly. The ladies will be happy to see you."

"I appreciate the invitation."

Carly followed her into a living room that had modern yet comfortable décor. On the glass coffee table, a white carafe, mugs, cream, and sweeteners rested on a colorful tray.

Dawn hugged Carly first, and then Klarissa did, and they all sat down. Carly was glad to see Klarissa's eyes looking clear and bright, although the pain of loss was still there.

Coffee was passed around, and Klarissa jumped right in. "Carly, I did something yesterday I should have done a long time ago—I paid a visit to Rose Manous. I apologized to her for my awful treatment of her. She was so gracious. I also let her know that I never refused to let her put out her pastries. That was all Auntie Meggs." She blew out a breath. "I realize now that Gordon and Tony meant everything to her. If I hadn't been thinking only about myself, I'd have recognized it much sooner."

Two days after entering the hospital, Gordon Manous passed away. A home security camera in his bedroom showed that he'd taken two extra heart pills himself, either out of sheer confusion or by design. Either way, Rose had been cleared of suspicion. Carly had been hugely relieved to hear that.

"I'm sure that was hard, Klarissa, but I'll bet Rose welcomed your visit. How is she doing?"

"Like me, she's devastated. In a way, we're in the same boat. She lost her beloved husband and her stepson. I lost my fiancé and…my aunt."

"Remember, honey, you don't need to talk about her," Ursula said gently.

"No, Mom. I want to. Ever since I can remember, Auntie Meggs has treated me like a precious, fragile object. I know she loved me, but it wasn't a healthy love. It was a…possessive, almost fanatic kind of love." She took a deep breath. "I'll never forget the day I told her Tony and I were moving to North Carolina. She looked at me like I'd physically assaulted her. When she ran out of the room clutching her stomach, I felt like the worst person on earth. I heard her throwing up in the bathroom, and I wanted to…to die."

"But you know that wasn't a normal reaction, honey." Ursula looked pained. "You never told me that." She looked over at Carly. "The truth is, Megan has suffered from emotional issues since she was a teenager. A failed engagement when she was eighteen threw her off course—emotionally, I mean. Everyone thought she'd recover, but somehow her mind went sideways. She couldn't keep a job and acted as if she hated the world. She was constantly getting pulled over for reckless driving. She got even worse after I married Klarissa's dad."

She'd been overwhelmed with jealousy, Carly surmised. Megan's behavior began to make sense, now—in a disturbed, warped sort of way.

"One night she got involved in a bad car accident," Ursula continued, "which triggered the severe travel phobia she's never gotten over. It wasn't until Klarissa was born that things started to change. While I worked, Megan took over Klarissa's care. I sensed she was getting too attached to Klar, but my husband and I were struggling to make ends meet so I needed to work. As a babysitter, I couldn't have asked for anyone more loving, more trustworthy than my sister. But as time went on, my beautiful baby girl became like Megan's own. I...didn't know how to intervene without hurting everyone involved, especially Klarissa." Her hand trembled on her coffee mug.

"Mom, stop blaming yourself. None of this is on you. You've always been a wonderful mom."

"But it is on me, honey. After that...incident with poor Nan, you shrank inside yourself. I couldn't figure out why it affected you so much. You wouldn't talk about it, so I asked the doctor to give you medication." Her eyes darkened. "But now I see what happened. You'd grown so fond of Nan that it infuriated Megan. Out of sheer jealousy, she decided to get rid of her."

Klarissa nodded slowly. "She must've remembered Nan telling her about her cow that almost died from eating the plant out in the field. She probably researched it, and then harvested it to use the same poison."

During the entire exchange, Carly observed, Dawn had remained strangely silent.

Now Dawn shook her head and murmured, "Cowbane. I heard Nan say the word that day as I was coming out of the bathroom. I had no idea what it meant. Good grief, I was only eight years old. I thought it was her way of cursing."

In a way, it *was* a curse. Carly had googled the word and learned that cowbane was another name for water hemlock. In her final moments, Nan must've realized what Megan had done.

"Tell them your other news," Ursula urged, smiling at her daughter.

Klarissa sat up straighter. "After...everything is settled here, I'm moving to North Carolina. The condo Tony and I rented is too large for one person, so I have a leasing agent looking for a smaller one. I want to start fresh, away from all the reminders of Tony, and…you know, my aunt." She gave Ursula a lopsided smile and nudged her arm playfully. "Mom's going to float me a few months' rent so I can look for a job as an aesthetician."

"I'll be sad to lose her, but I want her to be happy." Ursula squeezed her daughter's shoulder and pulled her close.

Klarissa's smile faded. "Tomorrow I'm going to visit my aunt in the hospital. It'll be the last chance I have before they send her to a psych ward for evaluation. I'm not even sure what I'm going to say to her, but, as the saying goes, I need closure."

"That's understandable," Carly said. "I wish you the best."

Ursula beamed over at Dawn. "Dawn, you have some news too, don't you?"

Dawn flashed a smile—a genuine one this time, not her usual forced grimace. "I'm moving out too. I found an adorable little apartment in a two-family house in Bennington. The house is old, but the apartment's been totally renovated. The appliances are brand new, and I'll have a little porch of my own."

"Wow, that was fast!" Carly grinned.

Dawn shrugged. "I had to work quickly before I chickened out. But I'm so glad I did."

"Tell her the rest," Klarissa prodded her friend.

"For years I've dreamed of becoming an architect. But lately I started looking at other options, and I'm thinking of studying graphic design. I've registered for some online classes—just to test the waters. If I like it as well as I think I might, I'll pursue a degree."

"That's wonderful, Dawn," Carly enthused. "What about your wedding planning business?"

"Oh, I'll still keep that. Tell you the truth, I do enjoy planning weddings. Besides, I gotta pay the rent somehow, right?" She laughed.

Klarissa's eyes filled. She hopped off the sofa and went over to hug her friend. "I haven't been a very good friend to you these past months, have I?"

Dawn swallowed hard. "It's okay. I told you, we're past that now. It's time for both of us to move on."

"I swear to you, Dawn, I'm going to make it up to you," Klarissa said. "But I'm really going to miss you too. I mean, *seriously* miss you."

"Yeah, me too," Dawn said with a smile. "But I'll visit you, and you'll come back for the holidays, right?"

"That's a given. Rose and I promised to keep in touch with each other too. I'm so glad she isn't mad at me."

Carly was happy to hear that. No longer a suspect in her husband's death, Rose Manous was now deep in mourning for the two people she'd loved most in the world.

Dawn turned toward Carly. "In case you're

interested, I have news about my mother. Believe it or not, she sought out counseling on her own—without anyone suggesting it. Not that she was responsible for anyone's death, but I think she began to see how her behavior affected everyone connected to her." Her voice softened. "Me, especially. I'm kind of impressed with her for doing it. I only hope she sticks with it."

Carly smiled warmly at her. "Dawn, that's really positive news."

"This is only my opinion," Ursula put in, "but I always thought Julie was looking for a man as perfect as she thought her father was. Needless to say, no one could ever fill his shoes. Not in her mind, anyway."

"That's very perceptive of you. I tend to agree." Dawn sipped from her mug and smiled. "And as always, Mrs. T., you make excellent coffee."

"Did someone say coffee?"

Dawn snapped her head around so fast she almost knocked over her own mug. "M-mother?"

Everyone's jaws dropped. Even Carly was stunned speechless to see Julie Chapin coming into the room.

Wearing a cream-colored winter pantsuit with navy trim, Julie paused for a moment and glanced all around. With her meticulously styled black hair and luminous makeup, she looked as if she'd stepped off the cover of a fashion magazine.

"I didn't mean to eavesdrop," Julie said sheepishly, her gaze resting on Dawn, "but I did hear a bit of your conversation. I know I have a lot to atone for, but I'm hoping this might be a beginning. And by the way, Ursula, you always have made the best coffee in town. Is there enough left for me to enjoy a cup?"

"Oh…my heavens, of course there is." Ursula got up and gave her an awkward hug. Julie looked around for a place to sit, but Carly hopped off her chair. "Sit here, next to your daughter, Mrs. Chapin. I was just leaving."

"Are you sure?"

"Totally sure. I have another appointment anyway."

Carly thanked Ursula for her hospitality, wished everyone well, and offered a round of quick goodbyes. Ursula fetched her coat.

As she was leaving, Carly saw Julie give her daughter's shoulder a light squeeze.

They're going to be okay, Carly thought. *All of them.*

~

Penny Harper was an entirely different person from the nervous, agitated woman Carly had met barely a week earlier. Her cheeks were rosy, and her smile was warm and welcoming.

They sat in her office, where a tablet was propped

on her desk next to a box of chocolates wrapped with a bow.

"Before we talk about the raffle," Penny said, "I want to thank you for everything you've done. But first—how are you feeling? I understand you got yourself a big bump on the head for your troubles."

Carly's head had felt the force of the blow for a few days after she was rescued. "Thanks for asking, but I'm great now. No more headaches."

"That's good. It hurts me, physically, to think of Gretel lying on that basement floor all those days, wondering if anyone would ever find her." Penny gave a slight shiver. "But you didn't give up. The police were close to figuring it out, but they'd have probably been too late. If you hadn't annoyed that videographer so much, I shudder to think how it might have turned out."

The same thoughts had haunted Carly over the past several days. "How is Gretel doing?"

Penny tapped her hand to her chest. "Oh, Carly, she's doing so well. She'll be discharged from the hospital tomorrow. Her cat will be waiting for her when she gets home." She lowered her eyes. "Not surprisingly, it's all over town about her...deception. She's given her resignation to the Board, but not all of them are willing to accept it."

"I can understand why, after the ordeal she's been through. Are there going to be penalties for falsifying her credentials?"

"They're looking into that. But you know what? No one I've spoken to seems bothered by Gretel's actions. She's receiving a huge amount of support from the locals. After all, she's done so much for Balsam Dell. That's what really matters, isn't it?" She gave Carly a hopeful look.

"I agree, totally, especially since she's been working so diligently toward her bachelor's degree. When will the Select Board make a decision?"

"They're meeting in one week," Penny said, twisting her hands. "I'm nervous. Only one member is hesitating, but the others are wholeheartedly supporting her. They've been bombarded with letters and emails demanding that she remain in office. I'm afraid it's turning into a big brouhaha."

In Carly's mind, it wasn't surprising. She only hoped Gretel would rethink her resignation.

Penny clasped her hands together and beamed. "I have a surprise for you." She pulled over her tablet and clicked a few keys. She turned it around and propped it on her desk so that it faced Carly.

The smiling face of Gretel Engstrom emerged on the screen. "Hi, Carly. So good to see you again. I'm sorry my voice isn't strong, but at least I look human this time." She chuckled.

"Gretel! Oh my gosh, it's so great to see you." Carly choked up. Gretel's face was thin, but her color was better, and her eyes were much more animated.

"I wanted to thank you," she said, "for finding me, for everything. Tell Grant I'm keeping his treat plate as a memento. Whoever my successor is, I'm going to encourage them to work with the School Board to get them in the school lunch programs."

"Grant will love that."

"I'm also going to visit your restaurant as soon as I'm well enough." She took a breath. "I've eaten your grilled cheese sandwiches many times, but always as takeout. Now I want to enjoy one in person."

The face of a nurse appeared on the screen. "Ladies, she needs to rest now."

"Yes," Gretel told them, "I have an interview later with the young man from the paper. See you both soon."

They waved their goodbyes and promised a reunion. Carly reached into her tote for the large envelope she'd been carrying.

"We sold every ticket," she said, giving the envelope to Penny. "There's three hundred twenty dollars in the envelope, along with the ticket stubs."

Penny looked thrilled as she peeked inside. "This is so exciting. This brings our total to well over a thousand dollars. Another volunteer and I have put together the raffle baskets, and they're gorgeous. But since it's the first year we've done this, we need to figure out where to hold the raffle, which is this coming Sunday. You don't have to be present to win, but people have been asking where it's going to be."

"You can't do it at the shelter?"

She sighed. "We thought about it, but they only have a small lobby. If gobs of people show up, there won't be enough room and it might be disruptive to the animals. And it's too cold to have it outside. We'll probably resort to doing it on Zoom."

With the restaurant closed on Sunday, it was Carly's one free day of the week. She'd spent her prior two Sundays undergoing interviews at the police station. She'd hoped to spend the next one with Ari.

"Penny, what if I open the restaurant for a few hours and you have it there? I won't be open for business, but I can serve complimentary cheesy snacks to anyone who comes in."

Penny pressed her hands together. "You would do that?"

"I would enjoy doing it," Carly assured her. "If you announce the time of the drawing, I'll open about an hour before that. After the names are drawn, I'll stay open another hour or so for people to mingle, then close up shop. It'll give the shelter volunteers a chance to chat with people about adopting too."

Penny jumped out of her chair and went over to hug Carly. She gave her the box of chocolates. "Then it's a plan. Here, these are for you. From me. For everything."

By the time Carly left, she felt lighter than a helium balloon.

Somehow, after the tragic events of the past week and a half, life was returning to normal.

CHAPTER TWENTY-SIX

"Hey Carly, did you read my article yet?" Don Frasco grinned from ear to ear as he held up Thursday's edition.

The interview Don had conducted with Gretel had gone extremely well. His questions had been insightful and thoughtful, and he'd told her story with sensitivity and empathy. It brought an unexpected lump to Carly's throat.

"Not only did I read it," Carly told Don, "I thought it was excellent. Thank you for showing Gretel to be the generous and giving person she is. I'm sure it meant a lot to her."

He shrugged, but his freckled cheeks flushed with pride. "I stayed up half the night getting the article ready for Thursday's edition. I didn't want to wait another week to publish it."

"That was good work, Don."

A decent crowd had shown up for the raffle—maybe forty or so. They gathered around in groups or in booths, munching on the goodies. With Valentine's Day only two days away, Grant had prepared miniature grilled cheese sandwiches cut into crisp heart shapes. Assisted by the dietary director from the school—a young woman he'd introduced as Isabella—he served each one on a recyclable plate with tiny candy hearts instead of chips. From the looks the two exchanged and from the glow in Grant's eyes, Carly suspected a romance was brewing. Despite the obvious difference in their ages, they clearly saw something in each other. If it was meant to be, Carly would wish them both well.

Suzanne wasn't able to make the gathering. She'd made plans with her family weeks earlier but gave her five raffle tickets to Carly for safekeeping—just in case she won.

All along the walls, poster-sized photos of animals awaiting adoption had been tacked up. Carly smiled when she noticed Dawn Chapin studying a picture of a small gray cat with white paws. "That one would be perfect for your new apartment," Carly stage-whispered to her.

Dawn turned and grinned at her. "You read my mind. Her name is Flora, and I'm picking her up tomorrow. Mother…I mean, Mom is coming with me. Isn't that, like, unreal?"

Carly was thrilled for her, for both reasons.

"I asked her if she'd give a donation to the shelter," Dawn went on. "Carly, she didn't hesitate for a second. My eyes almost popped out when I saw the size of the check she wrote. I'm going to give it to Penny Harper after the drawing."

"Dawn, that's great news. Be sure to send me a few pics of the kitty, okay?"

Valerie flounced over and joined Carly, her topknot held in place with a sparkly red heart. The flirty plaid skirt and white sweater she wore looked darling on her. She looked happier than Carly had seen her since the day she first hired her. "This worked out great, didn't it?" she chirped.

"It sure did," Carly agreed. "Is the chief here? I didn't see him."

Valerie's cheeks pinked. "He should be here any time now. After this, we're going to the opera. Your sister's beau is starring in *The Barber of Seville*!" She dashed off, leaving Carly's jaw hanging open.

The chief and Valerie. Who'd have thought it?

A grin glued to her face, Carly peered over at the chrome-edged counter. Rose Manous had delivered a tray of fancy pastries, and they were dwindling fast. She'd brought them over earlier but didn't want to stay. Her heart was broken, and she was still deep in mourning. She'd apologized for giving Carly the lavender-laden cookies. In her grief, she'd dropped the bottle of lavender into the cookie mix and stirred the contents into the batter. She realized later she shouldn't have given them to anyone, but her mind, so full of sorrow, had been elsewhere.

At the back of the restaurant, three spectacular gift baskets wrapped in cellophane sat on a folding table. Penny Harper stood behind the table and surveyed the room. It was obvious from her wide smile that she was delighted with the turnout. Everyone attending was a potential adopter.

Gretel sat beside Penny in a comfy padded chair, a cup of hot chocolate in her hand. A constant stream of well-wishers came over to shake her hand. Some leaned in for a brief hug or murmured something in her ear. Near the kitchen, Carly noticed two of the Select Board members speaking privately to one another. From their expressions, it was impossible to guess their thoughts, but she thought she saw one of them smile.

When Carly saw who'd sidled over to chat with Gretel, her jaw dropped again. Ron Benoit, looking sharp in a wool jacket and tie, was bending over Gretel with a huge smile on his face. It was the first time Carly had ever witnessed him smiling.

She couldn't resist. She wove her way through the crowd and stepped up beside him. "Hi, there."

Ron's smile collapsed. "Hello, Carly." He cleared his throat. "I don't know if you heard, but I'm teaming up with a drone pilot to form a new videography business. We're hoping that the *powers that be,* with Ms. Engstrom's encouragement, will commission us to do a promotional video of the town."

Gretel smiled up at him, then touched Carly's

hand. "I suggested that one of the shots on the video should be of this wonderful old building, including the sign over your restaurant."

Carly wondered if she'd fallen down a rabbit hole. Surprises were streaking at her faster than she could process them.

"Um, that…would be terrific."

"By the way," Ron said, "my buddy Adam told me to tell you that you can bring your dog back any time for a spa treatment. No hard feelings."

Gee, what a trouper.

"Well, that's nice to hear," Carly said. "Thanks for letting me know."

She glanced around for Ari, but she couldn't spot him in the crowd.

Gina and Zach breezed in and came up behind Carly. Gina's full cheeks were flushed pink. "Hey, we got a late start, but we made it. We had a bit of shopping to do."

"Shopping?" Carly's heart jumped in her chest.

"Get your head out of the clouds, lady. We were shopping for cat supplies. After this, we're going to the shelter to adopt a kitty. The shelter's open till five for adoptions."

"Yay!" Carly hugged her friend. "Be sure to tell Penny. She'll be thrilled."

Gina gawked at the gift baskets. "Man, look at all the goodies. I sure hope I win one of those." She looped one arm through Zach's and the other through Carly's.

"Hey, can anyone join this party?" Ari came up beside Carly, a happy-faced Havarti wriggling in his arms.

"Ari!" Carly squeaked. "I wondered where you were. Why is Havarti here?" She kissed Ari soundly on the cheek and then ruffled Havarti's fur.

He laughed. "Since this fundraiser is for the animal shelter, I knew he wouldn't want to miss it."

"Our very own poster dog for pet adoption, right here in person." Carly felt her eyes mist. "You thought of everything. But how did he get here?" She reached over and lifted her dog into her arms.

"Becca drove him over. I met her behind the restaurant."

Within moments, people began strolling over to pet Havarti. The dog, loving the attention, licked hands and gave out kisses with abandon.

Ari squeezed Carly's waist. "Look, Penny's spinning the ticket wheel."

The crowd cheered as three names were drawn. Two of the winners were present, and the third had been watching on Zoom. After the drawing ended, people trickled out of the restaurant. Ron Benoit kissed Gretel on the cheek before nodding at Carly and leaving.

The two Select Board members were still there, Carly noticed. When they ambled over to Gretel, Carly held her breath. One of them, a woman, spoke quietly to Gretel, then handed her an envelope.

Gretel smiled and pressed a thumb to her eye, and the two hugged.

"Is everything all right?" Carly asked Gretel after the Board members left.

Gretel swallowed. "The Board has refused to accept my resignation. They've asked if I will remain as town manager, on the condition that I complete my bachelor's degree and pursue my master's. All of which I was already doing, so it was really a no-brainer." She laughed.

"Gretel, I am so happy for you."

"I'm sure there'll be a few detractors along the way," Gretel said dryly, "but I'll deal with that as it happens. Don's interview went a long way in helping, by the way. I'm immensely grateful to that young man. I've been getting supportive letters and emails from people I've never even met."

"Be sure to tell him." Carly winked at her.

"Carly!" Penny shrieked, waving an envelope in the air.

Carly rushed over to her. "What's wrong? Is everything okay?"

Penny was trembling. "I just got this donation from one of your friend's moms." She showed Carly Julie Chapin's check. It was for ten thousand dollars.

Another surprise Carly didn't know how to process.

"Penny, that's amazing. How incredibly generous

of her," Carly said. "Wait till your friends at the shelter hear about it."

"She insists that it be anonymous," Penny declared, "but…oh goodness gracious! Isn't this fabulous?"

After everyone finally left, Grant helped Carly and Ari clean up the eatery. Isabella had another engagement, but she was meeting Grant later on.

Gretel's support for Grant's school project had him beaming like a chandelier. Before she left with Penny, he'd presented her with another healthy treats plate, this one shaped like a cat to represent Buttercup.

"Ready to head out?" Carly asked Ari, digging out her keys.

"Not yet." Ari went behind the counter with Havarti. Seconds later, the dog padded over to Carly, a small white box tied with a red satin bow dangling from his collar. "First I have to give you this."

Carly's heart did a broad jump. She loved Ari, but she wasn't ready for a ring.

"What is it?"

He flashed a mysterious smile. "Open it and find out."

She removed the box from her dog's collar, untied the bow, and lifted off the lid. Resting inside the box was a stone paperweight, deep blue in color and about the size of her palm. A message was engraved on the stone.

Grow old along with me, the best is yet to be.

"From the poem by Robert Browning," she murmured, swallowing back tears.

"Nah. It's from the video John and Yoko made. Haven't you ever seen it?"

Carly laughed and threw her arms around him. She didn't know if he expected an answer, but it didn't matter. There was no way she could utter a sound over the lump in her throat.

But if anyone could read her thoughts, Ari could.

When she could breathe again, she said, "Come on, let's go home. I think Havarti deserves an early supper, don't you?"

READ ON FOR A LOOK AT ANOTHER CHEESY MYSTERY FROM LINDA REILLY

CHAPTER ONE

Grant Robinson swept through the front door of Carly's Grilled Cheese Eatery and scooted behind the counter. "It's over, Carly. I finally did it. I gave my notice at the sub shop."

The grilled cheese Carly Hale was flipping did a slight wobble. Grant, the twenty-year-old food aficionado who'd been Carly's part-time grill cook since she first opened, also worked part time at Sub-a-Dub-Sub, a sandwich shop located across the town square. Or rather, he *had* worked there.

Carly shifted the grilled cheese back onto her spatula, then placed it, butter side down, on the grill. "Wow, you really went through with it. What did Mr. Menard say? Was he upset?"

"Upset? From the steam coming out of his ears, I'd say he was like a water heater about to burst."

Using her spatula, Carly slid the Sweddar Weather—a grilled Swiss and cheddar on marble rye—onto her cutting board. She sliced it in half, transferred it to a plate, and added chips and pickles to the dish, along with a cup of tomato soup. The heady aroma of melted cheese and butter-grilled bread never failed to delight her. It was the primary reason she'd returned to her hometown of Balsam Dell, Vermont, and opened her grilled cheese eatery. She'd taken over the space where a failing, decades-old ice cream parlor had finally gone belly up.

The other factor that prompted her return to her hometown was the death of her husband two years earlier. To escape the memories and start a new life for herself, she came home, as she thought of it, and opened her dream business. Sharing her favorite comfort food and earning a living from it was the best of both worlds.

Carly glanced around the dining room. At a bit past 2:00, only one booth was taken. Its sole occupant was Steve Perlman, a fortysomething man sporting rimless eyeglasses, a paperback book in front of him. Mr. P., as Carly referred to him, had been one of her high school teachers. Physics, her least favorite subject, she recalled with a shudder. But he'd been an earnest young man then, passionate about science as well as a good teacher. When he spotted Grant, he waved. Grant returned the gesture with a big smile.

Carly had opened her eatery earlier in the year, and though summer had brought in visitors galore, it was autumn that was proving to be her busiest season. While leaf-peepers descended on the town in droves, it was the high school that was turning out to be her best source of customers. The kids, and even some teachers, had been invading her restaurant daily after the last bell rang. They scarfed down grilled cheese sandwiches and cheesy dippers with gusto while they droned on about the disgusting food in the school cafeteria.

"Why don't you tell me all about it later," Carly told Grant. "Right now, you can give me a break before the hungry hordes come in, okay? Suzanne had to leave early for a meeting with Josh's teacher."

Suzanne Rivers was Carly's other server. With a son in fourth grade, Suzanne normally worked from 11:00 a.m. to 3:00 p.m. so she could be home for Josh after school. Lately she'd been putting in some extra hours to help Carly get through the midday rush. It helped that Josh had signed up for a few after-school programs, so on most days it worked out perfectly.

"Say no more." Grant hustled through the swinging door that led into the kitchen. He returned moments later wearing a crisp apron and vinyl gloves.

Carly delivered the sandwich plate to her sole customer. "There you go, Mr. P., and sorry for the holdup. Need a coffee warm-up?"

"I'd love one." He picked up a sandwich half and aimed it toward his mouth. "And Carly, please stop calling me Mr. P. It's been a long time since you were in my physics class. 'Steve' will do just fine."

"Force of habit," Carly said with a smile. She returned and refilled his mug. "By the way, how did you manage to beat the kids here today? School doesn't get out till two-thirty."

Steve swallowed a bite of his sandwich. "I had a doctor appointment, so I took the afternoon off." He winked at her. "Good excuse, right? Plus, it gave me a chance to pick up a few sci-fi books from the library. I read at least three a week."

"Ah. Got it." She smiled as if to assure him his secret was safe with her.

Carly went back behind the counter. Grant looked dismayed as he wiped down the grill.

Carly knew him so well. She was sure he felt both guilt and relief at having ditched his job at the sub shop. The owner's lackadaisical approach to food hygiene had, apparently, finally pushed him over the edge. Although Grant had only recently turned twenty, he was more mature than most thirty-year-olds and had a passion for all things culinary. He was also a gifted cellist, but to his musical parents' dismay, he was determined to become a chef.

With Grant's help, Carly had added some inspired new sandwiches to their grilled cheese menu, including their most recent offering—Brie-ng on the Apples, Granny. The new autumn sandwich was made by grilling creamy Brie, thin-sliced Granny Smith apples, and cherry relish between slices of raisin bread. After its debut in early September, it quickly became an eatery favorite.

Grant had also helped her design their entry in the town's annual Halloween Scary-Licious Smorgasbord competition, which was only two days away. *Yikes.* Aside from supplying light sticks to kids for trick-or-treat night, it was Balsam Dell's only concession to Halloween.

It would be Carly's first time participating in the event, and she was feeling more excited as the day approached. The competition, sponsored by the town's recreation department, was held every year on the Saturday before Halloween. Tables were set up on the town green, and local restaurants gave out samples of their creepy culinary creations. Attendees voted—one vote per ticket. After all votes were tallied, the winner was awarded a $500 cash prize, along with the coveted plaque engraved with the restaurant's name. Carly had already chosen a spot for the plaque, should it be awarded to her eatery.

"Carly, we're probably gonna be mobbed soon, so I'll tell you what happened real quick." Grant winced, then spoke in a low voice. "Mr. Menard is blaming you for my quitting. He thinks you put me up to squealing on him to the board of health."

"But...but...I would never do that! I would never try to influence you." She tried to keep her tone quiet, but she knew she'd hit a few high notes. Still, she was both aghast and furious at the man's accusations.

"I told him that. I defended you to the moon, but he kept ranting right over me." Grant shook his head. He looked worried. "At one point I got scared his heart would give out. He takes medication for it, even though he's only in his forties. His face got bright red, and he stumbled backward. His daughter, Holly, made him sit down and take a pill of some sort. She said he has angina."

"I'm sorry to hear that," Carly said. "I hope he's getting the proper care for it. But it doesn't give him the right to attack my character."

"It's weird," Grant said, looking puzzled. "He was blaming you more than he was me. Almost like... like he had a vendetta against you."

"I'm sure he was only lashing out," Carly said. "No doubt he's bummed about losing you right before the Halloween competition, but he has his daughter to help him. Once he calms down, he'll see that you had every right to give your notice and to tip off the board of health. Maybe it'll inspire him to clean up his act, right?"

Grant looked unsure. "Yeah, maybe."

"Hey, now that you're here, do you mind if I pop into the kitchen for a few? I need to make a call about my Halloween costume. I'm having it specially made for Saturday!"

"Take your time. I'll handle things here." He gave her a half-hearted smile.

Carly headed into her commercial kitchen. She fixed herself a quick cup of tea with one of the pumpkin spice teabags she'd bought earlier in the week. Though coffee was her normal comfort drink of choice, the Halloween season seemed to inspire cravings for anything pumpkin-spice-flavored.

She sat with her mug at the pine desk beneath the window that overlooked the small parking lot behind the eatery. Only four months earlier, she'd found a body out there. With her help, the murderer had been caught. Nonetheless, she hoped never to go through anything like that again. Pushing away the memory, she grabbed her cell phone and tapped a saved number.

"Miranda Busey. Can I help you?" came a squeaky, tired-sounding voice.

She sounded so young. Carly could hardly believe Miranda was a student who was taking design classes in college. "Hi, Miranda, it's Carly Hale. I'm just checking on my costume. Can I pick it up tonight?"

Carly and the man she'd been seeing, local electrician Ari Mitchell, were attending the Scary-Licious Smorgasbord competition dressed as Morticia and Gomez Addams. Ari's costume was finished, but Carly's required a slinky, lacy stretch of fabric over a full-length, gauzy black dress.

A long silence followed. "Miranda?" Carly prodded.

Miranda groaned. "Carly, I am so, *so* sorry. I was putting the zipper in the back of the lace overlay when my hand slipped and I tore the whole thing. I was so exhausted. I was practically seeing double. I was up almost all last night, sewing."

Carly's stomach dropped. She'd been counting on being Morticia to Ari's Gomez. With his dark eyes and neatly trimmed mustache, he fit the part perfectly—and much more handsomely than any Gomez she'd ever seen.

"It…it can't be fixed?" Carly swallowed.

"Unfortunately, no. I had to send away for that lace fabric. Even if I had more of it, I'm jammed up the wazoo with more jobs to finish. I guess I took on more than I could handle."

"Can I wear the dress without the lace?"

"Only if you want the entire world to see your

underwear." Miranda hesitated. "There's one thing I can offer, but I'm not sure you'll like it. I made a darling lady vampire costume for a customer who changed her mind. It's kind of a pale gray, with a filmy cape that extends out like bat wings. I think it'll fit you, and it's super pretty. Wanna try it?"

Carly was positive she didn't want the entire world to see her underwear. "Sure. I'll stop by after work and try it on."

Disappointed, Carly gulped the rest of her tea and returned to the dining room. As if a magic door had opened, in the short time she'd been gone nearly every booth had filled. The high school contingent had arrived.

A sudden burst of gratitude filled her.

With every passing week, her restaurant was gaining popularity. Only recently, an informal newspaper poll voted it one of the "coziest eateries" in southern Vermont. She had to admit, she agreed. With its exposed, pale brick walls, aqua vinyl booths, and chrome-edged counter lined with stools, it was exactly the way she'd hoped it would look when she first imagined the concept. In every booth, a vintage tomato soup can filled with faux flowers of the season graced the table. October's flowers were orange and yellow mums.

If she won the competition, it would add another feather to her culinary cap, so to speak. With luck, that would translate to an increase in business. It would be a perfect way to usher in the start of the holiday season.

Ferris Menard had won the competition the past three years in a row, according to Grant. It made Carly even more determined to emerge as this year's winner.

At one of the rear booths, a former middle school classmate of Carly's—Stanley Henderson—sat with books and notebooks spread over the table. These days he was preparing for the Realtor's exam and enjoyed reviewing his study notes while he scarfed down a sandwich and a cola. His current job as a guidance counselor at the high school was no longer "floating his boat," as he'd put it. He wanted to make his own hours and be his own boss, not to mention earn some serious commissions selling homes.

When he caught Carly's glance, he gave her a wide, pleasant wave. "Hi, Stan," she mouthed, then went behind the counter.

In the booth behind Stan's, Evelyn Fitch, a retired English teacher, sat with a book of crossword puzzles and a pink notepad. Carly had never had her as a teacher—she'd retired about ten years too early. Now somewhere in her eighties, Ms. Fitch spent at least three afternoons a week enjoying a late lunch of a Vermont Classic—sharp cheddar on country white bread—while she pored over a puzzle. "It's both my lunch and dinner," she'd told Carly one day, "which is why I always come here midafternoon." Carly suspected it was more a case of the lonely Ms. Fitch enjoying being around loads of people, but she'd told her, "Good plan," and let it go at that.

Carly's heart skipped when she saw Ari seated on one of the stools. She went over and leaned toward him. "Hey."

"Hey yourself." His smile warmed her, and she felt her cheeks grow pink. She gave him the bad news about the Morticia costume.

Ari reached over and squeezed her wrist. "Don't worry. It'll be fine," he soothed. "Actually, I'm sort of anxious, now, to see you in that lady vampire dress." His deep voice and stark gaze made her heart leap skyward again.

Carly grinned, and in the next moment the door to the restaurant swung open, hard. Ferris Menard stormed in, his blond brush cut gelled into porcupine quills, his face a scary shade of red. "Carly Hale," he boomed. He looked around, spotted her, and strode over to the counter. "Yeah, you. I heard about your little sabotage ploy. Well, it won't work—do you hear me?"

As if someone had turned off a switch, the dining room instantly quieted. Stunned by the verbal assault, Carly took a step backward. Grant, who had the protective instincts of a mother grizzly, moved to stand in front of her. "Mr. Menard," he said quietly, "what are you doing here?"

"My beef isn't with you, Grant. I know she put you up to it!"

"But—"

Carly shifted around Grant to face the man. "Ferris," she said tightly, "I will thank you to behave courteously in my establishment. Otherwise, you need to leave. Is that clear?"

"Oh, yeah? Well, I'll thank *you* to stop trying to ruin me." His small blue eyes blazed with fury. "I got a little visit from the health inspector this afternoon, but you already knew that, didn't you, *Miss Hale*. Unfortunately for you, I run a clean, sanitary operation. Oh sure, I got cited for one dumb thing, but it was ridiculously minor. As for this place"—his lip curled as his gaze flickered around the dining room—"suffice it to say, you wouldn't know an aged cheddar from a bale of hay. You're a fraud, and I'm going to prove it."

In the next instant, Stanley Henderson shot out of his booth and strode toward Menard, one fist curled at his side. Steve Perlman was right at his heels, and between the two of them, they blocked Menard's view of Carly.

With a shake of his head, Ari slid quietly off his stool. He went over to Menard and took him firmly by the arm, propelling him toward the door. "Time for you to go, Ferris."

Feigning bravado, Menard stumbled sideways a step, trying unsuccessfully to extract himself from

Ari's grip. "Let go of me," he hissed. Spittle formed on his lips, and he swiped at it with his free hand.

"Wait a minute, Ari." Carly circled around all of them and moved to stand directly in front of Menard. "Ferris, I did nothing to sabotage you, as you put it. But if you ever come in here and accuse me again, you can expect a visit from Chief Holloway. Is that clear?" She turned to her would-be protectors. "Stanley, all of you, go back to your seats. I appreciate your help, but I can handle this myself. Besides, Ferris is leaving now. Aren't you, Ferris?"

The rage in Menard's expression was so dense it could have been sliced up and served on a buttered biscuit. Stan flinched, and Steve took a step backward.

Menard wrenched his arm away from Ari, who was edging him closer to the door. Then, with a shake of his fist, he stalked outside into the crisp October day.

CHAPTER TWO

"IT WAS SO EMBARRASSING," CARLY GROANED TO her bestie, Gina Tomasso. "First Ferris verbally attacking me, and then Stanley and Mr. P.—Steve—jumping out of their seats to come to my rescue, like I was some damsel in distress. I swear, if they'd had pitchforks and torches, they'd have chased Ferris into the street, like the villagers who went after the Frankenstein monster."

Carly was seated at Gina's kitchen table in the apartment upstairs from her restaurant. She'd stopped in after closing time to give her friend the lowdown on the day's events. Glancing around, she saw that Gina's digs were really shaping up. Though she'd moved in only five weeks earlier, Gina was filling it with every 1960s artifact she could find. Gina's mom, who'd died when she was nine, had loved the décor of that decade. Carly suspected that her friend was sub-consciously choosing furnishings that would've pleased her.

Gina chuckled. "Well, at least they had your back, right? Gotta give them credit for that."

"They did," Carly admitted, "and I felt bad afterward for scolding them. I apologized later to both of them, and also to Ari and Grant, but they waved it off. Truth be told, I was relieved when Ari escorted Ferris to the door."

"It just infuriates me," Gina said darkly, "to think that Menard barged in like that and caused a scene in front of all your customers. Personally, I'd have wanted to sock him in the snout."

"I draw the line at fisticuffs," Carly said dryly, "but don't think I wasn't tempted. Now, though, I'm almost dreading the competition on Saturday."

"Why? You didn't do anything wrong."

"I know, but now it feels like there's a dark cloud hanging over me in the shape of an angry Ferris Menard." With a slight shiver, Carly plucked a handful of candy corn from Gina's candy dish and funneled them into her mouth. "You should've heard the sarcasm in his voice when he called me *Miss Hale*. I couldn't tell if he was being intentionally formal or if he doesn't approve of a woman keeping her maiden name after marriage."

Gina waved a dismissive hand. "Probably the first one, but don't let him intimidate you. Every year, Ferris Menard enters the same thing in the competition, with only a slight variation. I'm *so* over his sub sandwiches shaped like reptiles or zombies."

Carly had heard about Ferris's triumphs. His sub

shop was known for its special blend of dressing, created by Menard himself. It was used on all the cold subs they served.

Carly's own entry was going to be eye-catching, delicious, and tangy to the third power, as Grant had put it. In addition to the scrumptious grilled cheese he'd designed, he'd also created two dipping sauces—a ghoul green and a bloodred—both of which would be presented in hollowed out pumpkins.

Gina set her jaw and tucked a dark brown curl behind her ear. "If I were you, I'd just let Menard stew in his own juices. Or rather," she snickered, "in his own oil and vinegar dressing, which he thinks is so special. Anyway, just cross the jerk off your list of worries."

"I know you're right, Gina. It's just—"

"It's just that men are pros at making women feel guilty," Gina interrupted tartly. "You remember my ex-husband?"

Oh, Carly surely did. It was his body she'd found in her parking lot at the beginning of the summer.

In fact, it was only after the discovery of Lyle's body that Carly's defunct friendship with Gina had been reignited. In high school, the girls had been almost inseparable—until a huge misunderstanding over Lyle's pursuit of Gina had severed their friendship. Gina had married Lyle straight out of high school but divorced him three years later. By then Carly was living with her husband, Daniel, in northern Vermont—a good two-hour plus ride from Balsam Dell. Neither woman had attempted to contact the other, a mistake they now both regretted.

These days, having resolved their conflict, their friendship was stronger than ever.

"Well, that was one of Lyle's specialties," Gina went on. "That and cheating. Are you sure you don't want a cup of coffee?"

"No, thanks. I have to stop by Miranda's and try on the vampire costume. Plus, I have a dog at home who doesn't tolerate tardiness." She grinned at the thought of Havarti, her sweet little Morkie, rushing to the door to greet her. Half Yorkie and half Maltese, he was perky and funny and perpetually ready to shower everyone he encountered with kisses.

"I thought Becca took him outside during the day?"

Becca Avery, an army veteran, was the live-in caretaker for Carly's landlady, Joyce Katso. The pair lived in the apartment downstairs from Carly in Joyce's two-family home.

"She does, but Havarti has a sense of timing like you wouldn't believe. If I'm ten minutes later than usual, he does a circular dance around my feet and barks at my shoes."

Gina giggled. "I love that dog."

Carly glanced at the tangerine-colored Lucite

clock on Gina's wall. "Hey, I've really gotta run." She hoisted her pumpkin-themed tote bag—a gift from Ari—onto her shoulder and rose. As she did, a folded slip of pink paper fell out of an outer pocket. Smiling, she picked it up and handed it to Gina. "Look at the note that adorable Evelyn Fitch left in her booth this afternoon after she paid her bill."

Gina unfolded the paper and read: "'Carly's food is tempting and tasty. Always stuffed with melted cheese. Remnants of cheddar sizzle and brown. Leaving a flavor so unimaginably fine. You'll return again for more.'" Gina's face softened. "Aw, it reads kind of like a poem, doesn't it?" She raised a dramatic hand to her heart. "Ode to Carly's Grilled Cheese." She grinned and tucked the note back into Carly's bag. "You really do have a loyal posse of customers."

"On a different subject, are you seeing Zach tonight?" Carly asked her in a teasing voice.

Gina and Zach Bartlett had been an item for about four months. His job as an account manager for a national delivery service kept him on the road a lot, but he and Gina managed to see each other every chance they got. So far, they seemed to be nuts about each other.

A fierce blush colored Gina's round cheeks. "Can't. I've got a custom order for shower invitations that has me burning the midnight oil."

Gina owned a shop aptly dubbed What a Card—a gorgeous card shop located opposite the town green in the next block. Having mastered the technique of quilling, Gina was constantly filling demands for her custom-made cards—especially shower and wedding invitations. Carly worried that sometimes she took on too much work, but Gina never complained, even when she had grueling deadlines.

"So anyway, tomorrow night," Gina explained, "Zach and I are gonna see some new scary movie. I hope I don't scream as loud as I did at the last one. I felt like a total wuss."

"Not to worry. I'm sure Zach'll save you from any zombies."

"Are you kidding? He screamed louder than I did."

Carly laughed. "Later!" She waved and bounded down the stairs and outside to car.

RECIPES

Carly's Grilled Cheese Eatery has come a long way since those early days when she first opened for business. Some recipes have evolved from the classics. Others have been inspired by the change of seasons. And a surprising new recipe that initially had Carly scratching her head has proven to be an eatery favorite. But as she always says, "We prepare our sandwiches to please our customers. There's no wrong way to make a grilled cheese."

GRILLED CHEESE DONUT

When Carly decided to add grilled cheese donuts to her menu, she wondered if her customers would embrace the blend of sweet and savory in a grilled cheese or if the experiment would end up a bust. Fortunately, this simple-to-make twist on a traditional grilled cheese turned out to be one of her most popular sandwiches! This recipe is for one sandwich. Multiply as needed.

Ingredients

1 glazed donut (the bigger the better!)
Salted butter, softened
Shredded sharp cheddar cheese (as much as you can pile on!)

Directions

1. Using a serrated knife, slice the donut in half lengthwise. Spread softened butter on both *unglazed* sides.

2. Set one-half of the donut in a nonstick skillet or cast-iron pan, butter side down. Pile shredded cheese on top of the glazed side. (Don't worry about bits of spillage into the pan—they make nice little crusty edges!)

3. Top the cheese with the other half of the donut, butter side up. Grill over low to medium heat, pressing down lightly with a spatula. Carly suggests *not* using a grill press, as the weight will squish the sandwich too flat. Grill on one side until golden brown, then flip over and grill the other side.

Variations

When grilling, add pieces of crispy bacon or sliced tomato atop the cheese, if desired.

CARLY'S TIP:

- If you don't like using the shredded cheese, substitute with a few thick slices of your favorite sharp cheddar.

For this delectable treat, a cup of tangy tomato soup makes a perfect dipping sauce!

GRANT'S TOMATO SOUP

So many of the Eatery's customers have tried to pry Grant's tomato soup recipe from him! He has decided to share but emphasizes that, like making a grilled cheese, you can make your own variations to suit your taste. And though he prepares large batches at a time for the restaurant, he created this recipe to give you four servings.

Ingredients

4 tablespoons unsalted butter
½ large sweet onion, sliced thick or cut into chunks
3 cloves of garlic, minced (about a tablespoon)
1 (28-ounce) can of San Marzano tomatoes, crushed (undrained)
2 cups chicken stock
2 tablespoons sherry cooking wine (more if desired)

1 tablespoon sugar
1 teaspoon sea salt
A few hearty shakes of black pepper
¼ teaspoon ground thyme
¼ cup heavy cream

Directions

1. In a Dutch oven or large pot, melt the butter over medium heat and toss in the onion.

2. Sauté for a few minutes or until the onions soften, then add the minced garlic. Sauté only for another minute to ensure that you don't burn the garlic.

3. Add the tomatoes, chicken stock, sherry cooking wine, sugar, sea salt, black pepper, and thyme.

4. Bring to a boil and then simmer, uncovered, for about 40 minutes, stirring occasionally.

5. Add the heavy cream. Stir in and then remove from the burner.

6. Blend until smooth in a regular blender or using an immersion blender, taking care not to splatter the hot mixture. After tasting, add more salt and pepper if needed. Ladle into a

bowl and enjoy either alone or with a scrumptious grilled cheese!

CARLY'S TIPS:

- If it suits your fancy, top with a sprig of fresh thyme, a few sliced basil leaves, or a hefty sprinkling of Parmesan cheese.
- Want croutons? Make your favorite grilled cheese! Once the sandwich has cooled, use a sharp knife to cut into small squares and sprinkle them over the soup. Easy, cheesy, and delicious!

ACKNOWLEDGMENTS

I have been blessed with the best readers on the planet. To all of you who read or listened to my first Grilled Cheese Mystery, thank you for taking a chance on a new series.

To my editor, Margaret Johnston, and my agent, Jessica Faust, I have more gratitude than I can express. To the supportive, creative, and just plain wonderful team at Sourcebooks, I extend my heartfelt thanks.

To Judy Jones, thank you for being the voice of reason during my bouts of sheer panic. I can't imagine a better brainstorming partner. To June Butka, thank you for the grilled cheese donut idea and also for the delicious donuts!

And to my fellow authors on the Cozy Mystery Crew, thank you for always being there when I needed some sound writerly wisdom.

ABOUT THE AUTHOR

© Amelia Koziol

As a child, author Linda Reilly practically existed on grilled cheese sandwiches, and today, they remain her comfort food of choice. Raised in a sleepy town in the Berkshires of Massachusetts, she retired from the world of real estate closings and title examinations to spend more time writing mysteries. A member of Sisters in Crime, Mystery Writers of America, and Cat Writers' Association, Linda lives in southern New Hampshire with her husband and her cats. When she's not pounding away at her keyboard, she can usually be found prowling the shelves of a local bookstore or library hunting for a new adventure. Visit her on the web at lindasreilly.com or on Facebook at facebook.com/Lindasreillyauthor. She loves hearing from readers!